HOMERUNS

& Hearts

NIKKI RAE

ISBN-13: 9798991474160

Cover design made using Canva (canva.com) by: Nikki Rae
Graphics designs by: Nikki Rae
Library of Congress Control Number: 2018675309
Printed in the United States of America

From The Author

Dear Reader,

First I want to thank you for choosing to read Homeruns & Hearts. It means the world to me to know that you are taking the time to read my book. Before you read Emerson and Pacey's story I wanted to clarify a few themes featured here that could be upsetting or difficult to read. I want to make sure you, the reader, take care of your mental health first. No book is worth reading if it takes you down a dark path.

Homeruns & Hearts at it's core is a love story. However, you will see themes of sexual assault and abortion (mentioned and not in detail) and cancel society. As an author I use fictional stories to highlight real world events going on in our society. In no way do I believe that any of these subjects should be taken lightly. What I hope you will take away from Homeruns & Hearts is that there are two sides to every story.

I want you to know that if you have experienced any of the traumas mentioned above that you are not alone. There are many resources available to you, and I will list some of them below.

Sexual Assault Hotline: 1-800-656-4673 / rainn.org
Planned Parenthood: 1-800-230-PLAN / plannedparenthood.org

Once again, thank you for reading my book and know I'm forever grateful.

Love,

To those who have ever felt like the world was against them...

There's hope for a brand new day and a brand new start.

Keep on fighting!

Emerson

There were thousands of people in front of her and all Emerson

Holbrook could think was I have the best life ever. The crowd was

laughing as her friend, Laurel Adler, finished telling an embarrassing

story about her rockstar boyfriend, Zeppelin Foster. Along with

Emerson and Laurel was the third in their trio of fangirls, the OG

fangirl, Raelyn Burton-Jameson. If it hadn't been for her whirlwind

romance with her favorite actor, Austin Jameson, none of them would be sitting in this panel talking about their books.

The Red Moon convention had invited the three of them to have a panel and booths at multiple of their conventions. This was their first time talking about their collective books inspired by their real life relationships. Their moderator, Delaney Bishop, was a debut author herself and shared the same agent as the rest of them. Raelyn and Laurel both had told their stories about how their books, Project Fanfic and Project Rockstar were inspired. Now Delaney turned her attention to Emerson.

"Alright, so we've had our celebrity romance and our rockstar, friends to lovers romance. Now we're going to move to Emerson."

She smiled, "I guess I'm bringing the sports, fake dating romance."

The crowd cheered as Delaney chuckled, "First, I want to know how you went from working in a school as a social media coordinator to working for the Vancouver Explorers and dating All-Star, Pacey Tucker. Which you were a fan of before you ever met him."

"All true. As many of you know my dad is a retired pitcher from L.A. We always watched the Dodgers and from the first game

Pacey played in I was a fan of him."

"Were you nervous when you first met him?"

Emerson scoffed, "I was until he opened his mouth and was a complete jerk. You know what they say, never meet your heroes but what they don't tell you is how not to fall in love with them."

Raelyn and Laurel both said, "Preach sister!"

Everyone in the room was laughing and from her side of the stage, Emerson could see Pacey shaking his head. Zeppelin and Austin patted his back as they joined in with the crowd laughing.

"In all honesty, much like Raelyn and Laurel, our story is a whirlwind. We had a rocky start but in the end that became the strong foundation of our love."

The crowd awed as Delaney asked, "What was journey like? Working in a Chicago school district to moving to Vancouver, Washington to work for the Explorers?"

She glanced over to Pacey who was waiting patiently along with the crowd, "Do you all really want to hear this story?"

The crowd, Raelyn, Laurel and Delancy all responded at the same time.

"Yes!"

Emerson smiled, "Alright, well it all began on a normal day in March…"

Emerson

Ring, Ring, Ring

The first bell rang at Campbell High School and Emerson was settling into her makeshift office for the day. Her home base was the high school where she worked out of the Journalism classroom thanks to Mr. Daly. His students called him, Chief, for his titled as Editor-In-Chief for the school newspaper and yearbook, was kind enough to turn his extra storage space into a small office for her.

"Good morning everyone."

Emerson closed the door as Mr. Daly began his class. She popped in one of her earbuds and put on her most recent audiobook. The best part of her day was the first two to three hours when she could sit at her computer and lose herself in her work. Looking down at her planner, she went over her checklist of tasks to complete.

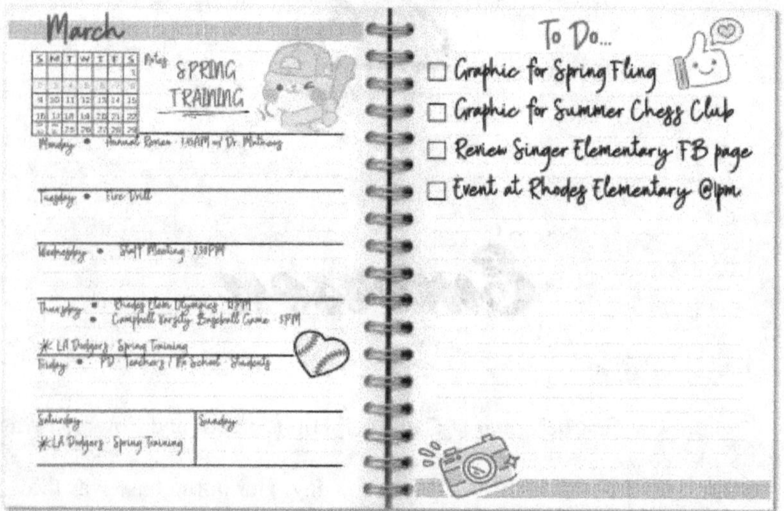

Emerson pulled up her design program and began working on the few graphics she needed to make. It felt good to let loose her creative side even if it was always in the same shades of purple and silver. A notification popped up on her computer with an email from her communications director.

Emerson groaned while pulling up Singer Elementary first since it was already on her to do list. Sure enough, Mr. Jay Walker had been posting rude comments about the district hating white people.

"People are truly crazy nowadays." She muttered hiding the comment he left and then blocking him from the page.

After an hour of going through all the elementary and intermediate school's pages, she needed a break. Peeking out her door, she found the students working independently at their desks. She gave

Mr. Daly a salute as she left his classroom and headed to the break room.

"Hey Emerson, how are you?"

Looking up from her phone she saw the newest teacher at Campbell High leaning against the door frame of the break room. Casey Mathews was charming, handsome and everything she should have found attractive in a man except she didn't. Whenever he came around her this year, her mind always threw up red flags and lit a neon sign saying *RUN*.

"Hi Casey, I'm doing good. You?"

A smirk appeared on his lips sending an uncomfortable chill down her spine.

"I'm good. Could be better though…"

"Oh really? How so?" She couldn't help being friendly even though he made her skin crawl.

He pushed himself off the door and sat down in front of her. His hand slid over hers, gripping it tightly.

"Well, you could say yes to having dinner with me tonight."

"Emerson, there you are! I need you in the office for a

moment."

She looked up to see the office secretary, Jacqueline, swooping in like a knight in shining armor.

"Okay, I'm on my way." She pulled her hand from Casey's grip, "Sorry, but I need to go. Also, I'm having dinner with my brother and dad tonight, sorry."

"Oh. Okay, maybe another time."

Emerson nodded without saying anything and followed Jacqueline out of the break room. Once they were in the office she leaned against the desk.

"You're officially my hero. Thank you."

The older woman patted her hand, "No problem. I've been having to save more female teachers from that guy than I care to admit. I think I'll have a conversation with Dr. Keller about him."

"I think that would be a great idea. I also think I'm going to head out to Rhodes before I have another run in with him. Tomorrow your morning coffee is on me." Jacqueline went to protest but Emerson held her hand up, "Nope, I insist."

"Thank you Em, that is very sweet of you."

Emerson spent her afternoon filming and taking pictures of the Rhodes Elementary Olympics. She loved seeing all the kids participating in the activities and how the older kids were helping the younger ones. She drove back to the high school parking near the baseball field. Memories of spending many nights at baseball fields with her dad and brother filled her mind. As if she had conjured her brother from those memories, her phone began to ring.

"Hey Em! Are you home?"

Her younger brother, Everett, was a student at Northwestern studying the get his second bachelor's degree in criminal justice while finishing his residency at Northwestern Memorial Hospital. He was coming home for the weekend to watch the first few games of Spring Training for the White Sox and Dodgers.

"No, I'm at the ball field. I need to get some shots of the baseball team for a post tomorrow. I should be home by the third or fourth inning."

"Will you pick up some dinner on your way? Apparently, dad is trying to burn the house down again."

"I even wrote down all the instructions for him this time," She groaned, "Yes I will pick something up. See you soon."

Ending the call, all she could do was laugh at the two men in her life. Her dad, Will, was an amazing father even if he wasn't always there. For most of her and Everett's childhood, their dad played professional baseball for the Dodgers. They had lived in Los Angeles for most of their lives until one fateful night when their world changed forever.

Emerson shook the memories of that night out of her head and she grabbed her camera. She couldn't think about her mom or the night she died. It had taken years of therapy to get her to where she was now in her grief journey. She wanted to keep herself from falling down that dark path again.

By the end of the third inning, Emerson was heading back to her car with some really great photos of Campbell High's varsity baseball team. A lot of the boys were talented enough to have scouts out in the stands. She was sure their names would be scrolling across her TV screen one day soon. Stopping by their normal diner for a takeout order the old cook only chuckled when he saw her walk in.

"Your old man called it in about an hour ago."

She thank him with a generous tip and headed home for the night.

Before she walked through the front door, Emerson could hear her dad and Everett cheering from the living room. Walking past them she made her way into the kitchen and started unloading their dinner. A louder groan echoed into the kitchen as she grabbed three bottles of beer from the fridge setting them on the serving tray with the food.

"How they looking?" She asked, sitting on her favorite chair.

Next to her was Everett and her dad on the couch, "Like they're two short of a World Series team." Everett grumbled.

"Sometimes, the players get a deal too good to pass up." Her dad took a beer and passed it to her brother then his plate of food.

Emerson looked at the screen to see the Dodgers were down 3-0 in the bottom of the sixth inning, "Wait… who got traded?"

Both men looked over at her conveniently taking a drink of their beers.

"No. You got to be kidding me?"

She pulled out her phone and started looking up the recent trade news from the Dodgers. Sure enough, three weeks ago her favorite player had been traded to the brand-new MLB team out of Vancouver, Washington.

"Oh, for fuc-"

"Watch it…" Her dad chuckled, "I really thought you knew already that Tucker and Knight had been traded to the Explorers."

She shook her head, "I've been busy and not regularly checking my MLB notifications. Honestly, I figured if any player was safe it would have been Tucker. He's been carrying the team for the last few years and Knight alongside of him."

Her dad leaned over towards her, "I spoke to my buddy, Nick, you remember him, right?"

She nodded, "Yeah, he was team manager for the Dodgers."

"Well, he is now GM of the Vancouver Explorers. He offered Tucker and Knight a hell of a deal to lead his new team. They're going to be a little green with a lot of minor leaguers coming up and he needed some seasoned players."

"Well, I guess I need to look up their jersey so I can get a new Tucker jersey. Do you know will he keep his number?"

Her dad nodded, "More than likely unless he wants to change

it. New team means he can have whatever number he wants."

Her dad turned his attention back to the pitiful game on the screen while Emerson looked up Pacey Tucker's Instagram account. He had no recent posts since the end of last season which wasn't unusual. One reason she liked him was because he kept his private life private. That and he was hot. She scrolled to one of her favorite pictures from last season. Pacey was standing in the on-deck circle getting ready to bat. He was mid swing when the photographer snapped the picture. Pacey had perfect form and when he was at bat he had hit a grand slam winning the game to get them into the Wild Card slot.

"Em, you're drooling." Everett chuckled as she threw a fry at him.

"And you're annoying as ever."

The next day, Emerson was thankful for there being no school due to professional development. This always gave her a day to catch up on any projects and edit photos for the social media pages. She was in the middle of going through comments on the high school page when her dad's name flashed on her phone.

"Everything okay?" She answered, hearing him laugh softly.

"Yes, everything is fine. I wanted to give you a heads up that there's absolutely no pressure to take what he's offering."

Emerson sat back in her chair, "What are you talking about?"

"My buddy Nick called me this morning about some issues arising with one of his players. He may be in the market to hire a social media manager for them. He asked me if I knew anyone and I…"

"You didn't…" She pinched the bridge of her nose, "Dad, please tell me you didn't offer for me to do it."

"All I said was you have worked in that field for many years in an educational setting. He asked for your number, and I gave it to him. Hear him out, he may be able to offer you a deal too good to pass up."

She sighed, "Fine, but I'm not making any promises that I'll take the job. You know how much I love my job."

"I know honey. Just after your mom's death, you stuck by Everett and me. I don't want you to miss out on living life."

Emerson's shoulders sagged, "I haven't missed anything, and I love my life. However, I'll hear him out and truly consider it if the deal seems right for me."

He chuckled, "Thanks Em. I'll see you later."

The call ended and Emerson let her head fall back against her chair. She was in her late twenties when her mom died, and her life had been put on hold. She had an entry level marketing job at a movie studio in Hollywood and had moved into her boyfriend's apartment. A year after her mom's death, her dad decided to move to Chicago to be closer to Everett and she moved with him. Never once had she regretted that decision or the life she built in Chicago. However, the closer to forty she was getting the more she realized how lonely she was.

Her phone chimed with a notification. "What the hell?"

Emerson opened the link from Google News however before she could read the article, her phone began to ring with a California area code.

"Hello?"

An older man spoke, "Emerson? This is Nick Steinberg, I'm

an old friend of your dad's."

"Hi Mr. Steinberg, how are you?"

He let out a long sigh, "Well I've definitely been better. I'm sure you've seen the news about Pacey Tucker."

She sat up straight in her chair. Was it possible he wanted her to be Pacey's social media manager.

"Yes, just now, but I haven't read the article yet."

"Well, that's why I'm calling you…"

Pacey

Pacey watched the clouds outside his window seat. Thankfully the

flight was enough time for him to play his current favorite playlist.

Sitting beside him reading one of the largest books Pacey had ever seen

was his teammate and best friend, Sam Knight. It was moments like

this that he wished his introverted friend was a little more talkative and social. He knew he could start up a conversation about everything going on in his head. He also knew this was Sam's favorite time to be in his own little world.

Staring out the window, he thought about the past month and how things had changed so quickly for him. When Nick had called him and Sam up to the GM's office they thought for sure they were going to get the retirement speech. Sure, he and Sam were a few years past the normal prime player age, but they could train and play as hard as any of their younger teammates. They were stunned when they offered them both deals for five years and $125 million to play on the newest acquired professional team out of Vancouver, Washington.

Guarantee five more years of playing professional ball was all Pacey needed to hear. The money didn't hurt either since he was already up for contract negotiations. He and Sam both spoke to their agents who went through all the fine print and before he knew he was planning to move some of his stuff from his home in Los Angeles to an apartment in Vancouver. He had spent some of the off season in his new place to get to know the city. Thankfully, Portland was only a twenty-minute drive from Vancouver for when he wanted a night out of fun.

There was a tap on his noise canceling headphones. He glanced over to see Sam putting his book back into his bag.

"We're landing." He said as Pacey noticed they were in fact descending through the clouds.

He quickly placed his headphones and phone into his bag while grabbing out his favorite hat. He chuckled as Sam placed his black rimmed glasses on.

"Clark Kent mode activated." He laughed.

Sam rolled his eyes, "I actually need them to see, dumbass."

There was all kind of press outside the airport as many professional players were flying into Phoenix International Airport for spring training. For once, Pacey was grateful that he wasn't flying with one of the most recognizable teams. He and Sam were able to grab their bags and find their driver before the press knew they were there. The drive to the hotel near Peoria Sports Complex was short and soon Pacey found himself alone in his room. It was still early in the evening when he walked down to Sam's room knocking on his door.

"No Pacey." Sam answered.

He walked inside, "You don't even know what I was going to ask."

Sam closed the door, "You're dressed in your normal going out to the bar clothes. So, again my answer is no."

"Come on Sammy, we need to go build moral with our new teammates. They need our guidance in all areas of being a professional baseball player."

His friend rolled his eyes, "You know I hate going out. I don't like bars or drinking or people."

Pacey slipped his arm around Sam's shoulders, "Two drinks, an hour tops. Come on, you know the first week of training sucks and we need one last hurrah before we whip these young guys into shape."

Sam groaned, "Fine. An hour and I'm bringing my Kindle with me."

Pacey went to protest but Sam narrowed his eyes at him, "Alright fine, bring your Kindle but then we stay for an hour and a half to have three drinks."

"Deal. Now get out of my room and I'll meet you downstairs in ten minutes."

"Perfect! I will text a few of the guys to see where they landed."

Within a half hour, Pacey and Sam found themselves sitting inside a crowded bar down the street from the hotel called Bats & Brews. Most of their team were spread throughout the bar playing pool or darts, laughing and enjoying their night. Pacey was sitting with Sam and their catcher, Jared Stanley. He had played with them a few times over the years from the minors.

"Heads up Tucker, cleat chasers at your six o'clock." Jared chuckled.

He glanced back to see three young ladies making their way towards their table. They were dressed to impress with short, skin-hugging skirts and tops that left little to the imagination. The leader of their little group had long, blond hair and enough make-up on to make it look like one of those social media filters.

"Are you Pacey Tucker and Sam Knight from the Dodgers?" She asked as her two friends giggled behind her.

"Guilty, however, we're now playing for the Vancouver Explorers." Pacey looked over at Sam who was trying to hide behind his e-reader, "I'm guess you ladies are big baseball fans."

They all giggled and nodded, "We sure are. Never heard of the Vancouver Explorers… I thought Canada only played hockey."

Pacey chuckled when Jared nearly choked on his beer, "They play all sports, but our team is in Washington."

The girls looked at one another for a moment, "So, like where the president lives?"

This time Sam laughed then took a long drink as Pacey stood up, "Um, no. As in the state of Washington. Anyway, ladies let me lead you over to the bar and buy you a round of drinks. I can introduce you to some other players who I know would love to be in the presence of three gorgeous ladies."

As the girls walked in front of him, Pacey turned around to his teammates, "You two owe me."

When he came back to their table after delivering the girls to the much younger players on the team, he found a beer and tequila shot waiting for him. They ended up staying at the bar until last call and then the three of them head back to the hotel for the night. Waving goodnight to Sam and Jared, he walked into his hotel room and decided a shower was needed before he went to bed. Washing off the stench of the bar and college girls who kept coming up to them. He dried off and climbed into bed knowing that the next morning was going to suck.

"Again!" Coach yelled.

"Fuck. Me." Sam gasped, wiping sweat from his forehead.

They were doing their second repetition of sprints running 127 feet and Pacey was feeling the full weight of his decision to go out the night before. Him, Sam and Jared were the oldest of the players and it was showing. The twenty-somethings were all bright-eyed and bushy tailed arriving to the training center. Meanwhile, Pacey, Sam and Jared all looked like extras for a zombie movie and now they were starting to smell like it.

"Next! Tucker!" Coached called out.

"Shit."

Pacey took off running from home plate to first base round it and pushing through to second and then finally third. He was standing next to the third base coach trying to catch his breath.

"Tucker, you gonna survive?"

Pacey nodded holding his thumbs up wheezing, "Y-Yep."

"Y'all know if some of your teammates hadn't posted on their night out online then he wouldn't be pushing you guys so hard."

Sam had stopped beside him falling to the ground trying to catch his breath. Pacey held out his hand to help him up, but Sam smacked it away.

"Just let me lie here and die."

The coach and Pacey both laughed helping Sam up, "No dying on us now, Knight. Why don't you two take a break and get some water to cool down."

"And show the younger guys we are weak, hell no. We got this, right Sammy?" Sam was already headed towards the bench and water station, "I guess a little break won't hurt us."

As the day went on, Pacey and Sam kept pace with one another as a competition like they had always done in years past. For Pacey, he felt like he had more to prove being one of the senior players on the team. He wasn't old by any means at thirty-two but in baseball he might as well have been in his eighties. He wanted to show not only the younger players but the fans and media that he was just as good as anyone else on the field or better.

When the day was over, he headed off to the ice baths where Sam and Jared were already soaking. Stripping down to his underwear he stepped into the large tub of ice water.

"Fucking hell!" He yelled before lowering himself completely into the tub.

"Did you hear Danny and Allen out there? They ran the full 344 feet three times before finally stopping. I don't think I can do that." Jared said before dunking his head beneath the water.

Sam shook his head, "We can't compare ourselves to them. They are all ten or so years younger than us. We were exactly like them at that age when we first moved up to the majors."

"Mr. Logical." Pacey mumbled trying not to chatter his teeth, "All I know is that the three of us will be setting the tone and pace of this team. We need to keep up and earn their respect."

Sam and Jared nodded as silence fell between them. Once they were dressed and ready to head back to their hotel, their team manager stopped Pacey.

"Hey, can I see you for a moment?"

Pacey followed him into a small conference room where Nick Steinberg was sitting in front of a laptop. He was talking to someone who sounded a lot like his agent, Marcus Thompson.

"What's going on?"

Nick looked up, "Hey Pacey, we need to discuss something that has come to light."

Pacey sat down next to Nick seeing that it was Marcus on a Zoom call while also talking into his phone, "Okay, what happened?"

Marcus sent a link in the chat then came off mute, "Pace, read this interview that your ex just release."

"Lyn? You're kidding me, right? We broke up years ago. What could this interview have to deal with me?"

Nick clicked on the link, "You need to read it, Pacey. Afterwards we'll discuss the next steps we'll be taking."

Suddenly, Pacey's stomach started to twist, and he started to read the interview.

"What the fuck?" He looked over to Nick then to Marcus, "What the fuck!"

THE STARS OF TODAY
WITH PATRICK WYMAN

SHE'S A SURVIVOR

My interview with actress, Lyn Dexter, talking about her new movie, life and how she survivor an abusive relationship.

Patrick: So, let's talk about this new movie you're in. It's a little darker character for you. How was it preparing for it?
Lyn: Well, not that I like to share my personal life too much. I really pulled from my real life experience of being in a difficult relationship with someone who was very much like the main male character.

Patrick: Wait, are you talking about your relationship with Pacey Tucker?
Lyn: Being with someone like him can be hard. His playing schedule combined with my filming schedule put a lot of stress on our relationship and in the end I think it changed him.

Patrick: How so, if you don't mind me asking?
Lyn took a moment to wipe away tears falling down her cheeks.
Lyn: I'm sorry, it's hard to think about that dark time in my life. Pacey was very hard person to be with towards the end of our relationship. I was starting to rethink my decision of being an actress because I really thought I wanted to start a family with him. Now looking back, I'm very thankful that I never did.

Patrick: Pacey didn't want a family with you? I find that hard to believe that someone wouldn't want to be with you.
Lyn: You're too sweet. Pacey was focused on his career and anything that could or did get in the way of that he would...

She paused to collect herself from the overwhelming emotions she was feeling.

Lyn: He would lash out verbally or sometimes even physically. He scared me at times especially the last few weeks we were together. There was a major shift that happened and made me realize he was not the man I fell in love with originally.

Patrick: Are you saying he hurt you? Physically?
Lyn: Oh no, he didn't lay a hand on me. However, if he was practicing his swing in the house sometimes the bat would accidentally fly out of his hands. Then there was the time I was in the hospital for a few days for a procedure.

Patrick: I remember that. The press release said you were out for a surgery. Was that a cover up for something else?
Lyn: All I can say is that Pacey was very adamant about not having a family at that time and he did whatever he could to make sure we didn't have one. Including making me have a procedure I didn't want.

Patrick: Are you saying that Pacey Tucker forced you to have an abortion?
Lyn: Like I said, he didn't want a family and I did, but that didn't matter to him. Whatever Pacey wanted to happen is what did. That's all I'll say.

"LIKE I SAID, HE DIDN'T WANT A FAMILY AND I DID, BUT THAT DIDN'T MATTER TO HIM. WHATEVER PACEY WANTED TO HAPPEN IS WHAT DID."

ISSUE
N.56
THESTAROFTODAY.COM
LIFESTYLEWITHPATRICK.COM

Pacey

His room was dark much like his mood. Pacey had his favorite Heartstrings album on repeat as the hard beats and angsty lyrics washed over him. He tipped the bottle of bourbon back absorbing the hot trail it left in its wake down his body. His phone lit up the room as it had for the last hour. Texts and calls from various family, friends, Marcus and the last string of texts from Sam. Pacey typed a reply back to Sam to make sure he didn't do anything drastic.

He turned off his phone unable to make himself even text his

mom. He shouldn't be sitting here feeling guilt for something that

wasn't even true. However, that was exactly what he was doing.

Drowning his guilt in bourbon when he should be letting off some

steam from the anger bubbling deep down in his gut. Pacey grabbed his

tablet and pulled up Lyn's interview again. Rereading her words fueled

his anger making his skin burn. He went to her Instagram page and saw

her latest post promoting the interview had thousands of comments in support of her.

"Doesn't anyone care what the fuck I think or feel about this?" He muttered, tossing his tablet beside him.

He took another long drag from the bottle as he thought back on his meeting with Nick and Marcus from early in the day.

***

"What the fuck!" He yelled.

"Calm down, Pacey." Nick placed a firm hand on his shoulder.

Marcus finally sat down in front of his computer, "Pace, I'm getting with the team PR team to get out in front of this. What we need from you is to not react to it publicly."

Pacey crossed his arms over his chest, "You want me to stay silent while she drags my reputation and name through the mud. I don't think so. I should respond to her and tell everyone that it's a load of shit. That she's the one who didn't want the baby and had an abortion without telling me."

He felt everyone looking at him when Marcus finally spoke, "You never told me that."

"I figured she didn't want everyone knowing about it and I honestly didn't want to relive it. That was the tipping point for me to end things with her."

"I'm sorry you went through that, but right now we need for you to keep quiet on this until the PR team can come up with a statement to release."

Pacey could tell from Nick's tone that it wasn't a request but an order, so he nodded then left the room before he truly let his anger get the best of him.

***

That was how Pacey ended up with a nearly empty bottle of bourbon in a dark room listening to emo/punk music. He looked back down at his tablet and with another swig of liquid courage he pulled up his Instagram account to post a video to his stories. He stepped out onto the balcony of his room and letting the city lights illuminate his face up.

"I know a lot of you have read the interview my ex recently posted. I want you all to hear directly from me and not some PR bullshit statement. What Lyn Dexter claims is not true. I would never,

never force a woman to do anything. A woman's body and what she does with it is her choice. I have always been a believer in that. So, just know that you can't believe everything that is released to the media. She obviously needed some pressed stirred up for her lack worthy career. Nice try Lyn but find another pawn for your game."

Pacey hit next and added the hashtag #thetruthbetold then posted the video. Immediately, his comment section began filling and the courage from the bourbon was wearing off. Tossing his tablet on the couch, he made his way to his bed and fell into it not giving Lyn Dexter another thought.

He thought for sure the loud banging was all in his head until he heard his hotel door unlocked. He sat up quickly only to have the room start violently spinning. His stomach lurched upward, launching Pacey off the bed and into the bathroom. What little food he had in his stomach from the day before all came up with a stench of bourbon. He heaved into the toilet as he heard Sam calling out his name.

"I-In here..." He quickly stuck his head in the toilet once more releasing more of his stomach into the porcelain bowl.

"Damn Pacey… you really did it this time."

He sat back against the tub holding out his hand, "Could you hand me that towel?"

Sam took the towel and ran it under water before handing it to him, "I'm guessing you haven't looked at your phone this morning."

He shook his head before placing the cool towel over his face, "No… let me guess Nick and Marcus are pissed at me."

"You've gone viral."

"What?" Pacey pulled the towel off his face to see Sam standing in the doorway, "What do you mean I've gone viral."

"Your little Instagram video has officially hit over a million views and is on every media outlet there is. I'm sure coach and a few others are going to want to talk with you when we get to practice. Also, your mom is threatening to fly down here if you don't call her back."

Pacey sighed, "Do I have time to shower and get my shit together?"

Sam chuckled, "Shower and call your mom, yes. Ain't nobody have enough time for you to get your shit together. I'll be down in the lobby reading. We have an hour before practice."

He waited until he heard Sam shut and lock the door before he stripped off his clothes and got into the shower. Letting the cool water beat down onto him for several minutes washing away the nastiness of being upset and hungover. He finally went through his normal routine and got himself ready for practice. He turned on his phone seeing all the missed calls and texts. He skipped them all and hit his mom's number listening to it ring once.

"Pacey Tucker, it's about time you called me back! I have been going out of my mind with worry!"

"I'm sorry mom. I really wasn't in the right head space to talk last night."

He heard her sigh, "That's obvious with that video you posted. You should have called me or your dad. You know we will listen to you no matter what. Angry, sad, or however you're feeling. You come to us; you got that mister."

He sat back against the couch unable to handle the guilt pressing into his chest, "Yes ma'am. I'm sorry I didn't call you or dad."

"You're forgiven. Now, how are you? Answer honestly, no matter what."

"I'm pissed and embarrassed. Most of all, I feel guilty for something that isn't even true, and I don't know how to deal with it." He closed his eyes letting his head fall back against the couch, "I just don't understand why she would bring this all up now after a decade."

The silence that came from his mom was deafening. He checked his phone to make sure the call didn't drop.

"It's not surprising that she is using you to get more publicity. Your last few years in L.A. have you in the spotlight and now you've signed an amazing deal to play for a brand-new team. She saw an easy opportunity and took it." She paused for a moment, "Pacey, I want to ask you something even though I'm ninety-nine percent positive I know the answer."

"Ask away." He said, sitting up and looking at his watch to see he only had a few more minutes before he had to leave.

"Is any of what she says in her interview true? I remember what your dad was like back in his prime and how the two of you were a lot alike."

The pain that pierced his chest made it hard to breathe. His own mom thought he could be capable of what Lyn accused him of.

That hurt more than the accusations themselves.

"You really think I would do that to someone? Mom, you were with me when I bought the engagement ring for her. I was willing to drop my career to take care of the baby while she had a career. I never even wanted her to have an abortion. I wanted the family."

The sigh of relief that came from her sent another painful stab into his chest, "I didn't think so, but I had to ask."

"No, I get it. You think because I lived with dad after your divorce and always hung out with his buddies that I would be some asshole." He stood up, grabbing his bag, "I have to go to practice now. I'll check in with you later."

"Pacey, I didn't-"

"Goodbye mom." He ended the call and headed out the door to meet Sam.

When they arrived at the stadium, the press was hovering around the entrance where security was making sure they didn't get in. He and Sam walked into the locker room to find the team all staring at him. Somewhere murmuring to one another while others stayed far away from him. He threw his bag in front of his locker before turning around to address the elephant in the room.

"Look, I know y'all have questions, concerns, doubts, whatever. No matter what your personal opinion on my personal life I want you to know this. I'm here to play ball and win. If you don't think you can do that because of what is going on then I suggest that you take that up with the GM. I'm not going anywhere and when we're on the field it is all about baseball and nothing else. Got it?"

Sam and Jared were the first ones to sound off, "Got it."

The rest of the guys all followed their lead and they all got ready for practice without another word being said. Once again, coach had put them all through the ringer. Running drills for their positions and then running sprints as a team. The sun was high in the sky as they took their lunch break. Most of the guys sat in the shade outside drinking Gatorade and water. Pacey was sitting with Sam and Jared when he saw Nick and Marcus walking onto the field.

"Oh shit." He muttered, as his friends looked to see who was coming.

"Damn Tucker, you really fucked up this time." Jared chuckled.

Nick smiled as he walked up to them, "Sam, Jared, how has practice been?"

"Nightmare-ish." Sam answered making them all laugh.

Pacey noticed Marcus was not smiling or even attempting to pretend to be in a good mood. He looked down at his phone and stepped away taking a call.

Nick patted Pacey on the shoulder, "Well, lucky for Pacey we are here to relieve him from practice for the day."

His friends looked concern for him, "Will he be back tomorrow?" Sam asked.

"Oh yes and I'm making sure coach has him make up whatever drills he will be missing today." Nick smiled, "Pacey, if you could come with me. There are some things we need to discuss."

"Yes sir, let me shower up and grab my things."

Jared leaned over whispering, "Good luck."

"Thanks, I think I might actually need it."

Within a half hour, Pacey was sitting in the small conference he was in yesterday. This time, Nick had Marcus and the head of PR with him.

"Now Pacey, I think you know why we're all here." He nodded as Nick continued, "We all understand that this is difficult for you. We hope you know that you have the support of the entire team and staff here behind you."

Pacey let out a shaky breath, "I feel a but is coming."

Marcus leaned forward, "No buts only an ultimatum to keep your spot on this team."

"Am ultimatum?"

"Yes, an ultimatum that I'm hoping you will find agreeable." Nick stated as Marcus pulled out a file folder placing it in front of him, "For the rest of this season, we have hired a social media manager to work for you. She will be in complete control of what posts go up on your social media pages so that we don't have any more viral videos. She will be attending every game and any events you are a guest of. You will go to her with all posts you want to do for your pages."

Pacey sat there dumbfounded for moment before the anger hit him full force, "You hired a fucking babysitter for me. Am I getting that right?"

Marcus smacked his hand down on top of the folder, "Pacey,

this is serious. This is the only way to keep you on this team and employed in professional baseball."

"So, if I don't agree to this then I'm fired. Those are my choices, a babysitter or unemployment?"

Nick nodded, "Yes. You have the rest of today to make your decision. Focusing on playing professional ball while someone else takes charge of the media part or not playing ball for anyone ever again. It's up to you and we'll respect your decision. Even if it's to tell us to fuck off."

Pacey scoffed as Nick continued, "Moments like this make me grateful that when I played we didn't have to worry about this kind of shit. From one player to another, let someone take this burden off your shoulders and focus on playing the best fucking game in the world."

He couldn't help but respect the man in front of him for being completely real with him. He held out his hand and Nick took it.

"Thank you. I will have my answer in the morning before practice." He shook his hand before heading to the door and taking the rest of the day to make the biggest decision of his life.

Emerson

Emerson was sitting on a box packed with books looking around her now empty apartment. The last couple of weeks had been a whirlwind for her. Accepting the position to work for the Vancouver Explorers and her favorite player. Saying goodbye to all her co-workers and students at school was more emotional than she thought it would be. Even Mr. Daly had given her a hug and shed a tear saying goodbye to her. Now sitting there, thinking about everyone at school getting ready for the Spring Fling dance brought tears to her eyes.

"Em, you okay?" Her dad asked, kneeling in front of her.

Her dad and brother had packed the last of her things that were going to Vancouver in the moving truck provided by the team. Now, they only had the things she was going to keep at her dad's house and the few personal items she was going to take with her as she road tripped to Washington state.

"I think so. Am I making the right decision, dad? I mean, my life here is good. Should I really be changing it up at my age?"

Her dad took a hold of her hands, giving them a tight squeeze, "We both know that you put your own dreams and wants on hold when you moved out here with me and your brother. Your mom would have encouraged you to go out and see the world. To live life to the fullest. I think you should as well, and I regret that it's taken me this long to realize how I have taken advantage of you being here for me."

"Dad, you know I wanted to be here, right?" She hated the look of sadness filling his eyes, "I have never once felt like I missed out on anything by being here."

He smiled but it didn't quite reach his eyes, "I know, but now

I want you to start living life for you and not worry about your old man in Chicago. I'll be fine here, and Everett is only an hour away. You have taken care of us long enough. Now, is your time to take care of you and see the world."

"By moving to Vancouver, Washington. I'm sure there is a lot of world seeing there."

They both laughed as he stood up helping her off the box, "Traveling with a baseball team will take you to many cities full of culture and crazy baseball fans. I'm sure you'll see more of the world than you think. Now come on, let's get this last box into your car and have one last family dinner together for the time being."

Emerson's last night in Chicago was filled with her favorite pizza and ice cream along with a lot of laughter reminiscing on fond memories. She and Everett slept out in the living of her dad's house like they did when they were kids. Watching old movies and eating popcorn getting more of it on the floor than in their mouths. The next morning came the tearful goodbyes with a lot of hugs. Getting into her brand-new Jeep Grand Cherokee, Emerson waved goodbye to her family and Chicago heading out into the world by herself for the first time since her mom had died.

Over the next two days, Emerson drove through seven different states and stopped at more tourist spots than she could count. She spent one night in Cheyenne, Wyoming where she was able to mail off a lot of postcards to her dad and Everett. It was late when she finally drove over the Washington state line and into Vancouver. She pulled into the Hilton Hotel where Mr. Steinberg had a reservation for her until her new home was ready. After getting settled into her room and taking a long, hot shower Emerson called her dad to let him know she had made it to Washington in one piece. She talked with him for about an hour before becoming too tired and falling asleep as soon as her head hit the pillow.

The next morning, she woke up having room service and getting ready to meet with Mr. Steinberg and the director of public relations for the team. Marine Stadium stood next to the park it was name after off of SE Marine Park Way. The stadium reminded Emerson of Guaranteed Rate Field where the White Sox play except for it looked like the stadium had a roof. Walking into the main office lobby, she checked in with the front receptionist and was led up to the top floor of offices. Walking off the elevator, she found Mr. Steinberg waiting for her.

"Hello Emerson, it's so nice to finally meet you."

She shook his hand, "It's nice to meet you as well, Mr. Steinberg."

"Please call me Nick, I'm not big on formality around here." He chuckled.

Leading her down the hall into a large corner office that looked out over the field, "How was your trip from Chicago?"

"It was a lot of fun. I visited way too many tourist spots and spent a little too much money, but it was worth it."

Nick pulled out a chair for her in front of his desk, "Trust me, life is too short not to have fun. I'm glad your trip out here was good. Your townhome should be ready this afternoon. My assistant will meet you over there to make sure you have everything you need."

"That sounds great, thank you. Am I still flying to Arizona at the end of the week?" She asked, hoping that maybe she wasn't going to meet her favorite player so soon.

He nodded, "Yes, on Thursday morning you'll be flying into

Phoenix and then picked up to go to Peoria to meet with Pacey, his agent, and team manager, Henry Morrow. Speaking of Pacey…"

Nick sat on the edge of his desk, "Pacey is apprehensive about having someone shadowing him and posting on his social media."

"I would expect nothing less. I can't imagine how strange it would be knowing a complete stranger is going to be around you most of the time, documenting your life."

"I'm glad you sympathize, however, I'm afraid that you may get some push back from him. He wasn't really given a choice about having a social media manager."

Emerson began to bounce her leg nervously, "Oh, well luckily, I've worked in education so I think I'll be able to handle any temper tantrums he may throw."

Nick smiled, "This is why I liked you for this job. I want you to know if Pacey becomes too much for you to handle then call me directly. I'll personally take care of him."

He handed her one of his business cards with his cell number written on it, "Let me guess, my dad put you up to this, didn't he?"

"Boy, can't get anything past you," He chuckled, "We may

have had a conversation about this, and I may have agreed to treat you as if you were my daughter. Again, if Pacey or any of the other players give you grief then call me."

"I can do that. Speaking of my dad," She looked down at her hands in her lap, "Did he happen to mention anything about my favorite baseball player? Other than him, of course."

Nick leaned down patting her hands, "He may have mentioned Pacey being your favorite player, yes. I have no doubt that you'll be able to remain professional."

"Absolutely, though when I'm at games it will be a little harder to do since I'm invested with this new team now." She laughed.

"Hey, for being our first fan I think we're the lucky ones. I'm looking forward to having you as a part of our team and seeing the work you do. As our team grows we may be able to find you a permanent spot here with our PR team. For now, stop outside and speak to Whitley about getting the address to your new place and set a time for her to meet with you there."

They both stood and she shook his hand once more, "Thank you for this opportunity. I'm looking forward to seeing a glimpse of what life was like for my dad when he played."

Nick laughed, "Oh the times they have a change, but the game… the game never changes at the heart of it. I'll see you soon."

Emerson walked out of his office and stopped at the young woman sitting at a desk just outside his office door, "You must be Whitley, I'm Emerson Holbrook."

Whitley Stanley was stylishly everything Emerson wanted to be. She was wearing an Explorers tee with a black blazer over it. Making her casual tee look professional and comfortable. Her make-up only highlighted her natural beauty bringing out her warm brown eyes and rosy cheeks. Her long, auburn hair was pinned back by a clip and a pen sticking out of the side of it. Round, golden rimmed glasses were dangerously close to slipping off the end of her nose.

"Oh yes! Hi, I have your address right here and the keys to your place. If I can say, it's pretty amazing. The furniture is provided but if you find you don't like something or need something then we can write down when I meet you there. Speaking of which, when is a good day and time for you?"

Whitley reminded Emerson of her childhood best friend with

her sunshine energy and couldn't help to think that maybe she would be a good person to get to know better. She could use some friends in her life especially girlfriends.

"Um, any day and time works except Thursday since I'll be flying to spring training."

Whitley looked down at her planner that was completely color coded and decorated beautifully. Emerson found herself a little jealous and impressed.

"How about tomorrow at five o'clock? I could stop to get us some dinner, and we can discuss what you envision for your apartment."

"That sounds great, thanks Whitley." She grabbed a sticky note from Whitley's desk writing down her name and number, "Here's my cell. Just let me know when you're on your way."

"Sounds good, see you tomorrow!" Her phone started to ring and she waved as she answered it, "Mr. Steinberg's office, this Whitley, how may I help you?"

Emerson made her way back to her car and put her new address into her GPS. Following the directions she found herself only ten minutes from the Marine Stadium driving into a gated community.

There was a tag on her keys that had the gate code and once she

punched it into the keypad she was making her way down the quiet

street. She noticed that most of the homes here were brand new condos

or townhomes which is what her GPS had her pulling up to at the end

of a cul-de-sac.

"Wow." She murmured as she parked in the driveway.

There was a one car garage attached to a two-story townhome.

It had a small front yard and a walkway leading up to the front porch.

Suddenly, she envisioned a small swing or chair outside that she could

read in. Emerson walked up to the front door and unlocked the door to

her new home.

The inside was as beautiful as the outside. She walked into a

small foyer that had the stairs leading up to the second floor. To the left

she found a small study or den with built in bookshelves. To her right

was the living room that had a couch with a chaise lounge and a love

seat. There was also a TV mounted to the wall with a small TV stand

beneath it. She walked past the living room into the kitchen and dining

area. There was a kitchen island and more cabinets than she could possibly fill up. Next to the refrigerator was a walk-in pantry and next to the pantry was a door leading to a small laundry room that led out to the garage. That is where she found all of her things she had shipped from Chicago. All of her boxes were organized and stacked nicely.

The dining room had a large bay window with a bench seat that overlooked the backyard and sliding doors that led out to a deck. Beneath the stairs was a door leading down to a finished basement and storage area. Emerson was overwhelmed by how amazing this place was. She made her way upstairs to find two bedrooms fully furnished.

The spare bedroom had a full-size bed with a small bedside table and dresser. The master bedroom was gorgeous, and she could imagine spending hours there. There was a king-size bed with a beautiful wood frame and end tables on either side of it. The walk-in closet had a full system of drawers and hangers that led into the master bathroom. There was a standing shower along with a large bathtub and double sinks. Her favorite part of the room was the oversized chaise lounge that was next to the large window overlooking the front yard. She sat down on the chair, pulling out her cell phone and calling her dad.

"Hey Em, how is Vancouver?"

"Dad, it's amazing here. I can't wait to tell you about this townhome they have for me." She told her dad about her new home, promising to send him pictures of her favorite spots.

"How did your meeting with Nick go?" He asked, hearing a loud clank from a pot hitting the floor, "Damn it…"

"For the love of all good things please don't burn the house down dad." She chuckled as he continued to curse.

"Don't you worry about me, Em. Now tell me all about your meeting."

She couldn't help the smile spreading across her face, "It was good. I'm sure you already knew that though, right?"

There was a long pause, "I have no idea what you're talking about."

"Nice try old man, I know you probably made Mr. Steinberg promise to call you as soon as I walked out of the door."

"I did not! I called him about fifteen minutes after your meeting."

Emerson laughed, "I'm proud of you for waiting at least

fifteen minutes. That must have been hard for you."

"Now you're patronizing me." He chuckled, "Nick said he was very impressed by you and thinks you're going to fit right in."

"Well, we'll find out at the end of the week when I fly down to Arizona." She paused as the butterflies began the flutter wildly in her stomach again, "I-I'm nervous dad. You know how socially awkward I am and there is going to be a lot of people around Pacey Tucker and what if…"

She stopped herself before saying what was really going through her head.

What if he hates me and makes my life miserable?

"What if…?" He dad prompted her but then continued, "Em I'm sure you're going to make at least one friend. If not, Pacey Tucker then one of the other guys or their girlfriends. You remember how much of a family a team is. All you can do is be yourself. Remember if any of those players, especially Pacey Tucker, gives you grief or gets to handsy then you call Nick so I can fly to you and kick their asses."

A burst of laughter came out, "No ass kicking needed dad but thank you for being willing to. I love ya."

"I love you too, kiddo. Now I'm going to finish cooking this mac 'n cheese without burning the house down. Remember to send me those pictures from my scrapbook."

"You don't have a scrapbook." She rolled eyes, smiling.

He chuckled, "Well I gotta get me some kind of a hobby now that my kids all abandoned me. Let me know when you get to Arizona and try to have some fun."

After ending the call, Emerson realized just how much she missed her dad and Everett. As she stood in her new home, Emerson was grateful that they pushed her to take this opportunity. She began unloading her car and organizing where she wanted certain things. She also knew that she would need to go to the store to get some essential food for the next couple of days. When she was about to leave, her phone buzzed with a text.

3605555062: Hey Emerson, this is Whitley. I wanted to make sure you found your place and were able to get in. Text me back!

Hi Whitley! Yes and you were right this place is amazing! I was about to head out for some grocery shopping. Any recommendations?

Emerson saved Whitley's number and waited for her reply.

True to her word, Whitley showed up at her doorstep in fifteen minutes and they headed down Lewis and Clark highway. Emerson found out that Whitley also lived in the same community with her husband, Jared, the catcher for the Explorers. Not only did she live in the same community, but she was only a few houses down from hers. By the time they arrived at the nearest grocery store, Emerson and Whitley instantly became friends. They both loved books, baseball and a little teen drama show, Red Moon.

After shopping and driving around, Whitley dropped Emerson off at home when it was nearly dark out. Spending the afternoon with Whitley was the most fun she had in a long time. It felt good to have a friend nearby and she hoped that this was a good sign of things to come when she finally met Pacey Tucker.

LynDexter

● ● ●

Eva: *#canceltucker* Let's ban together for women's rights and the victims of terrible men

MariJo: Thank you Lyn for being brave and speaking out especially for those who feel that can't speak out. You're the true hero! *#canceltucker*

JonnieB: I'm thinking there is more to this story like Tucker's side which we have not fully heard. Let's hear the man out and get ALL the facts. *#chillout #cancelculturesucks #hearthemanout*

OliviaD: *#canceltucker*

Mark: This was over a decade ago so why do we care about it now? Let it go, Elsa. *#getoverit*

MissRemi: This interview made me sad :(I always hoped Pacey and Lyn would get back together one day. They were so cute together. *#PaclynStan*

Jayme: *#canceltucker*

CeeJay: Man, I was hoping Pacey Tucker was different from all the other toxic men in baseball. I'm so disappointment *#StandWithLyn #canceltucker*

StanTheMan: Get over yourself and leave Pacey alone *#getoverit*

AngieH: I stand with the woman brave enough to stand up to the man. You go Lyn! Fuck you Pacey Tucker  *#canceltucker*

Mickie: *#canceltucker*

80.5K likes
2 days ago

☺ Add a comment...   POST

Emerson

The flight to Arizona wasn't long enough for Emerson to really do anything but listen to her favorite band, Heartstrings, and try to distract her mind from running wild. She had lived around baseball players and teams all her life. However, meeting and working for the player she admired the most was terrifying. Her favorite song, Mistress of Running, came on and Emerson turned the volume up as loud as she could stand it. Before she knew it the plane was descending, and she was grabbing her bags to make her way to the stadium.

"Miss Holbrook?"

An older man wearing khaki pants with a black polo shirt embroidered Explorers logo on it and dark sunglasses stood holding a sign with her name on it. He was built like a professional wrestler and looked as intimidating as one.

"Yes, that's me." She waved towards him nervously until a wide smile appeared on his face.

"Hi Miss Holbrook, I'm Ben and I'll be driving you to the Sports Complex." He took her suitcase from her hand, leading her towards the exit.

She let out a relieved sighed, "Please call me Emerson or Em. It's nice to meet you."

"You as well."

There was a SUV waiting for them outside the doors. Ben opened the back door for her shutting it once she was inside the car. Placing her suitcase in the back, he got into the driver's seat and taking off towards the highway.

"I'm part of the team's security team. I'm personally assigned to Mr. Tucker and you. If you ever have any problems or issues please come to me."

"Okay... are there security concerns or is Mr. Steinberg worried about me fangirling over Pacey Tucker?"

Ben chuckled, "He didn't mention you were a fan, but that's good to know. No, there are no security concerns. This is pretty standard while you're traveling with the team."

"Good to know. Well, I look forward to getting to know you Ben."

"Me as well, Miss Holbrook."

"Emerson, please."

He sighed, "Emerson, then. When we get to the stadium, I'll take you to the offices where you'll meet with Coach, Mr. Thompson and Mr. Tucker."

The fluttering butterflies in her stomach began raging knowing that in a few minutes she would be face to face with Pacey Tucker.

"Nothing like jumping right into the fire."

Arriving at the stadium, Emerson was taken back to memories of watching her dad during spring training. The cracking sound of hitting practice or shouts from the coaches during training. She stopped for a moment taking it all in. The sun shining, bats swinging, pop fly's being caught and players running the bases. She couldn't help the wide smile spreading across her face. She looked over at Ben who had a small smile on his face.

"Nothing better than the sounds of the greatest sport in the world being played." She said, taking one last look on the field before walking beside him.

"Couldn't agree more Miss Emerson."

She narrowed her eyes at him, "I'll accept that."

He chuckled then opened the door for the main offices for her. Further down the hall they walked the more her stomach twisted and churned. Other than meeting the stars of Red Moon at a convention a year ago, Emerson had never been this nervous. Ben stopped outside a conference room where she could see two men talking adamantly with Pacey Tucker.

"Shit." She muttered.

"Go get 'em, Tiger." Ben patted her shoulder then opened the door giving her a little push inside.

"Miss Holbrook?" A man in a Explorers jersey and ballcap stepped forward, "It's nice to meet you. I'm Henry Morrow, team manager, but you can call me Coach."

She shook the man's hand as her eyes drifted to the first baseman currently glaring at her and shift her eyes back to the coach.

"Nice to meet you, sir. I look forward to working with you this season."

Pacey scoffed loudly and she noticed him rolling his eyes.

"Tucker, knock it off." Coach turned his attention back to her, "I'm looking forward to it as well. Especially since I played against your dad back in the day. Good player and man."

Again, Pacey huffed as the other man smacked his shoulder hard, "Grow up."

He walked up to Emerson with his hand extended, "I'm Marcus, this asshole's agent. You'll hear from me a lot about different ideas and things that need to run on Pacey's social media. I'm available by text or email mainly." His phone began to ring, "Sorry, I need to get this."

Coach pulled out a chair for Emerson across from Pacey,

"And this is Pacey Tucker."

She held out her hand, "It's nice to meet you, Mr. Tucker."

He glared at her, "Let's get one thing straight sweetheart, I don't think you're needed here. I've handled all my own social media accounts for the length of my career and been just fine. I don't care if you like baseball or your daddy played back in the old days. I think all of this is a big waste of time for you and especially for me."

Her heart shattered as he stood up without a second glance back and walked out of the room. After all the interviews and events, she had seen him in where he was a complete gentleman. Now to find that he was actually a grade A asshole was sort of devastating.

"I'm sorry about him." Coach sat beside her, "He's been under a lot of stress with the whole thing with his ex and the weight of this new team on his shoulders."

She sighed trying to hold back the tears threatening to fall, "I understand. If you don't mind, I would like to walk around the field and get a feel for the team. I know I won't be doing their social media or the teams, but it will help me with what to focus on for Mr. Tucker."

"Absolutely. I'll have Ben walk with you while I make Pacey

do extra sprints for being a jerk."

She smiled then waved to Marcus who paused his conversation long enough to say, "I'll email you some ideas I want you to work on immediately. We need all the good press and stories we can get right now."

He went back to his call before she could respond and followed Ben back down to the field. Emerson was glad she decided to wear her Converse and comfortable clothes. She pulled her Dodgers hat out of her backpack and slipped her long ponytail through the back of it. She slipped on her sunglasses then took out her notebook to start taking some notes on the team.

As she walked the first base line, Emerson found Pacey talking to pitcher, Sam Knight and Whitley's husband, Jared Stanley. She noticed him pointing at her and throwing his arms up in the air before Jared jabbed his elbow into his side. She looked away as a cold wave of dread and regret came over her. Maybe she had made the wrong choice to take this job.

"Tucker! Two sets of sprints, now!" Coach yelled out.

"Coach, really?!" Pacey called back as he walked towards

home base.

"You want it to be three? Get going!"

Emerson was pretty sure Pacey muttered some curses before stepping on home then taking off to first base and back. She couldn't help to admire him as she stood near the batter's circle. His six-foot four body was in great shape. His sunkissed skin was glistening in the afternoon sun and his baseball hat with the Explorers emblem hid the bright olive eyes she knew he had and short dark chocolate hair. His training jersey was tight around his broad shoulders and chest along with his baseball pants that covered his long, muscular legs. She hated that he was even more handsome in person and an even bigger jerk.

When he finished his last sprint, he rolled to the ground near her feet panting.

"Take a picture sweetheart, it will last longer." He snapped.

She was taken back by his hostility towards her that all she could do was gawk at him even more. Sam walked over to him and helped him off the ground.

"Pacey, be nice. She's probably offended by the awful stench coming off you." He chuckled as Pacey shoved him.

"Like you smell like roses. Go back to pitching practice, Knight."

She saw a small glimpse of a smirk on Pacey's lips as he shoved his friend playfully. Once his back was to her, she wrote down a note about featuring their friendship on his pages. Emerson walked back to Ben who was standing in the dugout.

"I think I'm good here. Do you mind taking me back to the hotel so I can do some research on my own for the night?"

"Sure thing, Miss Emerson." He turned towards Coach who had down from the field for a drink, "I'll be back for the three idiots later, Coach."

He gave him a thumbs up before heading back out on the field. Ben led Emerson off the field, but she took one look back at Pacey, whose eyes were locked onto her. They stared at one another for what seemed like an eternity and then he turned his attention back to Jared who was talking to him. There was something about the way he looked at her that made her heart flutter. She pushed the feeling deep inside of her and followed Ben back to the car.

Once she settled in her hotel room, Emerson checked her

email to find a few from Marcus already. The first few were detailing Pacey's social media account information and allow her access to it. Then there were his sponsorships and endorsements that needed to be regularly featured. The final email had a few mediocre ideas of personal posts she could feature to gain some support from the whole ex-girlfriend interview.

She spent a good part of her afternoon and early evening reviewing Pacey's social media activity and the list of sponsors and endorsements he had. Branding was a key component to gaining popularity on social media. If you had a unique brand or feature then your page would do well. It was keeping relevant in a day in age of a society having the attention span of a squirrel. She decided to head down to the hotel restaurant for dinner and working on her laptop.

Emerson walked in and immediately recognized Pacey's booming voice from a table nearby. She saw he was having dinner with Sam and Jared. All of them laughing over something Pacey had said.

"If you don't mind I'd prefer not to sit by them." She said to the hostess who nodded and led her to a table in the far corner.

She had a direct line of sight to Pacey's table. The waiter took her order, and she pulled out her laptop along with her headphones. Putting on her favorite playlist, she pulled up the document she had started up in her room. She was trying to think outside the box of posts he had used regularly on his pages. Pacey was actively on the board for a non-profit who helped teens get the mental health resources they needed. He was also known for donating to various charities for homeless children and teens, youth baseball leagues in low-income communities and his alma mater, University of Texas-Austin, had the Pacey Tucker Baseball Scholarship for incoming freshman to play baseball for the school.

On the outside he seemed like a great man, but the man Emerson met today seemed the complete opposite. The waiter brought out her steak salad as her phone buzzed with a text.

Dad: How was your first day?

It was... eye opening...

Dad: Oh no. What happened?

"Stalking me already?"

Emerson looked up from her phone to see Pacey's dark eyes narrowed on her. She immediately shook her head.

"No, I'm having dinner and working on a plan to save your career."

"You? Save my career? Sweetheart, my career doesn't need saving and I don't need some cleat chaser stalking me pretending to do 'work'"

The way he called her sweetheart got under her skin, "Actually, your career in the public eye needs some superhero level rescuing. Lucky for you, I packed my cape. As far as being a cleat chaser, how would you even know if I was a fan of yours? Or does your over inflated ego make your think that every woman in the world is automatically chasing after you?"

He scoffed, "First off, I don't need rescuing. Second, the Dodgers hat you were wearing today had my number on the back of it so you made it pretty obvious that you're a fan."

Shit. Emerson forgot that she had ordered a special edition of her hat that featured Pacey's number on it. Well, no denying it now.

"Sure, I'm a fan of yours. I have been your whole career because my dad is a fan of yours. However, now I get to tell him that his favorite baseball player is nothing but a huge asshole."

Emerson stood up from the table without touching her food and grabbed her things, "Suddenly, I'm no longer hungry. Goodbye Tucker."

"Awe, don't go away angry sweetheart, just go away." He called out as tears began to stream down her cheeks.

Once she was in her room, she allowed herself to shed the tears freely before splashing cold water on her face. Her phone started to ringing and she saw a picture of her and her dad on the screen.

"H-Hey dad."

"What did he do? Do I need to fly out there and kick his ass?"

She laughed, "Oh dad, I think I made a huge mistake."

Emerson told him all about meeting Pacey and he had a few choice words for the baseball player who was his favorite.

"What do I do? I don't know if I can handle him mentally day to day with this back and forth hostility."

He grunted, "You hold your chin high and do the job. Prove to him that hiring you was the best decision the team made for him and save his ass from the court of public opinion. Take no shit from him and go toe to toe with him to put him in his place. You are strong enough to overcome some jerk baseball player with a bruised ego. I believe in you. You got this, Em so kick it in the ass."

She smiled, looking at her reflection in the mirror, "Thanks dad."

"Any time Em and if you need me to come kick his ass just say the word. I'll be on the next flight out there."

"I love ya, dad."

"Love you too, Em."

The next morning, Emerson sent an email to Marcus to have a meeting with him and Pacey before their afternoon game. She was going to do exactly what he dad told her to and not let Pacey Tucker get the best of her. She pulled out her favorite baseball themed tank top and pulled on her black blazer rolling the sleeves up to her elbows. She wore a pair of straight leg jeans and her Converse. To finish it off she pulled out her Dodgers hat and pulled her long hair through it the back of it.

Pacey and Marcus were waiting for her in the conference room when she arrived. Pacey was suited up for the game while Marcus was typing on his phone.

"Alright sweetheart, what am I doing here when I should be prepping for my game."

She smiled at him, "I wanted to let you know we got off on the wrong foot yesterday. I was a little star struck by meeting my favorite player in the league."

Pacey chuckled, "So, you've reconsidered your place here."

"I have and I wanted you to be the first person I told."

Marcus interrupted, "Miss Holbrook, please don't tell me you've reconsidered the offer you agreed to."

"Oh no, I haven't." She stared down at Pacey, "I want you to know that I don't care your thoughts or feelings on my job with this team. I don't care if you're going to act like a big baby and throw a temper tantrum. I'm here to do a job and I intend to see it through to the best of my ability."

Pacey started to say something, but Emerson continued, "That job, Pacey Tucker, is to make all the fangirls love you again and the baseball fans to take you seriously during this season. So, this is going to be how it goes from here on out."

"Oh please, tell me how it's going to be, sweetheart."

"First, any and all social media posts have to be approved by me first. No going rogue or late night, drunken videos that go viral. I agree that I will never post anything on your pages that isn't approved by you first. I will stay out of your way as much as I can and you will let me do my job to make you look good."

"You done?" He asked standing from his seat.

"No, if you don't play by my rules then I'll take over all your accounts and change the passwords, so you don't have access to them anymore. I will post whatever I feel will make your fans love and respect you again. Got it, Tucker."

He leaned forward mere inches from her face, "We'll see about that sweetheart."

"Oh, and one more thing." She smiled up at him, "Call me sweetheart again and I'll go out on the field and show them what a real first baseman looks like."

She turned away from him heading out the door before calling out, "See you on the field Tucker!"

"Yeah, you will fangirl!"

Emerson heard Marcus chuckling then say, "I like her."

She smiled, heading down to the field and taking her spot in the stands where she could capture some photos from the game.

Pacey

It had only been a little over a week and already Pacey was irritated seeing Emerson everywhere he was. She always had her phone pointed at him or her eyes locked onto him writing notes in her notebook. He felt like an exhibit at the zoo rather than a baseball player. With only two weeks until the home opener he needed to focus on his team and not the frustratingly sexy fangirl following him around.

He glanced up to see her walking towards Sam. She was comfortable around the players almost like she had been around a team before. She was wearing her normal outfit for taking photos out on the field. Her knee length black shorts hugged her body in all the right places especially her toned legs and perky ass. Today's T-shirt of choice was an Explorers baseball tee that was tied off to one side. Her long hair was wounded into a tight bun coming out the back of her baseball hat that his number was shining like a beacon in the night.

Pacey felt his compression pants tightening and adjusted himself. He hated that he was forced to have her follow him around but even more he hated the fact that he wanted her. He thought by now she would have giving up on her little no posting rules. Pacey had posted pictures and videos on his Instagram and other social media accounts without consulting her. She had done nothing but reminded him in passing to clear it with her first.

Sitting out in right field stretching and warming up for their last full day of training. He heard Emerson laughing at something Sam said. He had never seen his best friend willing talk with anyone let alone a cleat chaser. He seemed to be enjoying whatever conversation he was having with Emerson, and it was unsettling for Pacey. The sense of betrayal and jealousy was making his temper flair.

"Sam! Get over here!" He called out, as Sam waved goodbye to Emerson.

"What's up?"

"What the hell do you think you're doing?"

Sam stared him confused, "What do you mean?"

Pacey stood up, motioning towards his annoying shadow, "Talking with the enemy. Remember, I'm trying to get her to quit so I don't have to deal with her anymore."

His friend rolled his eyes, "You know, maybe if you were acting like a complete dickhead and got to know her you'd realize she's actually pretty cool."

Pacey barked out a laugh, "Cool? Her? She's a cleat chaser, Knight. A chaser who happened to get the opportunity of a lifetime to follow me around and get paid for it. That's not cool, it's stalkerish."

"Have you even seen the posts she's done? Or read the comments from fans? Before you judge her maybe take a look at what she's doing for you."

He watched Sam walk off, heading the pitcher's mound. Pacey could count on one hand the number of times Sam had stood up to him and he immediately felt guilty for even thinking Sam wasn't on his side. However, he didn't believe that Emerson could have made that big of a difference in such a short time. He made a mental note to check his socials closely to see what Sam was talking about. For now, he headed to first base as Coach called for the whole team to play a scrimmage game.

When it was time for Pacey to bat, he heard his walk-up song start to play from the dugout. Looking back, he saw Emerson fumbling with her phone to silence it. When she looked up her cheeks were a cherry red that brought out the natural glow of her skin. If she had been a normal cleat chaser, Pacey would have been all over her. Everything about her was his ideal woman. Her tall, slender figure made his fingers twitchy to reach out and caress her soft skin. Her light brown eyes were always covered by sunglasses or bright colored glasses. She was gorgeous… and frustratingly annoying.

"Tucker! Are you gonna bat or stare at your assistant all day?"

Hunter Rowe called out from first base.

Pacey flipped him off and headed to the plate. Sam was pitching against him and he adjusted his stance knowing his usual pitch rotation. Sure enough, he was going with the slider first and Pacey timed his swing perfectly to send the ball flying out into the open space between left and center field. He took off running to first base making sure he bumped into Hunter on his way to second. Looking at the third base coach he was calling him to keep going he pushed his legs to run faster and slid into third right before Grant's glove hit his shoulder.

"Nice job Tucker!" Coach called out as the next batter walked up.

The adrenaline coursing through his body washed away all the guilt and doubt he had been carrying with him since Lyn's interview dropped. His cheeks were hurting from the smile on his face and when he saw the ball fly into right field, he took off towards home feeling normal for the first time in weeks as his foot touched the plate.

That night in his hotel room, he pulled up his Instagram profile to see that Emerson had indeed been busy posting a lot of coverage from spring training. Photos of him playing first base during games or at bat. One photo captured his swing perfectly and had nearly five thousand likes on it and hundreds of comments. Every photo she posted only highlighted the best moments of spring training and in a lot of them she was able to tie in a lot of his endorsements. Pacey could admit that she was good at her job, but he still hated having her around all day, every day.

He went through the stories she posted including him walking up to bat with his walk-up song playing. She had posted a few videos of him stretching on the field and joking around with Sam and Jared. He noticed a comment on one video that had his blood boiling reigniting his hatred for having a social media babysitter.

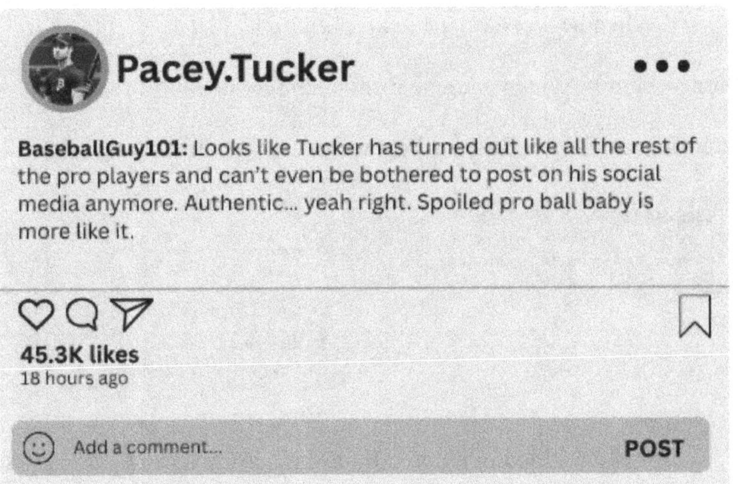

Pacey went to his stories and pressed the button to record.

"For anyone who thinks that this account is ran by anyone but me this is for you." Pacey flipped off the camera, "I'm all real and if anyone has a problem with who I am then I suggested you fuck off."

When he hit post an instant wave of relief washed over him. All the anger and resentment threatening to boil over was back to a hot simmer that he could handle. Not only would that video prove that the haters could hate all they want but it was probably the final push to get Emerson Holbrook to final quit. That was the last thought he had before falling into a peaceful sleep for the night.

When he woke up the next morning he had several texts from Marcus about his video and one from a number he didn't recognize. A victorious smile spread across his face as he typed his reply.

6305550612: Good morning Tucker, this is Emerson. I would like to meet with you this morning if you're available. 10am in the dugout. BTW, nice video

10am I'll be there and thank you

Pacey decided to ignore all of Marcus's texts and get ready to head to the field. He met Sam in the lobby whistling as his friend handed him a cup of coffee.

"You really had to go and poke the bear last night."

"I have no idea what you're talking about Sammy."

Sam rolled his eyes as they headed out to meet Ben and that's when he noticed a certain golden hair woman sitting in the front seat.

"Fuck." Pacey muttered as Sam chuckled.

"Serves you right, asshole." Sam opened the door behind Emerson, "Morning Em."

Pacey stared at his friend, "Em?"

Emerson looked over her shoulder at him, "It's the shorten

version of my name also known as a nickname and good morning Sam."

She went back to looking at her phone as he looked back at his friend who had a shit eating grin on his face, "Fuck you, Knight." He murmured.

Arriving at the field, Pacey noticed that Emerson headed straight to the offices while he and Sam walked towards the locker room. Her nonchalant demeanor on the ride there was unnerving. His only saving grace was that she was going to call Nick Steinberg to resign immediately.

"Why are you making her job so difficult?" Sam asked as they set their things down.

"Her job difficult? You try having a fangirl follow you around all the time taking videos and pictures of you. It's annoying. I want my socials to be the real me. I think fans respect that more than someone running them for me." He pulled off his t-shirt and pulled out his compression shirt from his bag.

Sam sat on the bench, "I think you should give her a chance and let her do her job. It can't hurt and Emerson is actually a really nice person if you get to know her. She knows the life and the game."

"So, what if her dad played ball back in the day. She doesn't know what it's like for us now or the stresses of a full season of pro ball. I think it's a waste of my time and the team's money to pay her to follow me around." Pacey finished pulling up his uniform pants and grabbed his jersey, "Now I have to waste time meeting with her before the game today."

Sam stood in front of him stopping him from leaving, "You know who her dad is, right?"

"Not specifically."

"Will Holbrook, ten-time gold glove player for the Dodgers."

Pacey's eyes snapped up to his friend's, "You shitting me? Didn't he retire after his wife died suddenly?"

Sam nodded, "Emerson's mom was on her way to pick her and her brother up from Dodger stadium when she was hit by a drunk driver. Will got the call…"

"In the middle of the fourth inning. I remember watching the game at home. Wow."

"So, before you go off and get his daughter fired or drive her to the point of quitting maybe have a little sympathy for her."

A deep ache spread over his chest. He couldn't imagine losing his parents even if they drove him completely crazy.

He sighed, "I will try but it doesn't change how I feel about her monitoring my life. I gotta go meet her in the dugout."

Pacey made his way up to the dugout where Emerson was sitting on the bench. Today, she had only a pair of black shorts and a golden tank-top covered by an Explorers jersey. Her normal Dodgers hat was nowhere to be seen replaced by an Explorers hat with her hair in a messy bun out the back of it.

"Alright, I'm here." He announced as she looked up from her phone.

"Great, I wanted to let you know I deleted the video you posted last night before it could go viral."

Anger rushed over him and out his mouth before he could take a breath, "What! Why the fuck would you do that? You had no right to delete anything from my page."

The smile on her soft lips infuriated him, "Actually, that is in my job description to monitor your posts. I also have asked you repeatedly to clear what you post with me first and you haven't even attempted to do so."

"I shouldn't have to clear shit with you. They're my accounts and I will post whatever the hell I want too. Regardless of what you, Marcus or anyone else thinks."

"I figured you would say something like that. I had a conversation with Marcus and Mr. Steinberg before meeting with you. We discuss a game plan moving forward for me as your social media manager."

He snarled his lip, "Does it involve you quitting and go back to wherever you came from?"

"No, however, I will make the same promise to you as before. I will never post anything that is personal and if I do want to share something more personal I will always ask your permission. However, anything related to you playing baseball or endorsement deals is fair game."

He towered over her trying to make himself look as intimidating as possible, "This has to be a breach of privacy or something. You shouldn't be posting about anything on my social media. You shouldn't even be here. More importantly, I don't want you here."

"That's too bad because I'm here to stay rather you like it or not. So, get over it and stop acting like a fucking child." She stood her ground with him.

"I don't need a fucking babysitter, fangirl." He seethed.

"Tucker, they don't pay me enough to babysit you, but since that's what you think my job is then I'll treat you as such. Now be a good little boy and follow the rules."

The smirk on her face had his fists clenching at his side, "Or what?"

"You'll find out soon enough. Have a good game Tucker."

She turned on her heel and head out of the dugout leaving him fuming. Pacey decided right then and there that Emerson Holbrook was officially the bane of his existence that needed to be dealt with. He pulled his phone out of his back pocket and went to pull up his Instagram.

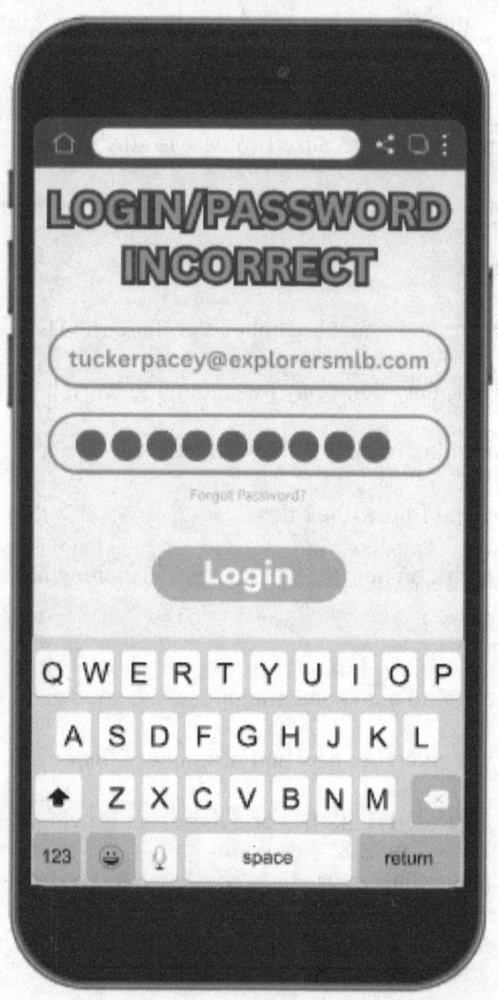

He tried logging in again and received the same message. He

knew he typed in his password correctly. Then it dawned on him as

Emerson caught his eye walking across the field. He tried logging into his other social media accounts getting the same login error.

"She didn't…" He said, trying to sign in one more time, "FUCK!"

He looked up to see Emerson smiling at him from the pitcher's mound where Sam was standing next to her. She waved her phone at him and flipped him off as Sam's laughter filled the stadium. Pacey narrowed his eyes at her as she high fived his former best friend.

"Oh, this means war fangirl."

Emerson

Being in complete control of a professional baseball player's social media accounts was a lot harder than Emerson thought it would be. Between scheduling, creating fun, interactive posts and graphics all while taking pictures of Pacey. She was passing out every night she returned to her hotel room. After her confrontation with Pacey, he had been playing nice but she was on edge waiting for the other shoe to drop. Keeping her word, she always consulted him before posting anything and took his suggestions or comments to heart. With only a week until the home opener, it seemed to her that he was more focused on his new team than her and she was thankful for that.

Sitting at the desk in her hotel room, Emerson was scrolling through the recent batch of photos she had taken during their game against San Diego. Pacey was on top of his game that day hitting two homeruns and making an amazing play throwing to Grant at third base. She looked at the photo on her screen of Pacey in the dugout icing his throwing shoulder after that play. There was a smile on his face but you could tell he was in a lot of pain. Emerson grabbed her notebook, writing down an idea of a feature on Pacey's pages.

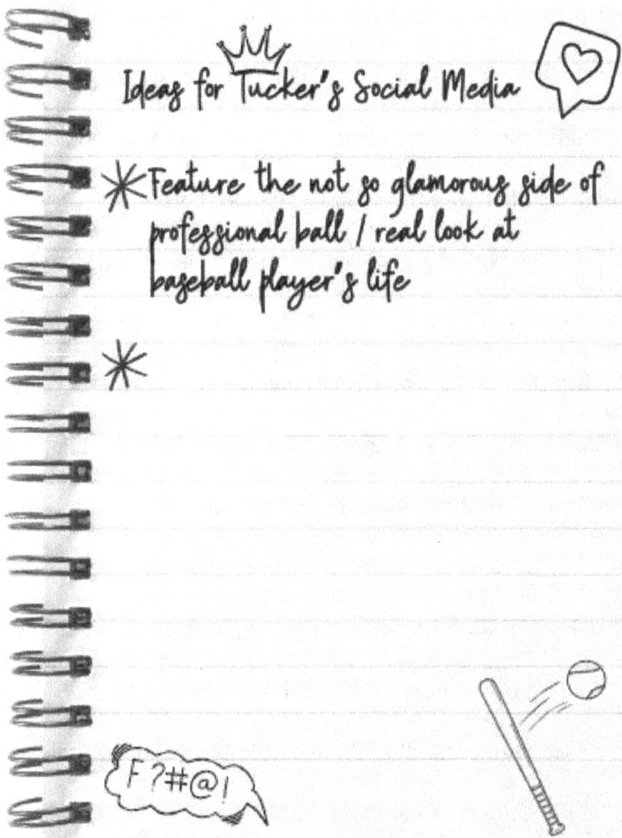

She wondered if Pacey would even go for that and made an additional note next to it to have Sam talk to him about it as well. She would never have believed that she would become close friends with quiet, reserved Sam Knight. He was known for keeping to himself and being an introvert. However, their common love for books had them talking for hours about their latest reads. She found him to be incredibly funny and smart as well. He reminded her a lot of Everett.

Leaning back in her chair, she sighed thinking about how much she missed hanging out with her dad and brother. Every Sunday since she left they would all get on Zoom and have their virtual version of Sunday dinner together. The Sundays where Everett was at her dad's were the hardest, making Emerson homesick. They were already making plans to visit her in Vancouver during one of the team's home game stretches. Until then, she was grateful for her Sundays with them on Zoom.

There was a knock on her door as Emerson looked down at her phone seeing it was nearly dinner time. Opening the door, she was surprised to see Pacey standing there and holding a bag of take out.

"Hello Tucker, what can I do for you?"

He rubbed the back of his neck, "I brought a peace offering and figured we could discuss a few things that will need to be addressed on my socials."

She chuckled, "That sounded like the most painful sentence you've ever spoken. Are you going to be okay?"

Pacey rolled his eyes, "Look, we can keep bickering in your door or I could come in and at least eat while we bicker."

Emerson stepped aside allowing him into her room. She did a quick scan to make sure none of her bras or underwear were out. She went to close her laptop when he stopped her.

"Why did you take that picture?" He pointed at the screen, "Do you enjoy seeing me in pain?"

"No, not particularly. I took that picture to show the authentic side of being a pro player. Everyone sees the homeruns, the double plays or sliding over home plate. We never see how throwing a baseball from first to third can hurt like a son of bitch. Also, it shows that even though you were in a lot of pain you were smiling through it. That is a lesson a lot of people need right now."

He turned towards with his eyebrows arched in surprise, "I guess I never realized you could get all of that out of a picture."

She took the food from his hand, a spark of electricity surging up her arm as their fingers grazed one other. Her eyes shot up to his seeing he felt it as well. Turning quickly, she headed to the small kitchenette to grab some plates.

"A random picture with the right message can tell any story you want it to. That's why I like social media. Ninety percent of the time people only share what they want you to see and know of their lives. It's the other ten percent that change the world."

Emerson saw her favorite order from the Chinese restaurant near the stadium, "How did you know this was my favorite?"

Pacey step beside her, leaning against the counter, "Sammy told me. You and he are like besties now."

She couldn't help trailing her eyes up his long, muscular body. He was in a simple, tight black t-shirt and black gym shorts leaving very little to the imagination of what was beneath the thin material. His soft laughter brought her out of her little moment.

"Once again fangirl, take a picture it will last longer." His low, raspy voice sent goosebumps over her body.

Shaking her head slight, she handed him a plate of white rice and bourbon chicken, "I have plenty of pictures of you. It's kind of my job. Speaking of..."

He pushed himself off the counter and headed towards the small couch in the room, "Yes?"

Taking her chicken and broccoli with fried rice to her bed, Emerson sat cross legged leaning against the headboard. She needed as much space between her and Pacey to keep her head clear of any sexy, intrusive thoughts.

"I have a few ideas for ways to get some positive press for you. However, I'm sure you're not going to agree with one of them, so I'll start with the one I think you will."

He opened a pair of chopsticks and expertly used them to pick up some rice with chicken. The way his fingers maneuvered had her mind racing with wild images. Deciding it was best for her not to look at him at all she reached over to the desk and grabbed her notebook. Glancing up for a moment, she noticed his eyes locked onto her. They were traveling up her chest and then looked away quickly when he realized he was caught.

Clearing her throat, "I thought maybe I could use a few of the pictures I took of you icing your shoulder, Sam having a bruise on his hip the size of Texas and Jared helping a San Diego player up after tagging him out. They show real moments with players, and that pro ball isn't all wins."

"I think that's fine. As long as you don't make us sound like wimps or anything." His eyes never left his plate as he spoke.

"It would be quite the opposite. I would probably schedule the post to go out after releasing your statement about your ex's interview. Once I have the draft from the PR team then I will come up with something similar that sounds more natural." She set her plate down making a few notes about checking in on the statement being released from the team.

"I would like to work on that with you, if that's alright."

Emerson nodded, "I think that would be great. We can schedule a time to work on it together."

"Now, what's the idea you think I'll hate?"

She looked over to see him smirking at her, "Vancouver has an independent minor league team that is more like a comedy baseball game. Right now, they are all the rage on Instagram and TikTok thanks to the Savannah Bananas team."

Pacey chuckled, "I've seen them before. It is definitely an entertaining game. So, you want me to go to a game and meet players or what?"

Emerson nervously chewed on her bottom lip, "They have special guests. Some throw out the first pitch and perform a dance with them. Others that are athletes will play in the game." She took a chance to look over at Pacey to see his reaction.

"You want me to play with the Vancouver team? Hmm…" He pulled out his phone typing something into it then laughing, "Vancouver Jesters, really? It looks like a ren fare and baseball had a love child."

She was surprised he didn't say no right away, but figured it was coming at any moment, "I figured it would look good for you being in a new city to support other teams there as well. I'm sure they have a jester's hat that will fit that big ole head of yours."

Pacey scoffed, "If and this is a big if, I were to do this when would it be and what exactly would I have to do?"

"Really? You're considering this?" she asked, stunned.

"Yes, depending on the when and what."

"The what is easy. You would play a couple of innings to bat and play first base. They will probably have you perform a dance routine with them which is usually something super simple. Then after the game would be walking with them to meet fans."

. "That sounds embarrassing but okay. When would this be?"

This was the part she knew he would balk at, "Next week. We would need to fly back to Vancouver on Wednesday, you would play Thursday night, and we would fly back early Friday morning for you to be here for your last spring training game."

His stare was making her uneasy, and she gripped the comfort beneath her bracing for him to start yelling. She watched him.take a deep breath as if to calm himself down.

"Do you think it's worth all the hassle for my public image?"

His question surprised her, "I think right now, any positive press is good for your image. However, I know that it's a lot of stress to put on you right before the home opener. I would understand if you didn't want to do this and I knew it would be a long shot for even suggesting it."

Pacey stood up, throwing his empty plate into her trash and braced his hands on her counter as he hung his head low. The urge to go to him and run her hand down his back, if only to let him know that someone was truly in his corner. She stood up, taking her plate and setting it on the counter beside him. Hesitantly, Emerson placed her hand on top of his.

"I can't imagine how tough it is for you to deal with your ex after all this time and carrying a brand-new team on your shoulders. I understand if you don't want to add anything else to your plate and we can keep to my posting schedule as is."

He rested his chin on his arm looking over at her, "I appreciate that. However, it might be fun to blow off a little steam before the home opener. I assume you'll be traveling with me."

She nodded, "Not as a babysitter though. Remember they don't pay me enough for that. Once we're in Vancouver, you'll be free to do whatever you want until the game."

He chuckled, "I mean blowing off that kind of steam would be great to, but I think I'll play it safe and stay in while we're there. Arrange the travel with Marcus and let the Jesters know that I'll be there with my Jester's hat and all."

Emerson laughed then noticed her hand was still on his and removed it quickly, "I will text Marcus right now. You should probably go get some sleep since you have an early training session."

"Wow fangirl, you even know my training schedule. Stalker much." He laughed.

"Why do you insist on calling me fangirl? Do you like the reminder that I'm a fan of yours?" She followed him to her door as he opened it and leaned against the door frame.

A breathtaking smile came across his face, "I like that your cheeks turn a glorious shade of red every time I call you that. Plus, you threatened me the last time I called you sweetheart, so fangirl it is."

She narrowed her eyes on him while smirking, "Fine. Goodnight Tucker."

"Night fangirl."

Closing the door, Emerson leaned against it trying to get the fluttering butterflies in her stomach to calm down. She hated the way Pacey could charm her in one moment and infuriate her in the next. After scheduling everything through Marcus, who was as surprised as she had been to hear Pacey had agreed to go. Emerson climbed into bed, falling asleep immediately and dreaming of playing a different kind of baseball game with a certain handsome player.

Marine Stadium • 1001 Marine Way • Vancouver, WA • 98660

OFFICIAL STATEMENT
IMMEDIATE RELEASE

First and foremost, I want to apologize to my team, those closest to me and most of all the baseball fans. My reaction to my ex-girlfriend's interview was harsh, rash and not thought through with a clear head. I'm sorry to anyone I may have hurt or offended with my behavior. I would like to think that most of our fans realize that even though professional athletes live a privilege life we are still humans. We make mistakes and at times hurt those we care about most. I am deeply sorry.

The allegations that have been brought to light are ones I take seriously and to heart. I was raised to respect others and especially women. I truly believe that they are the only ones who can make decisions about their bodies and should be the only ones to make those decisions. I hope that those who know me and the fans would see that what is being said is completely false. I'm hoping that a civil resolution between myself and Lyn can happen moving forward.

Finally, I want to thank my new team, my new city and all the fans who have been there from day one of my career. Your love and support through the good, the bad, and the ugly means the world to me. All I want to do is make you all proud and play a good game. I'm looking forward to this new season and I will see you out on the field.

Sincerely,
Pacey Tucker

 @vanexplordersmlb

 hello@explorersmlb.com

www.mlb.com/explorers

(360) 555-8269

Pacey

Pacey walked down the hall to Emerson's hotel room with his overnight bag in hand. They were flying into Portland early so he could have a little time off before playing with the Jesters. He knocked on the door unprepared to see Emerson when she opened it.

"Whoa…" His eyes took in the punk rock princess in front of

him, "Is this what you normally wear to fly?"

She was decked out in a Heartstrings band t-shirt with the sleeves cut off and a black tank top showing beneath it. Her long hair was in a high ponytail that gathered the wavy strands down her back. A pair of aviator sunglasses were resting on top of her head. She was wearing her normal, worn Converse that led his eyes up her toned, bare legs that ended with a pair of cut off, dangerously short, denim shorts leaving little to his imagination. He was more surprised to see her wearing black eyeshadow and dark red lipstick.

"No, but a friend invited me to the Heartstrings concert in Portland and I'm Ubering to it from the airport." She said, looping her arms through her backpack and carrying a duffel bag.

Pacey grabbed her duffel as she stared up at him, "What?" he asked.

"Nothing… um thanks for carrying that for me."

He watched her cheeks blossom into a rosy pink making his heart skip, "You're welcome. So, what exactly am I supposed to do while you're rocking out at a concert?"

She shrugged as they stepped into the elevator car, "I don't know. I figured you would go on to Vancouver and do whatever baseball players do when they have time off."

"Sleep. That's what we do." He smirked seeing the color on her cheeks deepen, "Get your mind out of the gutter, fangirl."

Suddenly, the air around them electrified as Emerson pulled her bottom lip beneath her teeth. Working with her the last couple of days, he had notice it was a nervous tick of hers and it drove him absolutely fucking crazy. Now, being in a small space with her, he could feel the strong pull between the two of them.

"My mind was nowhere near the gutter, Tucker. You obviously only have enough blood to flow one way and it's straight to your dick… like most men."

Well, it certainly was now as he felt his boxers-briefs get a little tighter. Of all the people for him to find fucking sexy as hell it had to be the girl he made the worst first impression on.

"No comment?" She joked as the doors opened, and they both took a deep breath as they walked off the car.

"Nope, because you ain't wrong."

Her laughter filled his chest with a warm, fuzzy feeling he

hadn't felt in years. Shaking it off, he placed their bags in the back of the SUV that Ben was in to take them to the airport. The flight to Portland wasn't long and they both spent it listening to their headphones. He had noticed that they both had similar taste in music which made sense since his favorite band was the one she was going to see.

Pacey tapped her shoulder to get her attention, "Who invited you to the concert?"

"I went to a conference for marketing and PR managers last year. One of the speakers was Thomas Reed, the manager of Heartstrings. During a social cocktail hour, we ended up talking and I mentioned that the band was my favorite. We exchanged info and he said if I ever wanted to go to a show to text him. I knew they were playing in Portland tonight, so I asked."

He stared at her in disbelief, "So, you're friends with the manager of Heartstrings? I gotta say, you are full of surprises."

She chuckled, "Good to know I can keep you on your toes. Anyway, Thomas gave me front row seats and backstage pass to meet the band."

Immediately Pacey remembered an article that recently was in Rolling Stone about the top five bad boys of punk rock. Zeppelin Foster was number one hooking up with fans and giving them one hell of night to remember then leaving them in the dust. Looking over at Emerson, he could feel his chest tightening with worry. He tapped her shoulder again as she took off her headphones again.

"If you interrupt my favorite song one more time I'm going to throw you off this plane."

He let out a halfhearted chuckled, "Duly noted. I think I should come with you tonight. You shouldn't go to a rock concert by yourself. You never know what douchebag will try something on you."

She let out a loud laugh, "Seriously? You're worried about me getting taken advantage of?"

"Yes. Unlike what my ex says, I'm not like other douchebags who see women as a piece of ass and tits."

Her smiled faded, "Pacey, I'm sorry. I didn't mean it like that, truly. I know you're not like that." Her hand gripped his for a moment, "But you don't need to worry about me. I've been to plenty of concerts by myself in Chicago. I'll be fine and I appreciate you offering to go."

He didn't accept her answer so he tried a different approach, "Okay, I'll be honest with you. It's not only because I'm concerned about your well-being. Heartstrings is my favorite band, and I would love to see them live. Not to mention the chance to meet Zeppelin Foster."

Emerson rolled her beautiful eyes, letting out a long sigh, "I will text Thomas once we land, happy? May I go back to my song now?"

"Rock on, fangirl." He held up the universal sign for rock on earning him a small laugh from her.

The moment they were off the plane, Pacey saw Emerson texting with someone. She looked over at him with a smile.

"Thomas sent their head of security to come get us. He'll have tickets and passes for both of us."

"Awesome, uh only problem is I didn't exactly bring concert clothes with me." He looked down at his gym shorts and hoodie, "We may need to make one stop before heading to the concert."

He watched as Emerson rolled her eyes but saw the smile on her face, "Let me guess, you only get designer brand clothes."

"Actually, I prefer Target. They usually have jeans that fit me perfectly and hold up well. I could care less about brand names."

She stared at him for a moment, "I guess I'm not the only one full of surprises."

He smiled, "No, you're not. Now come on, lets go find our ride."

Pacey picked up her duffel bag as they made their way towards the pickup area. There was tall, muscular man with short brown hair and sunglasses on holding a sign with Emerson's name on it.

"You must be Jake, I'm Emerson and this is…"

"Holy shit, Pacey Tucker." Jake said pulling his sunglasses on top of his head, "Huge fan of yours. I'm pretty sure the Dodgers are gonna suck this year without you and Knight."

Pacey shook the man's hand, "Nah, I think they'll be alright unless the come up against the Explorers then they're in for a world of hurt."

"I can't wait to see Alec and Rich's faces when they meet you. They're big fans as well. The car is outside waiting so we should go."

Jake led them outside to a waiting SUV.

"Jake, would it be okay if we made a stop at a Target along the way? We need to pick up a few things before the show." Emerson asked as they put their stuff in the back of the car.

Jake nodded, "Sure thing, we have a little time before I need to be back."

They stopped off at the first Target on their way to the concert venue. He pulled out his black ball cap and pulled it down enough that you couldn't quite see his eyes.

"You do know that doesn't help, right? You're a buff, six-foot-three man who screams professional athlete or douchebag actor." Emerson chuckled.

Pacey shook his head, "Ha. Ha. Help me pick out a shirt to wear while I go grab some pants."

He found his favorite brand of jeans and grabbed the darkest color they had. He made his way towards the shirts to find Emerson looking through the graphic tees. She picked up a tan shirt featuring three of the Care Bears. He stepped up beside her as quietly as he could.

"If it doesn't have Grumpy Bear or Bedtime Bear then I won't wear it." He laughed as Emerson nearly jumped a foot in the air.

She smacked his shoulder and Pacey felt a warm, tingling sensation spread up his skin.

"How is it a big buffoon like you can be so damn quiet!" Then her eyes snapped up to his curiously, "How do you know the name of the Care Bears?"

Pacey chuckled, "I may not know or like a lot of things but Saturday morning cartoons I'm a fucking expert in. Care Bears, Mutant Ninja Turtles, Ghostbusters. I watched them all with my bowl of Fruit Loops."

The smile that spread across Emerson's faces made his heart leap and it terrified him.

"Full of surprises, Tucker. Here…" she tossed him a black V-neck, "I was looking at the Care Bears for me."

She started to walk away as Pacey stared at her then picked up the Care Bear shirt and headed off after her. Once they were back on the highway, Pacey pulled out his clothes tossing them onto Emerson's lap.

"What the hell are you doing?"

He reached behind him, grasping the back of his shirt and pulling it over his head, "I'm getting dress."

Her eyes were wide staring at his bare chest, "Right now?!"

Pacey chuckled, "Yes. I don't want to carry my clothes with me at the concert. No one can see me back here except for you and Jake. I'm guessing Jake isn't going to sell my naked pictures to the press, are you?"

"Nope. If I wanted to do that then I would have sold Zepp's photos a long time ago." He laughed.

Pacey shrugged then lifted his hips to pull off his gym shorts. He swore he could feel the heat rolling off of Emerson as she pretended not to look at him. He purposely sat in his boxer-briefs pulling all the tags off his clothes.

"You… uh… should hurry up since we're almost there." Emerson stammered as her eyes went from his abs to his underwear.

Pacey leaned in towards her whispering, "If you want to snap a picture for your personal collection, fangirl then I could pose for you."

The gasp that came from her made him giddy as her hand shot up over her eyes, "Just get dress already you ridiculous man child!"

"Alright, if you insist."

Pacey pulled his jeans over his legs never once taking his eyes off of Emerson. He watched as she peeked through her spread fingers then all together dropped her hands from her eyes. When he pulled on his shirt he watched as her body fully relaxed against the seat.

"Was it as good for you as it was for me?" He asked pulling his ball cap on backwards. He smirked seeing her cheeks turn pink and his heart beat a little faster knowing he had that kind of effect on her.

"I hate you, Tucker."

"Love you too, fangirl." He smiled then saw Jake's shoulders shaking from trying to keep from laughing out loud.

Within an hour they were pulling up to the Moda Center where punk rock fans were lined up to get in. Jake pulled around to a private entrance where three tour buses were.

"Thomas is meeting us out here and will have your passes and tickets. It was nice meeting both of you." Jake said as he parked in front of the entrance.

"It was great meeting you as well. Hopefully it won't be the last time." Emerson's door opened revealing a tall, lean man, "Thomas!"

He watched her jump out of the car, hugging the man and suddenly Pacey was filled with jealousy. He extended his hand out towards Jake who shook it.

"Thank you for getting us here. Any time you want to see a game, let me know and I'll hook you up." He handed him a small card with his cell number on it.

"Thanks, I'll definitely keep that in mind depending on our touring schedule."

Pacey got out of the car, standing next to Emerson who was pulling her backpack on, "Thomas Reed this is Pacey Tucker, first baseman for the Vancouver Explorers."

"Hey, nice to meet you." He shook Thomas's hand, "Thanks for letting me tag along with Emerson here on such short notice."

"No worries, I'm glad someone will be there in case of a mosh pit break out. Zepp and I have a friend, Laurel, who is notorious for getting into them at shows."

Emerson laughed, "Sounds like a girl after my own heart."

Pacey tried to imagine Emerson in a mosh pit, thrashing around and he chuckled, "You know what, I would love to see that."

Thomas led them into the venue, giving them a tour of backstage and walking them out onto the stage. Pacey couldn't imagine standing in front of so many people performing even if he did it all the time on the field. Standing up above the seats with spotlights on was nerve wrecking. Emerson pulled on his arm as he heard a group of voice coming their way.

"It's them! It's them!" She whispered excitedly as Heartstrings walked up on stage.

"Holy shit!" The bassist called out, "You're Pacey Tucker… holy shit."

He chuckled as Emerson rolled her eyes then Thomas stepped beside the lead singer of the band, Zeppelin Foster.

"Guys, I would like for you to meet Emerson Holbrook and as Alec announced, Pacey Tucker. Emerson and I met during one of the conferences I spoke at. She's the social media manager for Pacey."

Alec and an older man who introduced himself as Rich, shook

Pacey's hand stating they were huge fans of him. Pacey kept his eyes on Emerson who was now fangirling over Zeppelin. He watched as the singer swing his arm around Emerson's shoulders and led her to the very front of the stage. It took everything in Pacey not to go stand beside her protectively.

"Don't worry, Zeppelin was warned not to do anything with Emerson. Thomas threatened him and Zepp usually listens to him." Rich mentioned to him.

"Good to know. Not that I'm one to judge but you hear and read things about rockstars."

Rich chuckled, "Oh and they're all true. We're lucky to have Thomas here to keep Zepp under control. They've been best friends since grade school and there's only one other person on this Earth who can keep Zepp in line."

"Let me guess, their friend Laurel. Thomas mentioned her earlier when talking about mosh pits."

"Oh yeah, she looks quiet and sheepish but deep down she is a true punk princess." One of the roadies called out to Rich and he excused himself giving Pacey the opportunity to head back over to

Emerson.

"You must be the baseball all-star Alec hasn't shut up about. I'm Zeppelin."

Pacey took his hand giving it a firm shake, "Pacey. He isn't the only fan here. Your song, Mistress of Running has been my walk-up song for two seasons now. Love your music."

Zeppelin looked from him to Emerson and back again, "That's amazing. I might have to watch a game with Alec and Rich then."

"I gave Jake my number if he or any of you want to catch a game just let me know. I'll give you the full experience like Thomas did with us tonight."

"You guys should absolutely come to a game. If Pacey doesn't hook you up then Thomas can text me and I will." Emerson said.

Zeppelin gave her a bright smile and Pacey could see her melt before his eyes in a pile of fangirl goo, "We definitely will now. You guys are welcome to stay for sound check if you like."

Emerson nodded excitedly as Thomas led them down to the pit area. Their music reverberated in his chest reminding him of when the crowd at Dodger stadium would cheer. He looked over at Emerson as her eyes were glued to Zeppelin and bopping her head to the music. He also noticed Thomas watching her and when he looked up to see Pacey staring him down he took a few steps away from her.

He wondered why it bothered him so much that Thomas or Zeppelin would be interested in Emerson. She was gorgeous and smart. For some reason, he couldn't shake the feeling that they were stepping in on his territory which was ridiculous. They were nothing but co-workers at best.

"Hey, you okay?" Emerson yelled up at him over the loud drum solo going on up on stage.

"Yeah, I'm good." He yelled back as she went back to jamming out to the song.

Halfway through sound check, Thomas showed them around the venue some more then led them out to the crowds where fans were buying merch, drinks and heading to their seats.

"Jake will come get you after the show and take you to the hotel for the night. It was great seeing you again Emerson." Thomas gave her a one arm hug then waved to Pacey, "Nice to meet you as well, Pacey. Enjoy the show."

"Wow, that was awesome! Zeppelin is such a cool guy. Definitely not what I imagined a rockstar to be like." Emerson gushed as they walked towards the merch booth.

Pacey waved down one of the workers, "Hey, could I get one of the trucker hats and whatever this fangirl would like."

She looked up at him, "You don't have to buy me anything."

He shrugged, "The least I can do for letting me tag along. Pick out whatever you want." Pacey handed his credit card to the worker.

Emerson ended up with a tour shirt and a hoodie. When they got to their seats, Pacey took off his ball cap and put on his new Heartstrings hat. Emerson scrunched her nose at him then took his hat off turning it around backwards on his head.

"Much better." She smiled then turned her attention to the stage where the opening act was coming out.

By the time Heartstrings hit the stage, Pacey was regretting his decision in coming with Emerson. Watching her rock out, swaying her hips to the beat of the drums and sweat glistening over her skin had his jeans uncomfortably tight. Zeppelin was in the center of the stage singing when Emerson started bouncing in her spot knocking into

Pacey. Her blistering skin set his ablaze and before he knew what was happening, Emerson placed herself right in front of him. Her body swayed and bounced against him. When the band started playing Mistress of Running, Pacey allowed the song to flow over him, and he started to head bang to the beat.

His hands instinctively went to Emerson's hips to keep her from bouncing into the person next to them. Unfortunately, it also meant her ass was in the perfect spot to press against his hard cock.

"Fuck…" He breathed.

Emerson leaned back against him yelling, "What?"

He leaned down pressing his lips to her ear, "Nothing."

Pacey felt her shiver and heat flooded his already too warm body realizing the effect she was having on him was vice versa. During the next song, Pacey placed his hands on the railing in front of them, caging her in. She lifted her arms waving up to Zeppelin, who was standing on the speaker holding the mic out for the crowd to sing. Hearing her scream out the lyrics, her body pressed against him, Pacey knew there would be a cold shower in his future.

When the concert ended, Jake took them back to the SUV and

drove them to a nearby hotel. The reservation was under Emerson's name courtesy of Thomas. All Pacey could think about was a shower and jerking off when he realized he would be sharing a room with her. Emerson swiped the card opening the door and they both stopped short.

"Seriously?" She muttered, "Well shit..."

Pacey groaned, "Let me guess, there's no other rooms available?"

She shook her head, "Nope."

"Just my luck." He stared at the one and only king size bed in the room.

Emerson placed her bags on the small desk, "You can have the bed. Not the first time I've slept on the floor."

Pacey shook his head, "No way I'm letting you sleep on the floor. I can sleep on the floor."

"You have a game to play tomorrow. No way I'm letting you sleep on the floor only to have you complain about how much your body hurts."

He stepped in front of her, "Then there is only one solution to this."

She looked up at him through her eyelashes and the urge to kiss her nearly got the best of him.

"What is that?" she asked.

He cleared his throat, "W-We're both adults and the bed is big enough for both of us. You stay on your side and I'll stay on mine. That way neither of us complains and I get to keep my gentleman card a little longer."

Her lip disappeared beneath her teeth and only a sliver of his will power stood strong, "You think about it fangirl while I take a shower." He grabbed his bag heading into the bathroom before he crossed a line he couldn't uncross.

Emerson

Emerson watched as Pacey closed the bathroom door letting out a long breath as she fell back onto the bed. The whole night felt like a fever dream. Between meeting her favorite band, trying to flirt with Thomas and then there was Pacey. Her body shivered remember how he had caged her against the railing and the way his muscular body had felt against hers. As much as she tried to be immune to his good looks and charm, there was only so much one hot blooded female could take.

"Fuck."

Emerson sat up hearing Pacey curse. Walking over to the door, she listened carefully in case he had fallen or something. The water was running then she heard him again.

"Fuck yes…"

Heat flooded her cheeks hearing Pacey moan. Emerson knew she should put her headphones on or turn the TV on, but she was frozen in that spot. She could her the water splashing slightly and a clear image of Pacey naked beneath falling water jerking off conjuring in her mind. Suddenly, a familiar ache started to bloom deep in her stomach.

"Yes, uh… fuck yes." A long relief-filled sigh filled her ears, and she heard the water shut off.

Her mind finally kicked back into gear, and she moved back to the desk slipping her headphones on like she was listening to music. She pretended to gather what she needed for her own shower when Pacey walked out of the bathroom. Nothing could have prepared her for the sight in front of her.

Pacey was standing before her with a towel wrapped around his waist and water rolling down his bare, well sculpted chest. His dark hair was sticking up from him running a towel over it and the dark ink covering his shoulder and right bicep stood out against his tan skin.

"Your turn." He said, walking over to his bag and unwrapping the towel from around his waist.

"What the hell, Tucker!" Emerson immediately averted her eyes as his laughter filled the room.

"Oh my god, fangirl. I have shorts on," She looked over at him seeing he indeed had a pair of gym shorts on then saw the smug smirk on his face, "Even if I didn't, it's not like you've never seen a naked man before. Or am I wrong?"

Emerson threw a pillow at him, "Like I would ever tell you."

She marched into the bathroom with her things and shut the door still hearing him laughing on the other side. She took a deep breath and immediately regretted going in there right after Pacey. His clean smelling soap filled her nose, and it felt like she was back at the concert completely surrounded by him.

"Fuck. My. Life." She whispered to herself as she turned the water on.

Stepping into the shower, the hot water hit her skin and muscles relaxing them instantly. She couldn't help letting her mind wander to the image of Pacey being in there and getting off. She ran her hands over her breasts with her loofa and down over her stomach. The ache between her legs was nearly too much for her to stand. She thought about giving Pacey a dose of his own medicine but decided that a cold shower was the more responsible thing to do. She let out a yelp as the cold water hit her burning skin.

"You okay in there?" Pacey asked through the door.

"Yes Pacey, I'm fine." She answered then muttered beneath her breath, "I'd be better if I could get off."

Quickly finishing her shower, Emerson did her nightly routine and made sure she was fully dressed before opening the door. She found Pacey lying on the bed flipping through the channels on TV.

"You know you could at least clean up after your shower. All your stuff was on the bathroom wall." She struggled keeping herself from laughing seeing Pacey's bright red and panicked face.

"I'm pretty sure it's shampoo… did you taste it?" He sat up

slightly, "Wait, were you listening to me in the shower?"

Her jaw dropped, "No! Ew, you're disgusting Tucker."

Emerson sat on the other side of the bed as Pacey chuckled, "You're the one commenting on my stuff being on the wall."

"Let's just go to sleep. We need to be up early to get to the Jesters stadium." She pulled back the covers to see Pacey was no longer wearing gym shorts but only a pair of black boxer-briefs.

"See something you like, fangirl."

His tone sent chills down her body, "Nope."

She decided two can play at this game. She slipped off her sleep shorts leaving her in a pair of hipster panties and a tank top. She could feel his eyes on her as she placed her shorts back in her bag. Looking up at the mirror on the wall, she found his eyes traveling the length of her body. The familiar electrical charge between them was tightening around her chest. Ignoring it, she went back to her side and got under the covers facing away from Pacey.

Feeling the bed move, she heard him mumbling, "Nicely played."

Doing a victory dance in her head, she fell asleep only to

dream about Pacey and her christening every surface of their room.

The next morning, they were both quiet and moving at a snail's pace. They called for an Uber to take them twenty minutes to the Jester's stadium. Emerson wondered if Pacey was always this quiet before playing or if she had crossed a line that upset him.

"You okay?" she asked.

He nodded without looking at her, "Yeah, why?"

"You're unusually quiet. Is this some pre-game, get your head on straight thing or are you upset?"

"Why would I be upset?"

He turned to look at her and her breath caught in her chest. His eyes were smoldering making her cheeks flare as flashes of her dream played in her mind.

She stammered, "I-I don't know, that's why I'm asking."

He finally smiled allowing her to release the breath burning in her chest, "I'm fine, Em. Getting my head in the game to not only play but perform for fans."

The way he called her Em made her heart skip, "Ah, that make sense. You could have just said that you know."

"And miss the way you were squirming in your seat. Ha! No way."

As they approached the stadium, Emerson noticed there was already a large crowd gathering. She instructed the driver to go to the east entrance as the Jesters manager had emailed to do. The security guard stopped them, and Emerson rolled down her window.

"Emerson Holbrook and Pacey Tucker to see Coach McKay."

The guard looked in the window as Pacey waved at him, "Go on through."

Coach McKay was not what Emerson was expecting him to be. He looked to be around the same age as Pacey dressed in a neon green jersey and jeans. He wore a hot pink baseball hat covering his long blond hair. He looked more like a surfer from California than a general manager of a minor league team.

"Miss Holbrook, I assume. I'm Stephen McKay." He shook her hand then looked over at Pacey, "No need for introductions from you."

The two men stared at one another before hugging each other, "How the hell are you Pace?"

"You two know each other?" She asked surprised.

"Oh yeah, Stephen and I came up in the minors together and played with the Dodgers for a year before he blew out his shoulder." Pacey explained.

Stephen rolled his arm, "Hard to be a pitcher when your shoulder pops and locks on its own. Worked out for the better in the long run. The team moved Sam up to the majors and I was offered a great spot on the coaching team."

Pacey threw his arm around his shoulders, "Let me guess, Nick gave you an offer you couldn't refuse and put you here."

"Actually, I asked to come here. It's much more relaxing and the fans are wonderful. All my guys are top notch as well. They're excited to meet you and kick your ass, Pacey."

They headed towards the locker room and Emerson suddenly found herself being the third wheel of their bromance. She also found herself in the middle of a locker room full of young, fit men in towels or various stages of getting dress. She tried to keep her eyes forward and not gawk but some of them were worthy of gawking at.

"You're drooling." Pacey whispered beside her ear.

"I don't care. Finally, some eye candy that isn't you."

As the words left her mouth she wished her brain filter had been working to stop them. A shit eating grin appeared on Pacey's face, and she knew she would never live this moment down.

"So, I'm eye candy." He said as they stepped in front of his locker for the day.

There were two jerseys waiting for him with his name on the back of them. The neon green was the Jesters home jersey while the more muted green was their away jersey. Pacey pulled his t-shirt off leaving him in a black compression tank clinging to every muscle of his chest and stomach. She turned away when he started to undo his pants.

"I think you already knew you were eye candy. You have millions of fans that tell you that." Emerson pulled her phone out and pretended to check her email.

"Whoa… what is a beautiful woman like yourself doing in this den of hooligans." One of the players stepped up to her smiling.

"Enjoying the view." She flirted, hearing Pacey grunt behind her.

The player laughed, "Well then you should come down to my

locker and enjoy the view from there."

She felt something covering her shoulders and saw the pale green jersey hanging off them. Looking up, Emerson found Pacey's dark eyes narrowed on the player in front of her. No words were spoken but Pacey's demeanor spoke volumes.

"My bad, I'll see myself to my locker." The player retreated flashing one last smile at her.

Turning to face Pacey she smacked his shoulder, "What the hell was that?"

She barely got the last word out when she realized he was standing before her in nothing but a pair of tight spandex boxer-briefs. Her eyes widened as they traveled down his well tone body to where God had obviously blessed him the most. Again, flashes of her and Pacey in the throes of pleasure rushed through her mind.

"Emerson!" Pacey's voice pierced through the memory, "You okay? You look like you're going to pass out."

She noticed the cocky smirk on his face, "I-I'm fine."

"Uh-huh. You can wear that jersey since they're the home team today. Unless, you would rather buy that other guy's jersey."

"No." Her answer came out entirely to quick making Pacey's smirk turn into a full blow grin, "I mean, I should probably wear your jersey since I'm here with you. I mean, I work for you."

His laugh infuriated her, "I'm going to be in the dugout. Whenever you're dressed come find me so I can snap some pictures of you for-"

"Your scrapbook of me?" He interrupted, laughing harder as she rolled her eyes.

"You wish, Tucker." She rushed out of the locker room and found her way to the dugout taking in a deep breath as the air hit her face, "Damn it, Em pull yourself together." She murmured to herself.

She dug out her camera and head up the steps to watch the fans filling the seats. Snapping a few pictures of fans with Pacey's Dodger jersey on, she remembered that his Jesters's jersey was still over her shoulders. Slipping her arms through the sleeves, she tied the ends of it into a knot at her waist. She saw Coach McKay coming out from the locker room and she walked down to meet him.

"I'm going to mostly take photos of Pacey for his social media, but if I have any photos that would work for your PR team, I can send them to you."

He smiled, "That would great, thanks. You know, I haven't seen Pacey this relaxed and happy since he was with Lyn. You two are good together."

"Me and Pacey? Together?" She scoffed, "Oh no, we're not together. Actually, we can barely stand one another."

He gave her a knowing smiling, "Oh, my mistake then. No matter, it's good to see him in high spirits with all the shit his ex is putting him through."

Emerson nodded, hearing the team making their way up to the dugout. Pacey was walking up with the player that had approached her in the locker room. They were laughing together like they were old pals. She snapped a picture of them then made a note in her phone about the sport that brings strangers together and makes them family. Pacey looked up at her with a breathtaking smile before walking up to her.

"You almost look the part, but you're missing one thing, fangirl." Pacey placed a Jester's hat on her head chuckling, "Perfect!"

"You're hilarious." She said flatly handing the hat back to

him, "Actually, I think I'll go purchase one of their hats so I can put my hair up. Be back in a bit."

Pacey called out to her, "I'm sure you could just ask for one!"

Emerson made her way to Coach McKay again, "If I wanted to change Pacey's walk up song, who would I need to see about doing that?"

He started laughing, "Let me lead the way."

Emerson had more fun at the game than she had in a long time. When Pacey went to bat, Katy Perry's Teenage Dream started to play, and Pacey looked around confused. Coach McKay and herself were nearly falling over laughing when he saw them he started to play into it. Singing and dancing his way through the chorus of the song and then hitting a homerun for the Jesters.

More importantly, the fans were cheering for Pacey and excited to see him perform. She had taken more pictures in the few innings he played than at any of his spring training games. Finally, when Pacey threw the ball to the catcher for the final out in the game the Jesters won four to three. They hoisted Pacey up and the crowd went wild for them.

Emerson waited for Pacey outside the locker room still wearing his jersey and looking through some of her photos. A new notification popped with from her Google search alerts on anything new dealing with Pacey. She figured it had to do with tonight's game and decided to ignore it for now.

"Hey fangirl, what'd you think of tonight's game?" Pacey had his bag slung over his shoulder as they walked up to the main parking lot.

Before she could answer they could hear fans chanting at the gate and the head of security stopped them, "We have a situation at the gate. Follow me so we can get you out of here safely."

Pacey wrapped his arm tightly around her shoulders, "What's going on?"

"We have protesters and media at the gate." The guard led them towards a car waiting for them.

Emerson could now hear what people were chanting and her stomach dropped. She looked up at Pacey, who had stopped, looking towards the gate.

"Cancel Tucker!"

"Her Body! Her Choice!"

"We stand with Lyn!"

"Cancel Tucker!"

Emerson grasped his hand squeezing it, "Pacey, we need to go now."

He didn't move and she stepped in front of him. Placing her hands on either side of his face she forced him to look down at her.

"Pacey, we have to go."

He nodded, grabbing her hand and getting into the car. The drive back to Portland was silent as Pacey stared out the window still holding her hand on his lap. She ran her thumb along his palm, hoping that it was helping to keep him calm. Once they were back at the hotel, Pacey was on the phone with Marcus to get them a flight back to Arizona as soon as possible. Emerson checked the alert on her phone from earlier.

"Shit." Emerson muttered as she looked up to see Pacey's pale face.

FRIDAY, MARCH 28TH
8:45
Lyn Dexter reveals that Pacey Tucker sexually assaulted her before forcing her to get abortion.
BREAKING NEWS

Fangirl Series Panel

Present Day - Red Moon Convention

"Wait, you knew Thomas before you knew me, and you were trying to

hook up with him?!" Laurel asked, interrupting Emerson's story

"I never told you that?" Emerson shrugged, "Now that you

mention it I don't think I've ever told Leigh that either. Oops."

"Uh, no! I think I would remember that. I can't believe you

were a fangirl of Heartstrings." Laurel laughed.

"Uh, so was I before I met you. Heartstrings was the

inspirational soundtrack to not only many of fanfiction I've written but

for Project Fanfic." Raelyn chimed in then turned her attention to

Emerson, "However you never mentioned about going to a Red Moon

convention and meeting the cast. I may be the original fangirl but

you're the ultimate fangirl."

The crowd was laughing as Emerson felt her cheeks burning,

"Honestly after getting to know you that first year while working with

you and hearing all about how Austin Jameson was like any other guy.

It kind of took away being starstruck from meeting him again. Now everyone is like family and less like celebrities."

Laurel's jaw dropped, "It's like I don't even know either of you anymore."

The four women on stage started laughing as Delaney asked, "It really seems like the universe conspired to making sure you three were in each other's lives."

"Apparently the universe forgot to give Laurel the memo though." Emerson joked.

"Continue on with your story. I need a moment to process all of this." Laurel put her head in her hands as the crowd chuckled.

Emerson patted her friend's shoulder, "It'll be okay. I don't think there are any other secrets I have. The rest of the story has pretty much been covered by every major press outlet."

Laurel waved her hand, "Still processing, don't mind me, keep going."

"Like I was saying, the flight back to Arizona was quick…"

Emerson

The flight back to Arizona was quick as Emerson worked on reading

the entire interview Lyn released. From what little she knew of Pacey

personally; she couldn't imagine him being the man Lyn described. She

had glanced over at Pacey to see him staring out the window in a

complete daze. She wanted to reassure him that he would get through this, and she would do everything in her power to help him. However, the distant look in his eyes and slumped shoulders kept the words from coming out. At one point, she simply reached over and squeezed his hand to let him know she was there for him. He gave her a sad smile, squeezing her hand back then went Back to looking out the window.

When they arrived back at the hotel, Pacey immediately went to his room while Emerson went to hers to work through the night. Her phone and email were blowing up from the Explorer's PR team and Marcus. Before the interview had dropped, Emerson had made some posts from the Jesters game that were now filled with comments for her to filter through.

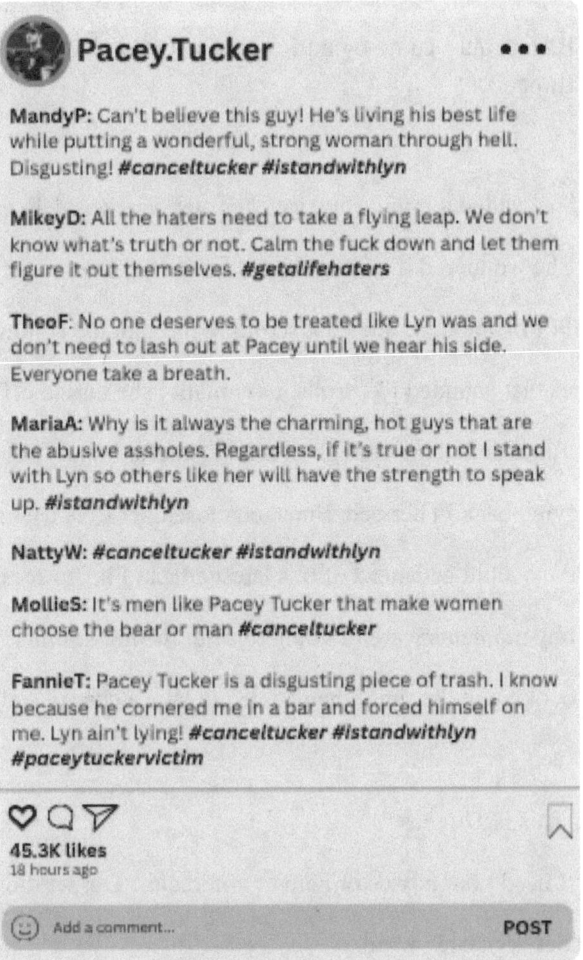

Pacey.Tucker   · · ·

MandyP: Can't believe this guy! He's living his best life while putting a wonderful, strong woman through hell. Disgusting! *#canceltucker #istandwithlyn*

MikeyD: All the haters need to take a flying leap. We don't know what's truth or not. Calm the fuck down and let them figure it out themselves. *#getalifehaters*

TheoF: No one deserves to be treated like Lyn was and we don't need to lash out at Pacey until we hear his side. Everyone take a breath.

MariaA: Why is it always the charming, hot guys that are the abusive assholes. Regardless, if it's true or not I stand with Lyn so others like her will have the strength to speak up. *#istandwithlyn*

NattyW: *#canceltucker #istandwithlyn*

MollieS: It's men like Pacey Tucker that make women choose the bear or man *#canceltucker*

FannieT: Pacey Tucker is a disgusting piece of trash. I know because he cornered me in a bar and forced himself on me. Lyn ain't lying! *#canceltucker #istandwithlyn #paceytuckervictim*

♡ ◯ ◁   ⊓

45.3K likes
18 hours ago

Add a comment…   **POST**

The last comment caught her attention, and she forwarded it to the PR team and included the head of security. Next she sent a text to Pacey.

She waited a minute and saw her message was delivered but not read. She wondered if he might have turned off his phone, which she wouldn't blame him. She kept scrolling through the comments noting ones that sounded like trolls. Eventually, she turned off the comment function having enough of all the hateful human beings online. Laying back in her bed, Emerson closed her eyes trying to think of a way they could get ahead of this latest attack. Fluff pieces and good ole boy moments weren't going to calm the masses this time.

Looking at the time, she decided to take a chance and call Thomas Reed.

"This is Thomas."

"I need your advice or help or a miracle." Desperation filled the space between each word.

He chuckled, "Em? I'm guessing your boy is in some deep shit now."

"The deepest. I'm emailing you an article."

She sat silently letting Thomas read the interview. She heard him mutter beneath his breath and then sigh.

"Wow, she's really got it out for him. This is his ex?"

"Yeah and she not holding back obviously. The good-hearted, All-American baseball player posts aren't going to work. I need something that shows his fans who Pacey really is. Short of him telling his side of the story I don't know what to do."

Thomas was quiet for a moment, "Yeah, the court of public opinion already has him charged, found guilty and wanting severe punishment. At this point, a statement from him would only play into the he said, she said of it. She's made her move and is about to checkmate him."

Emerson groaned, "Thomas what do I do? I've never had to deal with anything like this at school. I'm drowning here."

"Well, first take a deep breath and calm down. I can hear it in your voice that you're on the edge. You're no good to him if you're panicking."

She did as he said taking a few slow, deep breaths and clearing her mind. Years of therapy after her mom's death came in handy.

"Great, now here's my advice having to deal with a lot of heartbroken women and a famous best friend." She chuckled as he continued, "You need to do what is best for Pacey. Sometimes, that is creating a united front and having him tell his side. Other times it is taking him out of the spotlight all together. Having him sit out games and having no social media presence for a while."

"Neither of those sound like great options."

Thomas scoffed, "I wasn't finished yet. Personally, you need to think outside the box. Let his agent and PR team worry about the trolls and his ex. For you, start thinking of ways to counter what she's saying. If he's currently dating someone then show little personal moments of them together or who he's dating supporting him. Make it appealing to his fans and distract them from the hate spreading about him."

"Now that's the advice I was looking for. Thanks Thomas."

"No problem. If you need anything else don't hesitate to call or text me. For the time being we're home for a good stretch so I should be available."

She thanked him again and ended the call. A Google alert

popped up on her computer with Pacey's name. Clicking on it, she was prepared for it to be about Lyn's interview but was surprised when she saw it was a picture of her.

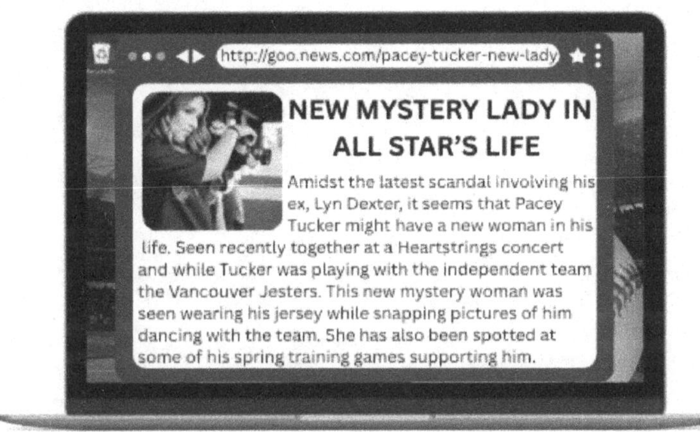

An idea popped into her head that was completely out of the box, but it might be the crazy miracle she needed. However, convincing Pacey of that was going to be a challenge. Deciding she couldn't wait, Emerson headed out of her room with her laptop and headed to Pacey's room.

Pacey

Pacey sat in his hotel room with the only light illuminating his face was from his phone. Lyn's interview was on the screen, and he was rereading it for the hundredth time. Little moments she warped into her only version was playing like a movie in his head.

In the whole interview that was the only part that was true. He had planned out the weekend and taken off a few days from spring training so it could fit into her filming schedule. They flew out to Aspen and spent the whole weekend in a little cabin watching it snow and making love on every possible surface they could. He couldn't remember a time when he had felt so much love in his life. The weeks after that trip were his own personal hell with her.

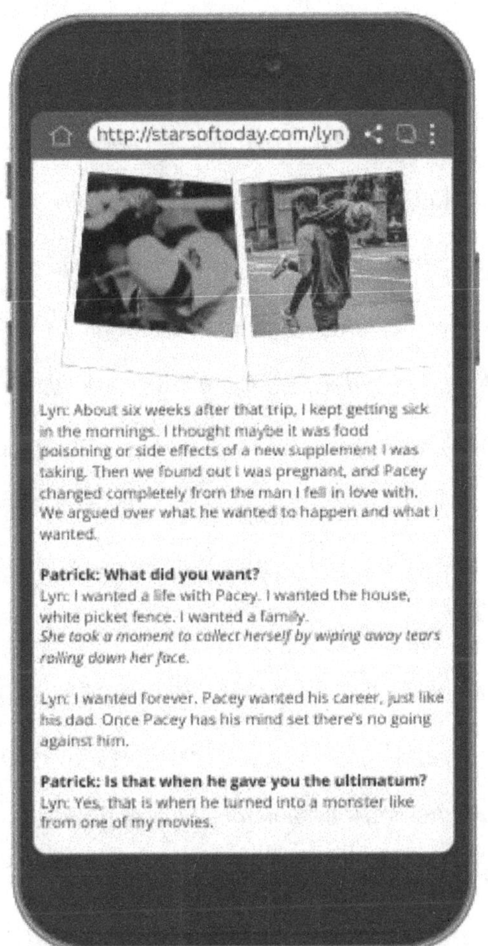

Pacey swiped out of the app on his phone and threw it on the

bed next to him. There was one memory from that time that would be forever etched into his brain until the day he died.

***

He stared down at the little baseball uniform onesie he had seen while out clothes shopping. He couldn't help himself to buy it even if they had a girl she could still wear it. When he found it, he had pulled out the small sonogram of the little person growing within the love of his life's body. Since that first appointment he often stared at the little photo not believing he was a dad. He walked into his shared home with Lyn and found her sitting in the living room watching TV.

"How was your doctor appointment? Again, I'm really sorry I couldn't come along with you. These negotiations with the Dodgers are getting ridiculous."

Lyn shrugged, "Everything went fine. I'll be cramping and bleeding for a little while but should be back to normal in a day or so."

"I thought the doctor told us that if you had cramping and bleeding to go see her? Is everything okay with you and the baby?" He asked, sitting beside her.

"Everything is fine. I took care of it. Now we can go back to

focusing on my career and our lives."

Pacey had a sickening feeling filling his stomach, "Lyn, what did you do? I thought you were going to see your OB."

She huffed turning the TV off, "Pacey we talked about this. We can't have a baby right now. My career is way too important right now and you're traveling all the time. We need to focus on ourselves and building the life I want for us. Maybe once you've retired from baseball and can stay home with a baby we can think about having a surrogate or something."

"Tell me you didn't do what I think you did. For the love of God, Lyn, tell me right now that our baby is still growing within you."

Her silence was the only answer he needed. Hot, molten rage flowed through his veins, and he picked up the remote from the couch throwing it at the TV.

"I can't believe you had an abortion without discussing it with me!" he yelled.

Lyn stood up, walking away from him, "I don't need to discuss anything with you when it concerns MY body. Your body was going to remain intact where mine was going to be destroyed. I can't offer for that to happen right now. So, yes I had an abortion because it's my right to make that decision for MY BODY!"

She walked upstairs while Pacey slid to the floor tears falling freely down his face.

***

The memory felt like ripping open an old wound. Fresh tears falling down his face as he thought about the onesie being packed away in his attic at home. The sonogram was still in the same place in his wallet. Worn and frayed around the edges from him looking at it over the years. Their child would be nearing ten years old if given the chance to see the world. That realization had Pacey gasping for air as overwhelming heaviness pressed into his chest.

When moments like this happened he would call the one person who knew the whole story. He and his mom had their difference but in the end he knew he could always go to her. Picking up his phone, he briefly saw a text from Emerson and ignored it hitting his mom's number.

"Hi Pacey."

"H-Hey mom…" He choked on the sob desperately trying to

escape his lips.

"What's wrong? Are you okay?" Her worried tone with the tipping point.

A rush was air and tears came out and he couldn't stop it from happening. He sat on the phone for several minutes crying before he could finally say anything.

"S-Sorry mom, just needed to talk to someone."

"You never need to apologize. Does this have to deal with Lyn and her interview?"

He nodded, knowing she couldn't see him but was unable to speak.

"Pacey, you know that woman is rotten to her core. She's probably doing this to get attention. You know what really happened and should pay no mind to her."

This was why he always called her. No matter what, his mom always knew exactly what to say to him. He was thankful to have her even if she could be a pain in his ass.

"I know, it's just hard. Brings up a lot of memories and then I realized that the baby would be turning ten this year. Double digits."

He let out a shaky breath.

He could hear his mom let out a soft sigh, "Do you remember how we celebrated you turning double digits?"

He chuckled, "Yeah, the only time you and dad were in the same room after the split. All I wanted was for us to go to a baseball game together as a family. You guys bought me anything and everything I wanted that day. It was like a boy's dream birthday."

"One day, you'll be able to give your own child that special kind of a day. It will happen; I know it."

"Yeah, have to find someone first to put up with me."

She chuckled, "Speaking of…"

"Oh no, mom I'm not looking for a hook up."

"I figured you weren't since you have some mystery girl now. She's very pretty, Pacey."

He was confused, "What are you talking about?"

"Don't play dumb with me. The girl wearing your jersey in all the pictures from the Jesters game. The media is going wild to know who she is and so am I. So spill it."

He was trying to think of who she could be talking about then

Emerson popped into his mind.

"You mean Emerson?"

"Emerson? What a pretty name. Pacey and Emerson, that has a good ring to it."

As much as he hated to admit, their names did sound good together. Then he thought back to sharing a hotel room with her and hearing her moan his name in her sleep. The way it rolled off her tongue had went straight to his cock and he almost went back into the shower to cool off.

"Pacey? Tell me more about this girl."

"There's nothing to tell, mom. The team hired her to be my social media manager. She's there to take pictures and keep a regular schedule for all my pages. That's all. We're just co-workers, I guess."

He could hear the disappointment in his mom voice, "Aw, I was hoping you finally found a good one. Maybe you should test the waters with her."

"And on that note I'm going to say goodbye and love you."

Ending the call with his mom, he immediately pulled up Google searching his name plus mystery woman. A bunch of pictures popped up of him and Emerson. A lot were from the Heartstrings concert and then several from the Jesters game. The most popular one was where her back was facing the camera while she took a picture of him dancing with the team. She was grinning from ear to ear as his name stood out on the back of the jersey she wore. Pacey could see why people would think they were together. As he was scrolling through all the pictures and saving them to his phone there was a knock on his door.

"Emerson?" He held in the small bubble of laughter.

She looked like a wild woman with her hair high on top of her head in a messy bun. She had her laptop held to her chest and she was breathing heavily like she ran to his door.

"Hi! May I come in? I have a wild idea that may be the miracle we are looking for."

Pacey stepped aside, flipping on the light and allowing his eyes to adjust, "I didn't know we were looking for a miracle."

She sat on his bed, opening her laptop, "Well I have been racking my brain to figure out the best way to help. Thomas gave me some great advice to think outside the box and well this idea might be far out of the box."

"Oh, I can't wait to hear this. Go on fangirl, tell me your idea."

She turned her laptop around to a post made by TMZ about new mystery girl in his life and a photo of the two of them watching the concert.

"We announce we're dating. We show everyone the real Pacey Tucker and how he truly treats a woman he's with and disprove Lyn's claims."

He stared at her from a moment, "You want us to fake date to disprove my ex?"

"Yes, we can go public, and I can show my complete support for you that none of what Lyn is saying is true. We keep posting all the normal baseball, endorsements, career things then throw in some real life, relationship stuff in there."

There were so many things that could go wrong with this plan, but at this point what the hell did he have to lose. Pacey leaned in towards her smirking.

"You know, if you wanted to go out with me you could just

ask. I mean we live in the age of girl power and women taking the lead."

She rolled her eyes making him chuckle, "Trust me Tucker, you're definitely not my type. I'm doing this because it is kind of my job, and I don't like it when women use hot topics to gain attention or popularity. It desensitizes the importance of those topics."

"And you secretly are in love with me and want to take your fangirl level up a notch."

Emerson smacked him on the shoulder, "Could you take this seriously for a moment? I'm trying to work this in your favor and you're poking fun at me."

Pacey sighed, leaning back on his bed, "Alright, alright. Serious Pacey it is then. So, what does fake dating entail exactly? What are the boundaries?"

Her eyes widen for a split second before focusing on her laptop screen, "In public we act like a couple. Holding hands, hugging, small PDA."

"Kissing?" He asked, truly curious how far he could push the boundaries she set.

"I think kissing on the cheeks is fine. I don't think we need to show any big PDA moments. Just enough to give the public the idea that we are together."

He nodded, "Okay. I assume we'll need to go on dates and be seen together at games."

She nodded, "Yes. I think if I start to post on my own social media about supporting you, sharing photos of us and what not then we should be able to create a believable story."

Pacey watched as Emerson nervously chewed on her lip waiting for his response. He made her wait another minute then finally couldn't take her fidgeting with the hem of her shirt.

"Okay, but I have one rule if we do this."

"What's that?" she asked, closing her laptop.

He leaned in closed to her, their lips mere inches from one another. He heard her suck in a breath that made him smile.

"You have to promise not to fall in love with me for real."

Emerson pushed him away, standing from the bed, "You don't need to worry about that Tucker. I promise I will not be falling in love with you."

She walked to the door then turned to face him, "We can make an announcement on our socials tomorrow before we head to the stadium. I will let Marcus and the team know about this, so they don't freak out."

"Sounds good babe. I'll see you tomorrow, love you!" He called out as she flipped him off letting the door close behind her.

The next afternoon, Pacey watched Emerson hover her thumb nervously over the post button. Her eyes scanning over what she had written once then twice. He still couldn't believe she was actually going through with this. He hoped she knew the moment she posted this her life was going to change forever. They had spent the morning calling their families, Emerson calling her dad and brother, to let them know what was going to happen so they weren't blindsided.

Looking at the photo she had taken of them this morning, Pacey couldn't help to smile. They were sitting outside on his balcony, when he pulled Emerson onto his lap wrapping his arms around her. He whispered in her ear to make her smile and took the picture. Right when her thumb hit the button, he kissed her cheek making her grin. They truly looked like a couple which had eased their worries that someone would find out it was all a hoax within the first twenty-four hours of their plan.

"Fangirl, hit post already." He nudged his knee against hers.

She laughed, "Here goes nothing…" she hit the post button.

She immediately went to her Instagram feed, finding the mirroring post she had posted on Pacey's page pop up first. The first photo was of Emerson from the Jesters game that they had sought out the original photographer to have permission to use it. The next photo was the one of them taking this morning. His post had similar wording to hers and she double clicked on his post to like it. Refreshing the page, they found her post was on top of his now.

 EmHolbrook • Following
Vancouver, Washington

Liked by **Pacey.Tucker** and **1,560 others**

EmHolbrook Cat's out of the bag! Yes, I'm the mystery girl supporting one of the best men I've ever known, Pacey Tucker. I know there are a lot of rumors going around about him and his past relationship. All I'll say is you can't believe everything you read. Pacey and I agree these are serious topics that should not be taken lightly. For me, I get to see a side of Pacey that few get to see and I'm hoping to share more of that now that we've gone public. I stand firmly in support of Pacey and will be here for him every step of the way.
#istandwithtucker

View all 20 comments

5 MINS

Pacey

The team filled the plane with a buzz of excitement. They were flying

to Vancouver for the season home opener. Pacey watched as the

younger players were talking about their chosen walk-up songs and

how they had family flying in for the game. Their excitement made him

excited for their first game as well, but the smile on his face was not entirely from the excitement of a new season. His eyes drifted back to his best friend who was sitting next to the woman pretending to be his girlfriend. Her head was thrown back in laughter as Sam leaned over pointed to something in the book he was reading.

Pacey took his phone out snapping a picture of Emerson laughing. He had been taking random photos of her that made him smile. Right now, the fact that Sam was not buried in his book with his headphones made Pacey like Emerson even more than he already did. Sure, they bickered and butted heads a lot, but it was part of what he liked about her. A week ago, when he made her promise not to fall in love with him, he should have made that promise to himself not fall for her. The more he got to know her, the more he was falling head over heels for her.

"Penny for your thoughts?" Her question brought him out of his daze.

"Gonna cost a lot more than a penny for what's up here." He pointed to his temple.

Emerson laughed, "I doubt that." She sat down in the sit next to him pulling out her headphones.

"I was thinking that it's nice to see Sam opening up to someone other than me."

She looked up at him, "Well, us introverts tend to either stick with like minded people or to ourselves. Which doesn't explain why he chose you as his BFF."

He acted offended, "Whatever do you mean? I'm a joy to be around."

"Uh-huh. I'm going to listen to my audiobook now. Do you mind if I rest my head against your shoulder?" She looked bashful when she asked.

"Of course, sweetcheeks. That is what boyfriend's shoulders are for."

"Add sweetcheeks to the list of nicknames never to be used again."

He sighed, "Seriously? I think that one is very fitting for you."

"Nope. I'd rather be called fangirl." She placed her headphones over her ears and rested her head against his shoulder.

She would never know how much comfort it brought him to have her leaning against him. Sure, he had dated a little bit after Lyn but nothing serious. He vowed after her to never let anyone get that close to him again. That is how he got his womanizing reputation. He only slept with cleat chasers or random hook ups from a bar. All of them nameless and faceless. Did that make him an asshole? Yes, but it also protected his heart from being shattered like it had been before.

With Emerson, anything that dealt with them being a couple came as easy as breathing for him. It was moments like this that he liked the most and scared him shitless. Being her fake boyfriend was too easy, and the line was getting blurrier with each passing day.

When they landed in Portland, Emerson and Sam took a different car from Pacey. He was staying in a nearby apartment building while Sam and Emerson were living in the gated community for the team. At the time, Pacey hadn't wanted to put roots down in Vancouver, but now he regretted that decision as Emerson kissed his cheek and got in the car with Sam. As he approached his apartment building, he could see a large crowd outside of it. A mixture of press and protesters were there and suddenly he wished Emerson was there with him. Security redirected his car to the private parking garage. Marcus was waiting for him by the elevator, and he knew nothing good could come from that.

"I'm sure you saw the crowd outside."

Pacey grabbed his bags from the back, "Kind of hard to miss them. Am I good staying here?"

Marcus nodded as they got into the elevator car, "For now. We can look at getting you into the players community if you like. Probably would be better for your 'relationship'."

"Don't start again. We know you don't like the idea. Get over it and move on." Pacey stepped out of the car heading towards his apartment.

Marcus was hot on his heels, "It will eventually blow up in your face and I'm going to be there to tell you, I told you so."

Walking inside, Pacey saw everything of his was unpacked and put away by the movers. He was thankful he didn't have to worry about that part of moving into a new place.

"Is the townhome next to Emerson available? You know I don't need a lot of space or anything." He asked.

"I'll look into it, however, according to Emerson there was press and protesters at the gate when they arrived. So, it looks like either way you're going to get bombarded." Marcus started typing on his phone.

"Let me know if the place is available. If there's nothing else then I would like to take a shower and get some sleep." Pacey said, walking back towards the door.

Marcus walked out the door, "I'll talk to you later."

Pacey closed the door and immediately pulled his phone out to text Emerson.

Pacey had debated on sending his last text especially now since there had been no response for a couple of minutes. It was enough time for the guilt to pile on top of his shoulders. Emerson never asked for her life to be in the public eye especially with a man that was currently in the middle of a scandal with his ex. Finally, Emerson texted him back.

> **Fangirl:** You should probably get some rest for the game tomorrow. I'll be fine and if I need anything Sam, Jared and Whitley are all nearby.

> **Fangirl:** No need for you to worry even though I appreciate you checking in on me. Goodnight Tucker

> If you change your mind just let me know. I'll be up for a while. Goodnight fangirl

He put his phone on the charger before getting into the shower and relaxing in bed for the night. His dreams were filled with him and Emerson bickering at one another until he kissed her to shut up leading to them in various wonderfully exhausting positions. When he woke up the next morning he found himself in need of a cold shower.

Once he was up, Pacey went through his normal game day routine. A light workout in his living room followed by a protein shake and some fruit. He packed his bag for the day and texted Ben when he was ready to leave.

He waited for Ben in the private garage seeing him pulling up. Pacey was surprised to see Sam in the front seat then opening the door to see Emerson sitting in the back. For a moment, he stood there staring at her. Her wavy hair was braided over one shoulder while she wore an Explorers hat with his number on it. She had on a pair of black shorts that showed off her long, toned legs. Finally, she was wearing a golden tank top and a new Explorers jersey seeing his name peeking out from the back.

"You know if you take a picture it'll last longer." She joked without looking up from her phone.

He smiled, taking out his phone and taking a picture of her, "You're right, it does." Pacey threw his stuff next to Sam's in the back then sat next to Emerson whose cheeks were pink.

Fans were already flooding the stadium as they drove around to the player entrance. A lot of them were wearing Tucker and Knight jerseys or brand-new team shirts. Ben stopped at the private entrance letting Sam and Pacey out.

"Aren't you coming?" He asked when Emerson didn't move.

"Nope, I'm watching from the family box today. Don't worry, I'll still get some great photos and videos of you."

Pacey was a little disappointed she wouldn't be down with him as she had been during spring training. He swallowed that disappointment down then was surprised when Emerson leaned over kissing his cheek.

"Go give 'em hell, Tucker."

Her smile took his breath away as she closed the door and Ben took off.

Sam was snickering next to him, "You got it bad for her."

"Shut up, Sammy. Come on, let's go rally the troops for our home opener." Pacey playfully pushed his friend towards the doors.

When Pacey walked through the locker room doors, he put his game face on. He could see and feel the nervousness from the other players. He focused on getting ready then stood up on one of the benches.

"Alright, this is what's going to happen. You're going to do whatever you need to get out all the nervous energy you have built up. If that's going to throw up, take a shit or jerk off then go do it. Within the hour, you need to be suited up and ready to play the best damn game of your life. Got it!"

Everyone agreed and then a few players headed to the bathroom, shower area. Pacey put in his headphones to listen to his normal playlist and get his head into game mode. He had finished putting on his new uniform when a text from Emerson came up. It was a picture from her seat next to Whitley.

Fangirl: Not too bad of a view. Also, I wanted to let you know that I have a little surprise for you during your first at bat. A certain band may or may not have written a song just for you. You're welcome.

I can't wait to hear it and thank Thomas for me. Also, the view could be a little better. It could have my favorite fangirl in it.

He knew there was a shit eating grin on his face, and he didn't care. He couldn't wait to hear his new walk-up song. A new photo appeared of Emerson smiling with Whitley. Her cheeks were bright red, making Pacey's heart skip.

Fangirl: How about two fangirls?

I mean, if you're into it then so am I

Fangirl: PACEY TUCKER! OMG you're unbelievable...

But you love me anyway

Fangirl: Don't you have a baseball game to get ready for? Stop texting me.

See you after the game fangirl

Pacey looked up to see Coach entering the locker room and he put his phone in his locker. Coach gave a more uplifting speech than

Pacey had. By the time they walked out onto the field for the first time, the Vancouver Explorers felt like home for him. They went through all the opening ceremony, National Anthem and player introductions. When his name was announced there was a mixture of cheers and boos from the fans. He tried to not let it affect him, but it had knocked him down a notch or two.

Finally, they headed to the dugout and the game started. Pacey walked up to the on-deck circle to warm up his swing. He paid close attention to the opposing team's catcher and pitcher. He found that they kept to a pretty clear rotation of pitches.

"Now up to bat, number 24. Pacey Tucker!"

The distinct riff of Heartstrings came through the speakers, and he stopped for a moment listening to the lyrics.

I notice the way I think about the game with a smile,

Curved lips I just can't disguise.

But I think it's winning making my life worthwhile.

Why is it so hard for me to decide which I love more?

Winning or...

The Game!

He smiled as he stepped up to the plate. Tapping the end of his bat against his shoe then the plate, Pacey took his stance keeping his eyes on the pitcher's hand. He switched his fingers from the two-seam fastball to the curveball. Pacey changed his grip slightly as the ball came barreling down at him. The loud crack resounded throughout the stadium. He dropped his bat, seeing the ball drop into the stands in left field, he took off running to first. The umpire signaled a homerun and the crowd went wild. Running the bases, hearing the crowd and seeing his team cheering for him. Pacey finally felt at home.

The Explorers ended up winning four to two and team morale was high in the locker room after the game. Jared had hit the winning homerun, and the other players were dumping Gatorade over him. Pacey and Sam were standing near their lockers laughing at the scene before them. After showering and changing out of his uniform, he checked his phone. Several texts from his mom and dad congratulating him on winning. Then he saw a post notification from Emerson's Instagram.

The picture made his knees wobble, and he sat down on the bench. It was Emerson holding her hands up cheering as he touched home plate for his homerun. His jersey on her stirred up a lot of emotions that had been simmering deep within him. However, it didn't begin to compared to the double speed his heart was beating seeing her cheer him on. He took a screen shot of the photo and saved it to his phone.

 EmHolbrook • Following
Vancouver, Washington

Liked by **Pacey.Tucker** and **3,720 others**

EmHolbrook HOMERUN BABY! My dear friend captured the moment my man hit the first homerun of the home opener. Explorers win! Great job babe!

#explorersmlb

View all 1.6K comments

20 MINS

He liked the post when Sam tapped him on the shoulder, "We're ready to head out."

Pacey nodded and followed his friend out to the car. He was expecting to see Emerson there, but her spot was empty.

"She rode with Jared and Whitley back to her place." Sam answered his unspoken question.

"Ben, could you drop me off at Emerson's?"

He nodded pulling out onto the streets where fans were celebrating. He noticed Sam snickering in the front seat and punched his arm.

"Not one word from you."

Emerson

Emerson sat on the floor in the middle of her office. While she had been gone, Whitley had come in and unpacked her things for her. Her office was everything she dreamed of with floor to ceiling bookshelves across one wall. She had a standing desk in front of a large window looking out over the backyard and her friend had even hung a few of her family photos for her. Emerson lay across the soft gray rug admiring her shelves trying to get the adrenaline to stop flowing throughout her body.

She always remembered watching her dad during home openers and the excitement she felt. However, she didn't remember feeling what she did today. It was a complete rush to watch Pacey and the team play. Seeing them give everything they had on the field then pushing it even further to give the crowd a great show. She couldn't help herself from screaming and jumping when Pacey hit his homerun. Reaching up on her desk she grabbed her phone and looked at the pictures Whitley had captured of her.

The one of her screaming as Pacey crossed home plate with his name clearly across her back was getting a lot of attention on her page currently. The other photo was one she saved for his page as soon as she showed it to him. He was standing at home plate watching to see if he had gotten the homerun then he pointed his bat up towards the stands. Whitley swore to her that he was pointing at her, but Emerson knew better. Staring at the photo now, she allowed her adrenaline fog mind to believe what Whitley said was true.

Emerson looked up when there was a knock on her door. Getting up to look out her master bedroom window she recognized the familiar black SUV in her driveway and panic surged down her legs to get to the front door. Opening it, she was shocked to see a freshly showered and dressed, Pacey standing there.

"H-How did you… what are you doing here?"

He chuckled, "Hello to you too. May I?"

He gestured to come inside, and Emerson stepped aside. It was then she realized that she was in her oldest pair of flannel pants and black tank top without a bra on. Quickly she crossed her arms over her chest after closing the door with her hip.

"Hello Pacey, nice to see you. What are you doing here?"

She watched as he walked down the small hall towards her kitchen, "You didn't stay after the game."

"I figured it would be easiest if I rode home with Whitley instead of waiting for you and Sam. Plus I figured you would be out celebrating somewhere with the team or whoever."

She had begged Whitley to leave early not wanting to deal with being around the whole team celebrating. Thankfully, Whitley used it to her advantage to surprise Jared when he arrived home.

"That's why I'm here. As your fake boyfriend there's only one person I would want to celebrate this win with and that's my fake girlfriend." He turned around, leaning against her island.

Emerson's eyes traveled from his boot covered feet then to the tight denim stretching over his muscular legs, skipping over the place she really wanted to look at. His dark button down was rolled up to his elbows and opened revealing a black t-shirt. Finally, her eyes made it over his smug smile and mischievous eyes.

"Fangirl, you're drooling."

"Am not." She narrowed her eyes at him, "I'm sure no one is going to notice that I'm not out with you and the team celebrating. Go, have fun and don't do anything stupid."

Emerson headed back towards her front door when Pacey gently grabbed her elbow and twirled her back to him.

"Sam is home celebrating the way he does with a bottle of scotch and a book. Jared has probably already blown his load and is sleeping blissfully next to his wife."

Emerson's laugh faded as Pacey's hand brushed down her

arm, "The rest of our team are young guys looking to nail every cleat chaser that comes their way. All I want to do is grab some dinner with someone without any pressure to be Pacey Tucker, baseball player and just be Pacey Tucker, normal dude."

She sighed, stepping out of his reach, "Give me fifteen minutes and we can leave."

"Really?" He asked, sounding bewildered.

"Yes and please don't make me regret going out with you instead of staying home to binge watch Red Moon."

Pacey's face scrunched up, "Not you too. Sam loves that damn show."

Emerson laughed as she walked up the stairs, "Oh I know, we talk about it all the time."

Walking into her closet, she quickly grabbed the one and only dress she owned. Slipping the simple, sage green sundress over her head, she grabbed her black flats and headed off to the bathroom. Emerson never really liked wearing make-up and had very little of it. Putting on some mascara, eyeliner and some nude color shimmer eyeshadow she finished the look with a simple pink lip gloss. Running a brush through her wavy hair, she looked in the mirror with a shrug.

"Good enough for a fake date with my fake boyfriend."

Grabbing her purse and her black denim jacket, Emerson headed back downstairs. She found Pacey sitting on her couch in the living room. He was looking at his phone as she stepped down the stairs.

"Alright, I'm as ready as I'll ever be."

He glanced up then his eyes widened.

"Is this okay?" She asked, suddenly unsure of her choices.

She felt the heat of his gaze spread over her body as his eyes trailed down her body. She was glad she skipped the blush since her natural heated cheeks would be all she needed.

Pacey stood, making his way towards her, "You're beautiful."

Her breath hitched as he stepped in front of her. No one had ever called her beautiful before. Sure, guys would say she's pretty, cute and sometimes even hot. For some reason Pacey saying she looked beautiful made her stomach clench and her heart race.

"T-Thank you." She whispered, taking the arm he offered to her.

They walked out to the SUV where Pacey opened her door helping her get in. That's when she realized that he was driving without Ben or any security.

"Is it alright for you to be without Ben or someone?" She asked, as he placed his hand on the back of her seat and looked over his shoulder to pull out.

"Where we're going it will be fine. He's with the guys bar hopping and probably wishing he was with me." Pacey chuckled.

Emerson watched as he pressed the gate button to open it then pull out onto the street, "Where are we going?"

He pressed the touchscreen to link his phone, and Heartstrings began to play through the speakers. Looking at him, she found a smile on his face as his eyes focused on the road ahead of them.

"Jared suggested a restaurant not that far from the stadium that overlooks the Columbia River. I made reservations before coming over."

"What if I didn't come?" she asked.

He shrugged, "Then I guess I would be having dinner alone, but I had a good feeling that you would come."

She rolled her eyes, "You're lucky I was hungry already or you would be Tucker party of one."

He laughed softly, "Well thank you for gracing me with your presence, fangirl."

"You're welcome."

Emerson was pleasantly surprised when they pulled up to a small restaurant with outdoor seating that looked out over the river and the marina. Pacey, once again, opened her door for her then held out his hand for her to take. Slipping her hand within his sent a current of heat up her arm and surprisingly a sense of comfort. Pacey gave his name and they were led to a small private dining table outside. Once the waiter brought their drinks, a Negroni for Pacey and glass of peach Moscato for her, they both sipped their drinks looking out over the water in silence.

"Tell me about yourself." Pacey broke the silence, "Something a boyfriend would know about you."

Emerson didn't quite know what to say, "Well, my dad, Will, is a retired pitcher for the Dodgers. I have one younger brother, Everett, who is only a few months older than you. He's finishing up his residency at Northwestern Medical in Forensic Psychiatry and has a second bachelor's degree in criminal justice."

"Whoa… overachiever?" He took another sip of his drink.

She smiled, "Partially. He was young when our mom was killed, and they never found the person who killed her. He kind of became obsessive about forensics and using profiling skills to find criminals from the evidence they leave behind."

She kept her eyes on the calming waters as she tried to hold back the tears from welling up. Even after years of therapy, she still had a hard time talking about her mom.

"I'm sorry about your mom. I remember when it happened, and when your dad retired." She looked over at him, "My dad played against yours and even had a kind of rivalry with one another. I remember him coming home and calling my mom to say he just wanted to make sure she was okay."

"She didn't live with you?" She asked, thankful for the distraction from her own mom.

He shook his head, "No. They got divorced when I was in middle school. They let me choose who I wanted to live with, and it was a no brainer. My dad not only traveled a lot, leaving me with a nanny most the time, but sometimes he would let me tag along to his home games. I would hang in the locker room and dugout then when the team would go celebrate I went with them."

She could see the regret in his eyes as he downed the rest of his drink, "And your mom? Did she live close by?"

"She stayed in my hometown of Oklahoma City." Emerson chuckled as Pacey asked, "What? What's funny?"

"Nothing. I could never figure out why, at times, you suddenly had a southern twang to your voice. Now I know."

He laughed with her, "I guess you can take the boy out of Oklahoma but can't take Oklahoma out of the boy. Anyway, she still lives there while my dad now lives in Florida in a nice retirement community."

Silence fell between them once more as the waiter brought out their food until Emerson was the one who broke it with a question.

"Tell me something no one else knows about you?"

Pacey leaned back in his chair, resting his fork against his lips, "I've never had anyone wear my jersey before."

"What?" She asked confused, "People wear your jersey all the time."

"True, but I've never had anyone in the family box who has worn my jersey before. When my dad came to games, he always wore one of his jerseys. My mom never comes to games and Lyn…" He paused, "Well, she only came to one or two games, and she was too self-absorbed to wear one."

"So, the fake girlfriend," She pointed to herself, "was the first person to choose to wear your jersey."

He nodded, "Exactly."

She pulled her bottom lip beneath her teeth, "Were you okay with me wearing your jersey?"

The smile appearing on his face filled her chest with a warmth she could only describe as pure joy.

"Absolutely. It was nice to know someone was up there rooting for me. Even if it was all for show."

"You know I was a fan of you before all of this. I've always rooted for you Pacey." Emerson reached over and squeezed his hand, "I always will root for you, no matter what."

"Thank you," He squeezed her hand back, "Okay enough mushy feelings. Tell me more about Miss Emerson Holbrook. Favorite color, food, drink, position."

She coughed, nearly choking on air, "What?!"

His laughed billowed out of him, sending his head back, "Oh man, the look on your face, fangirl."

Glaring at him she decided to answer him, "Green pepper and onion stuffed cheeseburger, Diet Dr. Pepper, and doggy style."

This time it was Pacey's turn to choke on air as Emerson took a long drink of wine. While Pacey collected himself, she felt her phone buzz with a text. Pulling it out from her purse, she found a text from a number she didn't know.

2135550105: You'll regret being with him

She ignored the text placing her phone back into her purse as the waiter brought out their dinner. As they ate, Emerson tried her best to be present and attentive as Pacey put forth his best boyfriend act. She knew that the night was only that… an act. Though her heart wanted

her to believe that it was the best first date she had ever had.

Once Pacey dropped her off at home, she immediately pulled

out her phone and sent a reply back to the mystery number.

Who is this?

2135550105: I think you know... you're a smart girl

2135550105: Top of your class at UCLA even as you grieved your mom's death

How did you get my number?

2135550105: : I have my ways and if you don't want everything I have on you to go public then you will help me destroy Pacey.

You need help, Lyn. Let me help you and then you can move on with your life.

2135550105: : Is that what your therapist told you when your mom died? I don't need help. I need revenge and once Pacey's life hits rock bottom then I'll feel just fine.

I don't care what you think you have on me I will NEVER help you

2135550105: : Oh yes you will, or every little detail of your pathetic life will go public. Your phone number, addresses, emails, school you worked at, your family's information, everything

2135550105: : I will have everyone calling you, emailing you, showing up at you and your family's houses. Everyone will know that you are helping an abusive, sexual predator

I think you're desperate and need more help than you're willing to admit. I'm blocking your number after this text. If you do have all my info then let me know when you're ready to get serious help

Emerson blocked the number, her hand trembling as she set her phone down. Even with a semi-famous father, she never once had to worry about any of her private information being public. She looked at her phone seeing it was nearly midnight and decided she would contact Mr. Steinberg in the morning about her run in with Lyn Dexter.

Emerson

One Month Later

Traveling from city to city staying in hotel rooms and watching games had been exhausting and all Emerson could think about was sleeping in her own bed. She was leaning her head against the window watching the city of Vancouver pass her by. Sam was sitting next to her while Jared was in the front seat next to Ben. Turning down their street, the car started to slow as flashing lights came into view.

"What the hell?" Jared muttered.

There was a large crowd of people with signs being held back by a line of police officers. Emerson gasped as she read the signs.

Emerson Holbrook loves an abuser!

Emerson Holbrook hates SA victims!

Cancel Tucker and Holbrook!

She looked over to Sam who was on the phone, "We have a situation at our gate. There are protesters and police here."

He paused letting whoever was on the phone speak, "Got it." He ended the call then tapped Ben on the shoulder, "Nick said they're aware of what is going on. The officers will let us through."

Sam squeezed her hand, "Everything will be fine."

"H-How did they know I live here?" She asked, remember her text conversation with Lyn a month earlier.

He shrugged, "It's no secret a lot of the team and employees live here. They probably got bored of protesting at the stadium and decided to come here. Nick said there are some at Pacey's building as well."

Emerson nodded as they pulled through the gate. Ben dropped her off first and promised to be back by to make sure she was alright staying there. Walking in through her front door, she dropped her bags at the door and headed to her kitchen. Her hands were trembling, and she needed something strong to take the edge off. Normally, she wouldn't drink to deal with her nerves, but she figured if there was ever a time to do that it was now. Pulling the bottle of whiskey from the top cabinet, she grabbed a glass and poured herself a shot. Downing it, she pour herself another drink and took the glass up to her room.

After a shower and the numbing effects of the whiskey, she felt almost normal again. True to his word, Ben had checked in on her and she had decided that she would be fine.

"Just call me if anything happens and I will come get you. We have a few hotels in the city that I can take you to that no one knows of."

She smiled, "Thanks Ben. Have a good night."

Emerson watched him back out of her driveway and grabbed

her bags to unpack. Going through her backpack, she grabbed her phone and turned it back on from being on the plane. Immediately it started buzzing and chiming with notifications. She watched as the screen filled with text messages from numbers she didn't know. Her stomach twisted as she began reading through them.

2065558959: What kind of women loves an abuser like Pacey Tucker

2525552541: I hope he sexually assaults you, so you know what it feels like

7175550007: Do all of us women a favor and jump off a bridge

4635555595: Do you even care about the victims of your boyfriend?

8045553015: You're a worthless loser!

3125558438: Just another attention whore fucking any famous guy she can

8165556050: What a waste of space!

Emerson stopped reading then noticed she had received forty voicemails. Scrolling through them, she read the first few and clicked out of the phone app. Tears were threatening to fall as her phone continued to fill with hate texts and voicemails. She couldn't delete them fast enough and ended up shutting off her phone. She headed into her office and pulled out her laptop. Checking her email, she found her inbox filled with hate emails. There was one email filtered into her family tag that was from her dad.

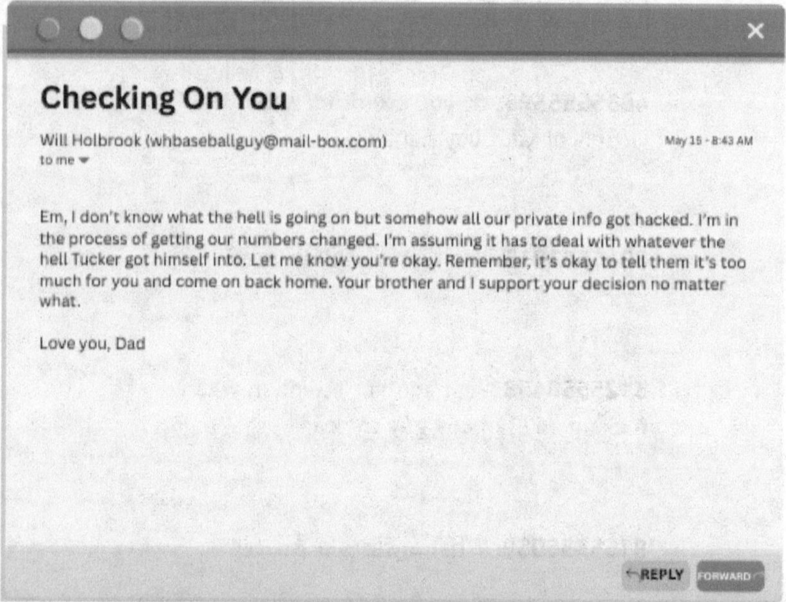

Tears flowed freely down her cheeks. She typed a short reply back letting him know she was fine, and she would handle everything. As she pressed send, the guilt tightened around her chest cutting off the air to her lungs. She tried taking a deep breath only to gasp. Emerson headed to the window and opened it letting the cool night air hit her face. Once again she tried to take in a breath and this time she coughed as the air filled her lungs. She looked out towards the front gate where she could hear the crowd chanting still. Slowly, she sunk to the floor and held her head in her hands.

"What have I done?" She whispered.

She pushed herself off the floor and sat at her computer again. Heading to her Instagram page, the notifications were endless but there was one DM that caught her attention immediately.

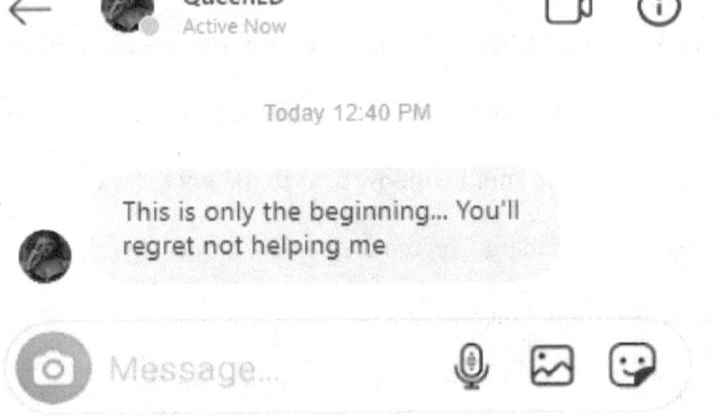

Rage burned throughout her body, and she slammed her laptop

shut. Letting out a primal scream, Emerson went over to her reading chair and punched the cushions. Anger was always the one emotion she could never control in therapy after losing her mom. It was always simmering beneath her skin and finally her therapist told her to let it out. They went into a room where there was one padded wall, stacks of paper and sound proofing. Her therapist left her in the room for ten minutes and simply told her to unleash all that anger building up within her. After that session, she never let her anger build up again. She would scream it out or hit couch cushions or when she had been back home she would go to the boxing gym her brother went to.

As she threw her fists against the chair, she could hear someone knocking at her door and her anger was quickly replaced with fear. She grabbed her phone in case she needed to call 911 or Ben. Looking through the small window next to the door she was shocked to see Pacey standing there. He knocked again, harder this time and calling out from the other side.

"Emerson! Emerson, please open the door!"

"Pacey, what are you-"

He rushed in, his handsome face riddled with worry lines as he shut and locked her door.

"You haven't been answering your phone or texts. I was worried and then Ben told me about all the protesters here. I wanted to make sure you were okay."

"I...u-um, I..." That is when everything hit her at once and suddenly she couldn't stop the tears springing to her eyes or the sob slipping from her lips.

"Oh Em, come here," Pacey pulled her into his arms, holding her tight against his chest, "Everything will be okay. I'll do whatever I have to in order to make this right for you."

Emerson could only continue to cry into his chest as he held her. It felt like they stood there forever until he led her over to the couch and sat them down. He kept one arm secured around her shoulders as his thumb swiped away the tears from her cheeks. It was a simple gesture that felt more intimate than it should have to her.

"I-I'm sorry." She whispered, pulling away from him.

Pacey kept his arm around her shoulders rubbing her arm, "You have nothing to be sorry for. You got pulled into all of this because of me. I'm the one who's sorry."

"This was all Lyn. She did this." Emerson turned her phone on again letting the notifications come through then showing Pacey the screenshot of her conversation with Lyn.

His eyes narrowed, "When was this?"

"The night of the home opener. She texted me when we were at dinner."

"Why didn't you tell me?" He asked, looking up at her then back down at her phone.

She watched as he scrolled through all the texts and voicemails from strangers that knew absolutely nothing about her. Emerson could see Pacey getting angrier with each message and she grabbed her phone from him.

"You have enough to worry about and I didn't want to add to it. I told Nick about it, and he said he would get someone on it."

Pacey stood, pacing in front of her, "Em, if they have your number then they could easily get your address. Gated community or not, they can find a way in."

"I'm sure they already have my address. My dad emailed me to let me know that him and my brother are getting harassed as well in

Chicago."

"Fuck!" he yelled making Emerson flinch, "I'm sorry. I just can't believe she is going through all of this to get to me and for what?"

Emerson stood next to him, placing her hand on his shoulder, "I don't know. She seems focused on getting revenge on you. Can you think of anything that you did or said that would make her hate you so much?"

He shook his head, "Right now, that doesn't matter. All that matters is keeping you safe from all the crazies following her. I think you should stay at my place for now."

"Spending one night at your apartment isn't going to change anything. Those people will still be out there when I come back."

"I didn't mean for one night. I meant for you to move your stuff in with me. I have a guest room that you can have, and my building has the newest security features. No one gets into that building who doesn't belong there. I think it's safest for you to stay there."

Emerson stared up at him in disbelief, "You want me to move in with you?"

Pacey

He couldn't believe the words coming out of his mouth. Did he really just ask Emerson to move in with him? When Sam had called him about the protesters, all Pacey could think about was making sure she was okay. After calling and texting her without any response, Pacey called Ben to drive him over to her place. Seeing the signs of the protesters only enraged him more. He saw an upstairs window open when they pulled up and his mind immediately went to the worst-case scenario. Now he was standing in her living room asking her to move into his apartment.

"Pacey, I really don't think I need to move. We'll be out on the road again and until then I can make sure to keep everything locked up."

He ran his hand through his hair, "Fine, but for tonight I'm going to sleep on the couch."

Emerson rolling her eyes quenched the fiery rage in his chest, "You need to get a good night's sleep for this six-game home stretch. I will be fine."

She tried to push him towards the door, but he stood his ground, "You think you get a choice in this, fangirl. I'm staying rather you like it or not."

"For god's sakes Tucker! I'm a big girl and can take care of myself. I don't need some big, strong Neanderthal playing bodyguard for me!" She yelled, shoving him back exactly one step.

Pacey grabbed her shoulders finally snapping at her,

"Emerson, shut up or I'll give your mouth something to occupied itself!"

Shit.

Had he said that out loud. By the silence and wide hazel eyes staring back at him, he had.

"Did you just threaten to occupy my mouth?" Emerson asked, her eyes now narrowing on him.

It took Pacey exactly ten seconds for the burning rage from earlier to turn into a flood of desire. He closed the distance between them grabbing either side of her face, crashing his lips against hers. Her lips were as soft as he imagined them to be. He could feel her hands grasping the front of his shirt before sliding up over his shoulders and into his hair. He backed her up to the couch as her lips parted enough for him to deepen the kiss. They fell with a slight bounce on the couch enough to knock them apart and for reality to set in.

He quickly pushed himself off her sitting on the opposite side of the couch, "Emerson, I-I'm so sorry. I-I didn't mean…"

"I think you should go." She whispered.

Her fingers were touching her lips but her eyes wouldn't meet his, "Emerson, please…"

"Pacey, I'm fine. Just… just please go." She got off the couch walking up the stairs and he heard her close the door.

For a moment, he thought about leaving. He walked to the door, looking up the stairs then turned back walking back to the couch. If he left and something happened to her then he would never forgive himself. He kicked off his boots and laid down putting his arm over his eyes. Their kiss replaying in his head on repeat. Turning on his side, he closed his eyes counting to one hundred before falling into a restless sleep.

The delicious smell of caffeinated beans filled his nose, and he opened his eyes to the most beautiful sight. Emerson was standing over him in an oversized baseball tee and shorts, holding a steaming cup.

"Is this heaven?" He murmured.

"No, but I can make hell for you if you like." Her sass game was on point this morning, meaning she had probably been up for a while.

Sitting up, Pacey rubbed the sleep from his eyes then stretched out his aching muscles, "Is that cup for me? Or are you going to pour it over my head?"

Her soft laugh brought a smile to his face, "Now that is a good idea unlike you sleeping on my couch before a game."

Pacey took a long drink allowing the hot liquid warm his body and fire up his brain cells. Emerson sat down on the opposite side of the couch pulling a throw blanket over her legs. A moment of disappointment washed over him then he sat back enjoying his coffee.

"Why did you stay? I mean, it's obvious that no one was going to get into the community, let alone my house. So, why stay?"

"Have you ever played the what if game?" He asked, holding the cup with both hands to warm them.

She nodded, "Who hasn't."

"The only thing going through my mind was, what if something happened to you. That would be on me, and I couldn't live with that."

"And exactly what were you going to do? Fight them off? That gives you even more bad press, and the team definitely doesn't need that. Don't you see how ridiculous this is? Going out of your way for someone you don't even like or want here."

There was a sharp pain in his chest as her words sliced through him. He knew his reactions when she was first hired were not the best and sure he had been against her working for him. Now, he couldn't imagine her not being there and he didn't know exactly when that changed but it had.

"You're wrong." He set his cup on the small side table and moved to sit beside her, "Sure, my first impression was terrible…"

"You were an asshole."

He chuckled, "Alright, I was an asshole. It's different now."

"How so? What changed? I'm still the same girl that walked into that office meeting her favorite baseball player and you're still you." She was looking down at the mug in her hands.

He took the mug from her making her look at him, "I think you can feel what's changed. Our bickering back and forth and power struggle is all a screen for what's really going on between us."

She swallowed hard, "There's nothing going on between us. You're my employer and I'm your employee. That's all."

"Really? That kiss last night says otherwise…" He gently

gripped her chin, leaning in toward hers, "I think if I kissed you again it would prove otherwise."

As if the universe was telling him to cool it, his phone started to ring, "You should get that." Emerson whispered.

She got up, taking their mugs into the kitchen as Pacey grabbed his phone, "Hey Nick, I'll be at the stadium soon."

"That's not why I'm calling, Pacey. We've found a leak within the team that is feeding information to your ex. We have a private security firm looking into it. For now, we're going to move Emerson into one of the hotels nearby. I wanted to let you know before I call her."

Pacey leaned his elbows on his knees, "I'm with Emerson now. What happened that makes you want to move her?"

"Look outside her front window."

He got up, looking out the window and saw a large crowd of people standing in front of her house. Police were keeping them at bay, but the crowd looked like it was growing.

"Pacey!" Emerson called out from the kitchen.

"Hold on Nick." He headed into the kitchen where he could

see a group gathering in her small backyard.

"H-How did they get in?" she asked, wrapping her arms around herself.

"I don't know, but you need to go pack up some of your stuff."

Emerson continued to stare out the window as police were herding the crowd towards the front. Pacey placed his hand on her cheek gently pushing her to look at him. Her wide eyes were filled with fear, and he felt a crack in his heart.

"Em, go pack enough clothes for a couple of weeks and whatever else you need."

She nodded before walking off towards the stairs. Pacey turned his attention back to Nick on his phone.

"Emerson can stay with me in my building. The security is top notch, and we can have Ben add some extra guys there just in case."

There was silence on the other end, "Do you think that is a good idea? I'm worried that this fake relationship is no longer fake."

"Look, she's in this mess because of me. I want to make sure she is taken care of. She's staying with me. End of story."

"Alright Pacey. Ben should be there to pick you and Emerson up. I'll keep you updated with what we find on the leak." There was another pause, "I have to ask, are you able to focus on the game or do I need to get Hunter to play the next few games."

For a moment he considered having Hunter play, "No. That gives Lyn exactly what she wants. I'm good to play."

"Alright then. I'll let Coach know you'll be arriving late. I'll see you in the dugout."

The call ended as Emerson walked back into the kitchen dressed for the day. She was wearing an Explorers t-shirt with jeans and her hair braided down her back. He could see her suitcase, duffel bag and a laptop case sitting by the front door.

"Ben will be here soon to take us to my place." Emerson went to say something, but he stopped her, "Please don't argue with me. If anything, do this for my peace of mind. Please?"

She smiled, "All I was going to say was thank you."

When Ben arrived, they grabbed Emerson's things placing them in the back then Pacey got in the backseat with her. His phone started to ring again surprised to see it was his lawyer.

"Hey Jake, what's up?"

"Pacey, we've been given a heads up that Lyn Dexter is pressing charges against you."

The air in his lungs evaporated, "W-What? What kind of chargers?"

He looked over to Emerson who was staring at him curiously.

"Second degree sexual assault and emotional abuse. I'm flying out this afternoon to meet with you and the team's lawyers. I've contacted Mr. Steinberg to let him know. I wanted to give you the heads up to prepare for the press that will come from this."

Pacey felt like his world was spinning out of control, "Thanks Jake. I'll see you later then."

"Pacey, don't say anything to anyone or post anything on your social media until after we've talked."

"Got it." Pacey ended the call the call staring down at his phone.

"What was that about?"

Emerson's soft tone almost broke the dam of tears threatening to fall. Never did he think Lyn would go this far and now she was not only dragging his name through the mud but Emerson's as well.

"Pacey?" He looked up at her, "What's going on?"

"That was my lawyer giving me a heads up that Lyn is officially pressing charges against me. He's flying out today to talk with me and the team's lawyers about it. You should probably sit in on the meeting as well." He explained still not believing the words coming out of his mouth.

"Are you sure?"

He nodded, "At least be available because I'm sure they are going to be stricter about what is posted on my social media from here on out."

Arriving at his building, they went in through the private garage and took the elevator to his floor. Even with his world falling to pieces around him, Pacey couldn't ignore the electric charge between him and Emerson in the elevator car. He wanted nothing more than to lose himself within her again. To pin her against the car wall and kiss her until neither of them could breathe. To feel her hands tugging his hair and her body against his. When he thought his willpower was going to fail, the doors opened, and he saw her let out a long breath before walking out.

His apartment was tiny compared to his home in L.A., but he loved the view here especially with Emerson standing in front of the floor to ceiling windows. They overlooked the Columbia River and were high enough that no one could peek into them. All the furnishing was simple and nothing like the style he had at his house. Everything was in shades of gray where back home everything was in warm browns and creams. His apartment felt cold until Emerson stepped inside. An overwhelming sense of home washed over him and it scared him.

"Wow, this place is…" She looked around as if searching for the word within the room.

"Yeah, I didn't choose anything in here. The apartments come furnished and I figured I wouldn't be here enough to change it."

"Ah. Well, it's good to know you're not as cold as this room seems to be." She chuckled, "Where should I put my things?"

He led her down a small hall where there was a bathroom at the end of it then a door on the left which he opened for her. Inside there were exactly three pieces of furniture. A full-size bed with light gray bedding, a dresser and a bedside table.

"If there's anything you need just let me know and I'll order it for you." He said as she looked around seemingly unimpressed by her new living quarters.

Her smiled didn't reach up to her eyes as she said, "This is fine, Pacey. I'm assuming you need to head over to the stadium soon."

He nodded, checking his texts seeing a response from Nick after he had spoke to his lawyer.

> **Steinberg:** I've placed Hunter on the roster for the next three games as precaution. Be in the offices by 5pm

"Actually, Hunter is playing the next three games. We don't have to be there until five o'clock." He leaned against the door sending Nick a reply back.

He looked up at Emerson who was sitting on the bed biting her lip, "Oh, well then I guess I'll get settled in."

"My room is across from yours and you can use the bathroom in the hall. I have one in the master. Let me know if you need anything."

She nodded putting her suitcase up on the bed with a long sigh. Pacey walked into his room, flopping face first onto his bed. Guilt, anger and exhaustion hitting him hard. Before he knew it, he was dozing off.

Emerson

Between sleeping in a strange bed and dreaming of protesters screaming at her, Emerson hardly slept. She saw it was after ten in the morning when she finally walked out into the living room. Pacey's apartment was quiet, and she found a note on top of a new iPhone box.

Em, I had to head to the stadium for a meeting with Steinberg and Coach about the next few games. There are menus for places that deliver to our building and feel free to use my card info at the bottom. Since your number was made public I figured you would need a new phone. I know you'll argue with me about getting it for you but just accept it as an early bonus for putting up with all my bullshit. Spend the morning setting it up and relaxing. I'm still benched for the next couple of games.

See you later,
Pacey

She smiled, rereading the note one more time then opened her

new phone. It was the latest model with the largest storage space. It had

to be at least fifteen hundred dollars or more. He had been right when

he said she would argue with him. The least she could do was help pay

for it. Looking through his menus, she decided on ordering from a local

Chinese place for lunch. She was getting ready to place her order when her phone started to ring. The picture of Pacey standing with his back to her in his spring training uniform popped up.

"Hi Pacey."

"Good afternoon, sleepy head. I see you have you phone set up." He chuckled.

Emerson curled her legs beneath her on the couch, "Yes and you're right I am going to argue with you about at least helping pay the bill or something."

His groan made her laugh, "I expect nothing less from you, fangirl. Sam and I are on our way back and were wondering if you had ordered lunch yet."

"No, I was going to order from the Chinese restaurant down the street."

She could hear Sam in the background, "Well you just made the pitcher very happy. Text me your order and we'll pick it up. We went back to your place and grabbed a few more things for you. Hopefully, it will help make my dingy place feel more like home for you."

A soft smile spread across her face, "Thank you. I appreciate everything you're doing Pacey. I'll text you right now. See you guys soon."

The call ended and she sent her order to him. Deciding she needed a shower and to get dressed, she headed down the hall. By the time she was dress in her favorite jeans and band t-shirt, Emerson could hear the guys walking in. They were laughing and arguing about the best dish from the restaurant.

"Smells good, I'm starving." Emerson said walking into the kitchen.

She noticed both of them were staring at her. Sam was grinning from ear to ear while Pacey's eyes were trailing down her body. She felt the heat spreading over her skin and she distracted herself by emptying the food bags.

"You look different." Pacey commented.

She arched an eyebrow at him, "Good different or bad different?"

He shrugged, "I don't know... just different."

She laughed, "I have my contacts in. I noticed my frames are getting a little loose because I need to get a new pair. I don't particularly like wearing contacts, but they come in handy."

"She doesn't have the hot librarian look any more. Now she looks like a punk rocker." Sam laughed as she threw a chopstick at him.

"Ha. Ha. Very funny. I like punk rock and I take that as a compliment. You're delusion if you think I look like a hot librarian."

Sam grabbed his food, heading towards the couch. Emerson could feel the electric aura that surrounded Pacey raising the hairs on her arms. His firm body pressed against her back while his arms caged her to the counter.

"I don't know, hot librarian is fairly accurate description of you. I could think of a few things we could do in the stacks." He whispered against her ear.

She sucked in a breath before turning around to face him, "You wish, Tucker." She ducked under his arm with her food going to sit next to Sam.

After lunch, the three of them brought in the things they had grabbed from her house. Sam had brought a lot of her books from the TBR cart next to her bed. She was grateful for him grabbing them. Pacey had grabbed some bedding from her closet and her favorite blanket, pillow and cat body pillow. She noticed he had also packed some pictures from her office of family and friends in Chicago. The small gesture meant a lot to her as she set them up on the dresser.

The guys had decided it was pizza and movie night, heading out to grab all the necessary supplies. While they were gone, Emerson decided to change into a pair of Dodgers pajama pants and her favorite school hoodie since Pacey kept his apartment at arctic temperatures. When they returned, Sam was carrying three pizzas, and several bags of chips. Pacey had a case of beer and bottle of whiskey that matched the one she left at her place.

He handed her the bottle, "Noticed it on your counter and figured it couldn't hurt to get you one for here."

She chuckled, helping them unload everything. She made sure to keep some distance between her Pacey. She conveniently always had Sam as a buffer between them. Thankfully, Sam seemed to get what she was doing and was her knight in shining armor until they moved into the living room.

Emerson curled up in her blanket stretching her legs out while Sam sat on the floor on the opposite end of the couch. Pacey sat on the floor as well with a beer and box of pizza in between him and Sam. His long, muscular arm stretched along the couch brushing against her legs. Emerson became hyper focused every time his hand rested on top of her shins, bouncing his fingers against her skin.

The boys had chosen a new horror movie to watch while Emerson curled even further into her blanket. She hated horror movies however her pride would never let her tell the guys that. She watched Pacey and Sam laugh and heckle at the TV while she would shield her eyes from the horrors on the screen.

"Fangirl, are you scared?"

She pulled down her blanket far enough to see Pacey's bright eyes staring up at her, "Nope. I'm inspecting the thread count of my blanket."

"Pacey, leave her be…" Sam warned, chuckling.

She watched as he stood up, lifting her upper body off the couch and then sitting them both back down with Emerson cradled into his arms.

"Don't worry fangirl, I won't let the boogeyman get you."

She rolled her eyes getting off his lap and sitting next to him,

"I think I can handle a fictional horror character, but your beer breath is the true horror story."

Bellowing laughter erupted out of Sam while Pacey's jaw dropped. Emerson sat a little taller with a smile on her face as she turned her eyes towards the TV screen once more. Surprising to her, Pacey never moved back to the floor and now ran his fingers along her arm. Trying to pay attention to the gruesome murders instead of daydreaming about how his fingers would feel on other areas of her body.

By the time the movie was over the three of them were full of pizza, beer and appalling murders. Thankfully, Pacey put on Sports Center to catch up on the latest scores and she bid them both a goodnight heading to bed.

Emerson shot up from her bed after dreaming of a madman trying to kill her, "Damn movie…" she muttered.

Walking out to the living room, she was surprised to see Pacey still awake and drinking from the bottle of whiskey. She walked up behind him grabbing a hold of the bottle making him jerk it awkwardly from her.

"Think you had enough, Tucker." She motioned with her hand to give it to her.

A challenging smile curled on his lips, "If you w-want it then come… come getsit."

She walked around stopping in front of him. His long legs were spread wide enough for her to step between them. She watched as his eyes focused on her and she snatched the bottle from him.

"No-No fair." He pouted, "Using your woman-ly p-powers onsme."

Emerson rolled her eyes, "Where's Sam?"

Pacey pointed to the door, "Ben got him. Took him home."

"Come on, I think it's time for bed you drunken fool." She set the bottle down then tried to lift the 240-pound first baseman off the couch.

He shook his head, "Nope. I will not let you take ad-advantage of my drunken state of mind. Do you know that is consider sexual assault offense? Yep. Any time someone is not in their right mind or 'fluence and someone has sex with them they can be charged with it."

"Pacey…" She said softly, sitting next to him.

"I'm just tellin' ya what I learned from the law people. Apparently, the emotional abuse I put Lyn through made it to where the last time we had sex it was considered sexual assault. She wasn't in her right mind, and we had sex. So now I'm a bad, bad man."

Her heart was breaking for him, "I don't think you're a bad man."

His low chuckle was unnerving, "You don't know me or maybe you do. You think I'm an ass-hole. I am. I'm the ass-hole who fucks cleat chasers for sport, for the shits and the giggles. I'm the ass-hole that fell in love, wanted a family and got his heart fucking smashed to pieces catching her with another dude. She fucks a co-star in our bed, in our house and I'm the ass-hole, sex offender."

Pacey tried to push himself to stand but ended up sliding onto the floor with a thud, "I'm the ass-hole who is ruining your life. You… Miss Perfect, Miss Gorgeous and I'm fucking up your life."

Emerson moved from the couch, sitting cross legged in between his outstretched legs. She placed her hands on either side of his face making him look at her. His glossy eyes were filled with unshed tears and his shoulders were slumped forward in defeat.

"You are not fucking up anything. Not my life and definitely not hers. None of this is your fault, Pacey. I don't blame you for any of it. You shouldn't blame yourself either. The only person to blame is Lyn. She is the one causing all this hell and for what? To get her name in the spotlight for five minutes. She's an attention seeking, entitled, bad actress and a bitch. She doesn't deserve your guilt or tears or your drunken confessions."

His bottom lip was trembling, and Emerson knelt in front of him, wrapping her arms around his neck. His arms wrapped around her waist. She pressed her lips against his temple.

"You can let go. This is a safe place for you to just be you and feel whatever you're feeling. I've got you. I'm right here. I'm not leaving. I've got you."

His arms tightened around her then his body began to shake when a heart shattering sob broke out of him. She held him, letting him get out everything he needed to until his arms finally loosened from around her. Her shirt was soaked with his tears and snot, but she didn't care. It was all worth it to see the clear, shining green eyes locked onto hers.

"Feel better?" She asked, slipping her shirt over her head leaving her in a tank-top.

His eyes widened for moment and suddenly the room was instantly warmer. The dark sweatpants he had on was doing very little to hide his hardening cock. Emerson quickly got up, tossing her shirt on the couch and crossing her arms over her chest.

"B-Better." He cleared his throat, "Though I'll probably have a raging headache in the morning."

"Yeah, well you kind of deserve that from drinking almost entire bottle of whiskey." She helped him get to his feet, "Think you can make it to your room?"

"Nope. Thinking the couch is going to be my bed."

He sat down rubbing his hands over his face. Emerson started to go back to her room when he reached out grabbing her hand.

"Do you think…" He bit his bottom lip, "Would you mind staying out here with me? I… I don't want to be alone."

She sighed, "No funny business?" Her eyes immediately went to the long, thick length in his pants and heat rushed to her face.

"Promise. No funny business."

His serious tone took her by surprise, and she believed him. Emerson went to the other end of the couch, laying down spreading her legs enough for him to lay down on top of her. Pacey slipped his arms behind her back and rested his head just below her breasts. Taking a shaky breath, she ran her fingers through his soft hair like her mom would do whenever she was sick or upset. She chuckled seeing him contour his six-foot four frame on half the couch. Soon, his breathing was even and deep. She closed her eyes trying to focus on anything but the incredibly hot, literally and figuratively, man laying on top of her. Eventually, she was able to fall sleep only to dream of Pacey throughout the night.

The morning, she could feel sweat trailing down between her breasts. Opening her eyes, she found they had moved in the middle of the night. Pacey's back was against the back of the couch while one arm was wrapped around her waist holding her body tightly against his. One of her legs was hooked around his hip and his hand was holding it there. Waves of heat were coming off of him which was making her sweat but that was not the only thing making her sweat. Pacey shifted slightly bringing her leg tighter around him and his hard cock was pressing against her thigh.

"Fucking hell…" She muttered, trying to untangle herself from the massive man and his cock making her stomach clench in ways they hadn't in a long time.

"Five 'ore minutes…" He mumbled against her shoulder.

"Pacey, we need to get up or I need to get up."

He groaned, "Fine."

He loosened his grip on her and she not so gracefully fell to the floor. His raspy chuckled sent waves of desire over her body and she took her frustration out by hitting him with a pillow. Deciding she needed a cold shower, she headed to her bathroom before he could say or do anything else. When she emerged fully clothed and chilled, Emerson headed back to the living room to see it had been cleaned up and coffee made. Pacey was sitting at his kitchen island, sipping from a steaming mug in only his sweatpants and no shirt.

Emerson took a deep breath then focus herself on an idea she had while showering, "I think we should see about us posting a statement together. Showing a united front against the charges and showing the fans that the rumors are just that."

Pacey nodded without looking up at her, "I'll make a call to my lawyer to see if we can today." He got up, leaving his mug on the island, "I'm going to take a shower and sober up."

The tension between them was palpable and it worried Emerson. She was hoping it was only the hangover getting to him, but the dread pooling in her stomach told her otherwise.

"Hey everyone, I know I've been fairly quiet on my socials the last week. I wanted to come on here with Em to address the elephant in the room."

Emerson rub his back supportively as Pacey continued to

speak into the camera.

"There are a lot of rumors, speculation and honestly just a lot of hate being spread around about myself and Em. We wanted to come here to all of you, face to face, and tell you what's what straight from us."

Pacey took a deep breath as Emerson squeezed his hand, "You got this babe."

He nodded, "I will get the tough one out of the way first. Yes, my ex-girlfriend, Lyn Dexter has filed charges against me. What those charges are I will not say, but they are serious. I, Em and the team are taking them seriously and are hopeful of a civil resolution. There is a lot of behind-the-scenes things going on that we cannot speak about on the advice of the attorneys. Please know, whatever may come out of this that I am not taking any of this lightly."

"As many of you know, mine and my families personal information was leaked to the media for people to use. There's nothing that can be done about that, only that I ask for anyone with that information please do not use or share it. A lot of people know that my father is a retired MLB pitcher for the Dodgers and after tragically losing my mother, he has led a very private life."

Emerson took in a shaky breath, "People showing up at his house, harassing him about me, my boyfriend and my life is not fair nor right. If you want to post hateful comments about me then that's your prerogative. Please leave my family alone."

Pacey placed his arm around Emerson's shoulders as she rested her head on his, "The rumors of sexual assault and emotional abuse being spread are simply ridiculous. They are an attempt to get attention and I'm asking everyone who is a fan of myself and my team to please not play into it. There are real victims of these terrible acts that need help and need support. Emerson and I want to make sure that you have the information to do so instead of spreading wild accusations."

"We have a link to the National Sexual Assault Hotline below. It's available twenty-four hours a day, seven days a week. If you are the victim or know someone who is being sexual assault. Please call that number and speak to someone immediately. You are not alone, and we both encourage you to reach out to professionals or a trusted person in your life for help."

Emerson laced her fingers with Pacey's as she continued, "Lastly, I wanted to make it very clear that I am in support of Pacey fighting the charges against him. I will be by his side every step of the way. Never once have I believed in any of the rumors or accusations being spread about him. I know a lot of you know him as a golden glove, first baseman, Pacey Tucker. To me, he's a loving, kind, big-hearted, caring boyfriend. We are going to stand together and come out the other end stronger than before. Right Pacey?"

He looked at her with a soft smile, "That's right. I know this video has been a little rambly but we both felt it was important to show a united front. It's her and I against the world and I couldn't ask for a better partner by my side."

When he glanced at her again, Emerson leaned in and kissed him.

"Me neither. Thank you all for listening to us and we will see you at the next Explorers game. Bye everyone."

Pacey

"Are you TuckerGirly, fangirl? Come on, you can be honest with me."

Pacey chuckled, sitting at the kitchen island reading fan reactions to their video yesterday.

"Not even, Tucker. Now do you want your pancakes with or without spit in them." She looked over her shoulder at him with a smirk.

"Ha. Ha." He rolled his eyes, "Are you almost done? I'm starving and those smell delicious."

She held up her spatula, "Patience, youngin'. Perfect pancakes take patience."

He scoffed, "Youngin'? I'm not that much younger than you."

"Anyone my brother's age I consider a youngin'. Now stop distracting me or your pancakes will be extra crispy."

Pacey continued to scroll through the comments on their video seeing one about their kiss.

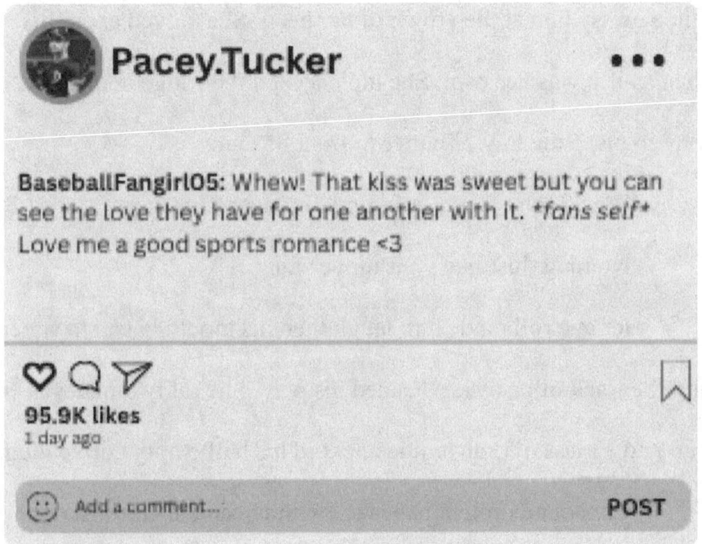

He had thought about that kiss on and off since yesterday. He hadn't expected her to kiss him. His lips tingled now thinking about her lips pressed against his. He was pretty sure he could spend hours kissing her soft, full lips and it still wouldn't be enough for him. However, the fan's comment about them loving each other was giving him heart palpitations. Love? Was that what was going on between them?

Pacey looked up to see Emerson swaying her hips to the music quietly playing in the background. She was in her pajamas still with her hair in a messy bun at the crown of her head. She moved about his kitchen as if it was her own. She hip checked the fridge door close, turning to place the tray of butter in front of him.

"What?" she asked, bringing him out of his daze.

"Nothing, just like your moves fangirl."

Her eye roll made him laugh then his mouth began to water seeing the stack of pancakes headed his way. She sat two plates in front of him and a glass of orange juice next to his half empty coffee mug.

"Chocolate protein pancakes with chocolate chips, scrambled eggs with shredded cheddar and an obscene amount of bacon. Bon Appetit!" She announced with a curtsy.

Pacey buttered his pancakes then pour an unhealthy amount of sugar free syrup over them. Cutting into them with his fork he took his first bite and fell into food heaven. He moaned, closing his eyes and savoring each bite.

"Do you need some alone time with those pancakes?" she asked.

He opened his eyes to see her eating a bowl of oatmeal with peanut butter and banana. Stuffing his mouth with another bite he pointed to her bowl.

"Why you 'ating that when you can 'ave he'ven in your 'outh?"

"Pacey, for the love of everything good in this world please chew and swallow before speaking." She took another bite of her breakfast, "I'm a creature of habit or as my therapist would tell you I tend to be on the scale of obsessive compulsiveness."

He swallowed his bite then took a drink of his coffee, "Meaning?"

Emerson walked over next to him, leaning her hip against the island, "This was the breakfast I was having when I found out about my mom. She would make it for me when I was a kid, and it stuck. Grieving is different for everyone. My brother became the overachiever, my dad is the hermit, and I tend to obsess over things. There is no logical reason behind it but if I don't eat this for breakfast then I feel like my day will go to shit immediately."

"Oh." He put his fork down for a moment then held up a small bite towards her, "Try one little bite then go back to eating your normal breakfast. It would be a crime if you didn't at least try your perfect pancakes."

He watched her stare at his fork for moment. Her eyes darting back and forth between the pancakes and her oatmeal. Her shoulders were tense, and he wondered if maybe he crossed a line. He was about to take his fork back when she opened her mouth. Watching her lips wrap around his fork added with her satisfied little moan when she pulled the pancake into her mouth had instantly sent his blood flowing straight to his dick.

"Hmm, you're right those are some pretty damn good pancakes." She smiled.

He cleared his throat, "I, uh… I think balance is key here. Having your traditional breakfast and adding small changes when you feel ready."

She pointed her spoon at him, "Since when did you get smart? Here I thought you were just a dumb jock."

"Don't let anyone know. I have a rep to protect." He laughed.

She pretended to zipper her mouth close, "Your secret is safe with me."

After breakfast, they each went to their rooms to pack for the away series in Chicago. He could hear Emerson rocking out to Heartstrings, singing and what he could imagine dancing in her room. He enjoyed having her in his apartment more than he ever thought he would. After living with Lyn, he swore off ever living with another woman unless they were marriage material. With Emerson, everything was simple. It felt right like she belonged there the whole time.

"Ben is here!" Emerson called out.

"Be right there!"

Pacey threw any last minute items in his carry on. He went over his mental checklist making sure he had his headphones, chargers, and tablet in his backpack. He slipped on his old Dodgers hat and slipped his sunglasses down the front of his V-neck. Walking out, he found Ben and Sam talking with Emerson.

"About time slow poke. Let's go!" She bounced on her heels excitedly.

"I think she's excited to get out of here, Tucker. Have you been locking her away like some book villain?" Sam joked.

"She wishes. I think she's excited to see her family."

Emerson pointed at him, "Ding! Ding! Ding! Wow, twice in one day you have been right. Must be a new record."

Sam and even Ben chuckled as Pacey flipped all of them off, "Come on, let's go so we don't miss our flight."

The rest of the team was loaded and ready to go when they arrived. Emerson opted to sit next to Sam so they could watch Red Moon together. Pacey sat across from them next to Jared who was already asleep in his seat. Slipping on his headphones deciding that some ambiance music and sleep was a good idea. Pacey felt like he had just fallen asleep when Emerson was shaking him awake.

"Sleeping beauty, we're here."

He stretched his arms over his head, slipping his headphones around his neck, "Thanks for the update, fangirl."

The team was making their way out of the airport when a couple of girls recognized him and Emerson. They politely asked for a picture which Emerson offered to take for them.

"Um, well… we were hoping to get one with both of you. We just love you two together. Much better than Lyn Dexter." The fan explained.

"Oh, okay then. Everyone squeeze in." Emerson handed the phone to Pacey who stretched his arms out to their full length to get the four of them in the selfie.

"Thank you so much! I would say good luck tomorrow, but we're Sox fans." They giggled.

Pacey chuckled, "I understand. Well, I hope it will be a great game to watch. Have a great day ladies."

He gave each of them a hug before slipping his hand in Emerson's. At first she stiffened then immediately relaxed squeezing his hand. Once they were in the van with Sam, Jared and few others they dropped each other's hand.

"Almost forgot to play my role. That's why I was always on the set team for drama club than acting." She joked.

Pacey let out a half-hearted laugh realizing he hadn't grabbed her hand to sell their fake relationship. He simply just wanted her to be close to him and that realization was all he thought about on the ride to the hotel. When they arrived, Ben pulled Emerson off to the side then he high pitch squeal echoed throughout the lobby. Immediately, Pacey turned around to find her and make sure nothing was wrong. That is when he watched her jump into the arms of an older man hugging him. Beside him was a younger man who looked like he could be Emerson's twin.

"Is that her dad and brother?" Sam asked.

He nodded, "Sure is. You're not going to fanboy all over Will Holbrook, are you?"

"Why? You think it would make a bad first impression for your fake future father-in-law?"

Sam dodged Pacey's shoulder punch as Emerson led her family towards them.

"Dad, Everett this is Pacey Tucker and Sam Knight. Guys, this is my dad, Will and my brother."

The men shook one another's hands. Pacey noticed that both her dad and brother tightened their grips when shaking his hand.

"It's nice to finally meet you. I kind of feel like I watched you grow up since following your career with the Dodgers. You and Sam."

Will said.

"It's an honor to meet you, Mr. Holbrook. Sam and I were big fans of yours as well. Hopefully, we make you proud out on the field tomorrow."

Will nodded without saying anything more and turning his attention back on his daughter. Pacey hadn't seen Emerson smile this much in the months he had known her. Her whole face lit up when she smiled and it made his heart skip.

"Em, we wanted to take you and Pacey out for an early dinner if that's alright. We made reservations at your favorite restaurant."

Emerson hugged her dad, "Awe, you didn't need to do that. It should be fine, right Pacey?"

The eager look in her eyes had him answering before he could think about it, "Absolutely. Ben will probably have to tag along but other than that should be fine."

Now her radiant smile was pointed at him. He decided there was nothing on this earth that would keep him from making her smile like that again and again. Will and Everett headed back home to let Pacey and Emerson get settled in their rooms. That is when Ben came up to them with a weary look.

"Um, for security purposes, we've put you two in the same room. However, there was a little mix up with the room."

Pacey took the room keys from Ben asking, "Mix up?"

"Yeah." Was all he said as they rode the elevator up to the fifth floor.

When they walked into their room, Pacey felt every muscle in his body tense up, "Fuck. Me."

"You have to be kidding me?" She said, dropping her bag to the floor.

The room itself was a decent size. There was a large window overlooking the Chicago skyline. Walking in was a small kitchenette and living area with a couch and TV. Next was a barn style door that opened to the single, king size bed and large bathroom. Pacey and Emerson were both focused on the single bed in the room.

"This was the only rooms available, I'm sorry." Ben said before walking out of the room.

Emerson sighed, "I guess I'll be on the couch."

She walked over sitting on the obviously uncomfortable

furniture. He picked up her bags and took them into the master suite.

"Honestly Em, I think we can handle sleeping next to each other. As long as you promise to stay on your side of the bed with no funny business."

"You wish you could do funny business with me." She snapped playfully, "It's you who needs to stay on their side of the bed. No drooling all over me… again."

His drunken night sleeping on her was still fuzzy except for the epic breakdown he had. She never brought it up and he was thankful for that. However, it had been the moment that he was most grateful for having her in his life. Emerson was one of the few people who saw him as a normal guy, and he appreciated that more than he could ever express.

"I promise." He held out his pinky to her.

She hooked hers with his, "Promise. Now, I need a shower to get the travel yuck off me."

"Ladies first. I will take mine after." He stepped out of the room closing the door behind him.

He pressed his forehead against the door flashes of listening to

Emerson in the shower the morning after his drunk night. The soft moans echoing as she pleasured herself. Often his dreams were filled with her and him, but that morning was on repeat. Even now, he could feel his cock getting hard and he forced himself to step away and flip on the TV. Finding a news station, he focused on the reports of crime in the city to distract his mind from wander to the beautiful woman naked in the shower.

Once Emerson was done getting ready, Pacey took his time letting the hot water beat against his tense muscles. Regardless of their relationship being fake and her family knowing that, having dinner with her family was intimidating. He needed to be on his A-game. Not knowing what kind of restaurant they were going to, he decided on a nice pair of jeans, dress boots and a navy button down. Running his fingers through his damp hair, he called it as good as it gets and walked out of the master suite.

Emerson was sitting on the couch in a knee-length, pale yellow skirt and plain black blouse with her hair cascading down her back and over her shoulders. He was so used to seeing her with a hat on and hair pulled up that seeing her now was like seeing a whole new woman. The way his heart thudded against his chest had him reconsidering his promise to stay on his side of the bed tonight.

"Ben is waiting for us downstairs. It's about a half hour drive to Elmhurst from here so we should go to hopefully beat some of the Chicago traffic." Emerson grabbed her purse, slipping her phone inside of it, "You look really nice, by the way."

There was a faint pink shade over her cheeks as she helped straighten out his collar. "Thank you. You look beautiful especially with your hair down."

"Thanks, it will probably be up before we get to the restaurant. It drives me crazy." She laughed as Pacey opened the door for her.

The drive to Elmhurst was filled with Emerson giving her tour guide impression. Pacey even caught Ben laughing at moments. He wondered if Emerson knew the effect she had on the people around her. Always making them feeling comfortable, safe and happy. He made a mental note to tell her that whenever they got back to the hotel. They drove down a small-town road with a lot of small businesses and restaurants. The small-town look like it was straight out of a Hallmark movie.

"Turn right at the light. The parking lot is on the left." Emerson directed Ben.

Pacey chuckled seeing the 50's style diner with drive up order stations and teenagers on skates delivering meals.

"I feel a little over dressed." He said as they parked, and he helped Emerson out of the car.

"I think you look fine. Plus, it's just dinner with my dad and brother. No need to impress since they know the truth about us."

Every time Emerson brought up how their relationship wasn't real a piercing pain would flare in his chest. He knew she didn't mean anything by it, but it was a constant reminder that he wasn't dating the most beautiful, perfect woman the world ever created. That fact hurt him deep in a spot of his heart that had been dormant since Lyn.

He put on his most charming smile holding his arm out for her. She took it without a second thought seemingly. They saw her dad and brother sitting at a table with three beers waiting for them and water for Pacey.

"Figured you wouldn't be drinking before a game." Will said with a small smirk.

"You would be right." He took a long drink wishing it was whiskey to calm his sudden onslaught of nerves.

Pacey sat back silently letting Emerson catch up with her family. Every once in a while his dad would direct a comment or question towards him, or his brother would glare daggers at him. He was resting his arm on the back of Emerson's chair absentmindedly twirling a strand of her soft hair with his fingers. When she went to pull it over her shoulder their hands brushed against one another. The spark made them both flinch and the only other person who seem to catch it was Will. His eyes were locked onto Pacey making him shift uncomfortably in his seat.

"Pacey, would it be alright to walk down to the ice cream parlor?" She asked as they were all standing to leave.

"Sure, I'll text Ben to let him know."

She hooked her arm with her brother as they started to walk down the street. They were about a foot or two ahead of him when Will dropped back walking next to him.

"So, this fake relationship…" he started to say.

"I know it's not ideal, but so far Emerson's idea has been

working. I'm incredibly grateful for her working with me. I know I wasn't at first, but I promise, I definitely am now."

Will nodded, "Well I'm glad you realize how lucky you are to have my girl in your life. I'm sure you've noticed that she loves people with her whole being. She is the fiercest protector and the most loyal woman you will ever meet. Em is a lot like her mom in that way."

Pacey let the silence fall between them watching as Emerson pulled her brother into the ice cream shop. Will stopped him from following her.

"Can we keep this between you and I?" he asked as Pacey gave him a nod to continue, "Don't hurt her. I can see it in your eyes and hers that your relationship is getting more real. Don't hurt her. She's been through a lot and if she lets you in then you thank your lucky stars for that opportunity. Understand?"

"Sir, I won't promise you that I won't hurt her." Will's eyes narrowed on him as he continued, "I will promise you that it will never be intentional. I'll do everything in my power to protect her even if it's from me. I'll do whatever Emerson wants or is best for her."

Will patted his back, "Thank you."

Emerson and Everett walked out each holding a cup of ice cream. Emerson handed him a small cup of chocolate ice cream with a smile.

"Balance." she said smiling.

His lips curled into a smile, feeling like a lovesick fool as he took a bite, "Balance."

Emerson

"I don't like him." Everett whispered to her as they walked back to the restaurant parking lot.

Emerson rolled her eyes, "Well maybe if you stopped glaring at him and got to know him you would like him."

Her brother scoffed, "I thought this relationship thing was

supposed to be fake. Doesn't seem so fake to me."

"Trust me, Everett. It's all completely fake. Do you really think someone like Pacey Tucker, who can have any woman he wants, would be with someone like me. I think not."

"I think he likes you. I think I want to punch his pretty face in and tell him there's more to come if he breaks your heart." Everett punched his fist into his palm.

"No punching him. Seriously, there's nothing to worry about. He can't break my heart because it's all fake. Now act normal or he'll think you're some kind a deranged lunatic." She smacked the back of his head.

He playfully pushed her back before he could say anything Pacey was strolling up next to them.

"I let your dad know that Ben is going to come get them in the morning for the game. That way you guys can get to the family box before the crowds."

Emerson smiled at the thoughtful gesture then looked over to see Everett's eyes narrowed on Pacey. She elbowed him in the ribs breaking his death glare and making him gasp for air.

"That's very thoughtful of him, right Everett?" She said his name through gritted teeth.

He nodded, mumbling, "Yeah. Thoughtful. Thanks."

Her dad slipped his arm around her shoulders bring her in for a hug, "Em, we'll see you tomorrow. You kids have a good night."

"Goodnight dad, see you tomorrow." She hugged him tighter then pulled away slugging her brother in the arm, "Change your attitude or I'll do it for you tomorrow."

Everett gave her nod, "Got it. 'Night."

Emerson noticed Pacey chuckling to himself as he held out his arm for her again. Something had changed between them tonight. Slipping her arm with his, she couldn't place what it was, but something was different. He opened the car door for her then got in the front seat with Ben.

"Fun night of meet the family?" He asked, heading back out onto main street.

"I had fun." Emerson said with a smile.

She meant it. She loved being with her family again, but she loved it even more that Pacey was with her. That is when it hit her. She looked up at him, his green eyes on hers as he looked back at her. A soft smile was on his lips.

"I had fun as well. Dare I say, I would do it again something."

He turned back around in his seat, and she slumped back against hers. There was only one thought running rampant in her mind.

Shit, I'm in love with Pacey Tucker.

They walked up to their room in silence, Emerson too absorbed in her revelation and forgetting that she now had to share a bed with him. Walking in, Pacey kicked off his shoes and fell face first onto the bed. She stood near the small kitchenette, frozen in her spot as her quickening heartbeat echoed in her ears.

"Emerson?" Pacey's voice knocked her back to reality, "Are you okay? You look like you're going to pass out."

"I-I'm fine, promise, Just tired."

He stood up, walking to her then placed the back of his hand on her forehead, "You sure? You do feel a little warm."

"It's summer in Chicago. Everyone is hot." She shivered as his hands ran down her arms, "We, uh, we should get some sleep."

Pacey nodded, taking a step back from her then unbuttoning his shirt. His fingers took their time slipping each button loose and he slowly unrolled the sleeves down his arms. Her mouth became suddenly dry as the desert watching him. Rolling his shoulders back, he tugged down on the sleeves and the shirt fell free from his body. Emerson felt her knees wobble as Pacey stood in his jeans and white tank. Her eyes focused on his hand unfastening his belt then unbuttoning his pants. She sucked in a shaky breath right before hearing his low chuckle.

"Once again fangirl, if you take a picture it will last longer." He took a step towards her, reaching behind him and pulling his tank top over his head.

Emerson's mind had gone completely blank staring at the achingly beautiful man before her. Her eyes took in every line and muscle of his well tone body. His jeans hung low on his hips and his black boxer-briefs were peeking out. The tips of the V lines visible above the waistband leading down into what she could only assume would be a bliss filled oblivion. His fingers pressed beneath her chin, raising her eyes to his. They were dark, shining with desire.

"What are thinking right now, fangirl?" His voice was soft, deep and sent waves of heat over her skin, "Tell me, please. I'm dying to know."

She swallowed, "You're beautiful." It came out breathless but earned her a charming smirk.

"Been called a lot of things, but beautiful isn't one of them. Especially not from an equally beautiful woman." His fingers brushed her hair back behind her ear before cupping the side of her face, "I'm going to kiss you now."

He started to lean in towards her when Emerson turned her head into the palm of his hand, "Y-You shouldn't do that. We're not… this isn't real, Pacey. You don't have to keep the act up when we're alone."

Pacey stepped back from her, and she felt like she could finally breath again. His jaw set into a firm line as he ran his hand through his hair.

"Do you really think this isn't real? That this is all an act?" He asked, his body tense suddenly, "I feel like I'm going fucking crazy. I mean, do you not feel the tether tying me to you? Pulling me to you in every possible way. Feel how natural it is to be around one another."

She could see the line between real and fake fading fast. Emerson didn't know what to do then her mom's voice rang clearly in her mind.

Honesty is always the best policy, Em. Especially when it concerns your heart. Never settle for less than the best and always be honest with whom you're with. Don't toy with men's hearts, they are more fragile than they allow themselves to be seen to be.

"Yes." She whispered.

"Yes what? That I'm crazy or you know that this fake relationship is no longer that?"

Her natural reaction to tense, uncomfortable moments was to make a joke of it, "I mean the answer is all the same. Yes, I feel this between us and yes, you're bat shit crazy."

His jaw slacked for a moment before a bellowing laugh erupted from his lips. Emerson's tense body relaxed enough for her laughter to join him. As suddenly as his laughter started it faded.

"Wait, if you feel whatever this is too then why are we still standing here like awkward teenagers on prom night and not naked in bed?"

The thought of Pacey naked made her cheeks burn, "This between us is nothing more than raging sexual tension from two people who obviously haven't had sex in a while. Sure, would it be a great and exhausting time? I have no doubts, but then what? Awkward morning after when you realize that it was nothing more than sex and you move on to the next girl. I… I can't just have sex and move on."

"You think I'm only in this for the sex? Emerson, if I wanted sex only then I would sleep with the cleat chasers. I thought you of all people would have known that by now."

The hurt in his voice broke her heart, "Pacey, I know it's not only that. I'm sorry if I implied differently. All I was trying to say was what happens when we give in, and you realize it's not enough… I'm not enough. You can go out and be with any woman you want. I, on the other hand, am one very short step away from my crazy cat lady membership."

He let out a half chuckled, "Only missing the fluffy pink robe and cute cat slippers."

"I have both back home."

They both laughed then Pacey let out a long sigh, "Well, this moment is officially ruined."

"I think it's probably for the best that we keep this relationship fake…" His shoulders sagged as her words sunk it, "at least for now."

His head snapped up then a small smirk played on his lips, "Can I ask you one question?"

She nodded, "I'm sure I'm going to regret this, but go on."

Pacey stepped in front of her again, his hand slipping behind her neck pulling her lips close to his. She sucked in a breath staring into his dark eyes.

"If I had kissed you, what would have happened?"

Honesty is always the best policy, Em…

"There probably would have been a lot less talking and more ripping each other's clothes off." She whispered, desperately wanting him to put her out of her misery and kiss her.

She was close enough to feel the rumble in his chest as his jaw tightened then his low voice sent goosebumps down her arms.

"Next time, I may not have the willpower to not follow through." He let go of her, walking into the bathroom and shutting the door.

Emerson grabbed a hold of the counter to keep her knees from giving out, "Fuck. Me."

She took a deep breath then forced her legs to move to her bag. She heard the shower come on and she decided that her own willpower was not strong enough to keep her from going to him if she heard him getting off. Placing her noise canceling headphones on, she played her favorite playlist as loud as she could stand it while getting ready for bed. Between traveling, seeing her family again and the unsatisfied ache deep inside of her, Emerson fell into a deep sleep before Pacey came out of the bathroom.

Her alarm began to ring on her phone. Peeking one eye open, she pressed the off button then tried to get up only to find she was being held on to. Looking down, Emerson found a large, tan arm wrapped around her waist. Her legs were entangled with two very long, strong legs keeping her pressed against a very firm body. Pacey stirred behind her, groaning and pressing himself against her. Emerson bite down on her lip to keep the moan from escaping as Pacey's hard cock rubbed against her ass.

"Five 'ore minutes…" He mumbled.

If she stayed for five more minutes, she would be riding that cock within three, "P-Pacey, I need to get up. I… I have to use the bathroom."

He buried his face between her shoulder blades groaning again, "Hold it… comfy… warm…" A soft moan slipped from him.

"Fucking hell…" She muttered, trying to think of anything that fucking sexy man behind her, "I swear to god Pacey Tucker, if you don't let me up then I'm going to pee all over this bed."

The deep, raspy laugh against her hot skin nearly sent her over the edge, but then he loosened his grip on her. She nearly jumped out of the bed and ran to the bathroom. She could hear him laugh as she slumped against the door. After one very cold shower that included one satisfying, yet slightly disappointing orgasm, Emerson emerged from the bathroom wrapped in one of the towels. In her rush, she forgot to take her bag in with her and now she had to face her sexy fake boyfriend practically naked.

"You're testing my willpower, fangirl."

She shivered, "Sorry, I forgot my bag. Let me grab it and get decent."

"Please, don't on my account. I'm all for my willpower failing and fucking you into oblivion."

Emerson's jaw dropped, "I… did you… what?!"

Pacey picked up her bag holding it out for her then snatching it back when she tried to grab it, "You heard me." He winked at her then handed her the bag.

"You're unbelievable, Tucker. Fucking unbelievable." She slammed the bathroom door on his laughter filling their room.

When she came back out, she was dressed in her normal game day attire, denim shorts, tank and hat with braided hair. She was only missing one thing.

"Pacey, did you see my jersey? It wasn't in my bag."

"You mean this?"

She looked up to see him holding an Explorer's away jersey, but it wasn't hers, "Whose is that?"

"Your new jersey." He said with a smirk.

Emerson took the jersey, looking over it. She noticed it was bigger than the jersey she had purchased. It had patches on the sleeves and the official MLB logo on the back collar.

"Pacey, is this your jersey?"

He nodded, "Yep. Benefit of being my fake girlfriend is you get to wear the real deal. Go on fangirl, put it on."

Emerson slipped her arms through the sleeves, and it fit almost like a dress on her. She caught his eyes traveling up her legs to the shorts that were now barely visible beneath his jersey.

"Looks way better on you than me." He cleared his throat, "Ben and your family are waiting down in the lobby. I'll see you after the game."

She picked up her backpack then set it back down, going up to Pacey and hugging him. She pressed herself up on her toes, kissing his cheek.

"Thanks, fake boyfriend. It means a lot to me to wear your actually jersey."

His smiled took her breath away, "Anything for you, fangirl. Now get outta here, so I can mentally prepare for the game."

Emerson saluted him, "Give 'em hell out there, Tucker." She yelped as he playfully swatted at her ass as she headed out the door.

Arriving at the stadium, Emerson took her family up to the box reserved for them. During away games, their box was usually empty and today was no exception. Only a couple of the players' girlfriends were there and Emerson was thankful to have her family next to her.

"Wow… if we get seats like this all the time then I can get used to Tucker dating you."

Emerson loudly whispered, "We're. Not. Dating. Not shut up and enjoy the game."

She sat next to her dad, who was staring at her jersey. She could feel her cheeks heating up and not from the sun.

"You know he could get in trouble for giving you that jersey. One thing Nick hates is players losing or giving away their uniform and having to order them new ones."

"I'll make sure he gets it back and without a mustard stain on it." She laughed.

Her dad leaned in towards her, "Seems to me, your brother is right. Less fake boyfriend and more real boyfriend."

Emerson sighed, "Not you too. I swear…"

"Well, all I'll say is if he breaks your heart then I'm going to let Everett break his face."

Her brother smiled, "Yes!"

"I'm starting to think every man in my life is ridiculous and delusional. Not eat your hot dog, old man and watch the game." She joked, making her dad laugh.

The Sox's were kicking the Explorer's asses. Pacey seemed off his game, striking out twice when he was at bat. Then the shortstop threw a sloppy ball to him and hit the top of his mitt causing the Sox to gain a runner on second and third. They were headed into the seventh inning when Emerson's phone started to buzz non-stop.

"Is the world ending?" Everett asked as she looked at the notifications.

WEDNESDAY, JUNE 10TH
5:23
Pacey Tucker in fake relationship as reported by someone close to Tucker
BREAKING NEWS

MLB's golden boy, Pacey Tucker, is creating his own love story straight out of the rom-com play book. A source close to Tucker reported that the first baseman is apparently fake dating his social media manager, Emerson Holbrook. When Tucker's ex, actress Lyn Dexter, started throwing allegations of forced abortion and sexual assault the source told TMZ exclusively that a plan was hatched for Tucker to pretend to date Holbrook. The two have been taking to social media on the regular posting about their "relationship" and how they support one another fully.

"They don't even like each other. I can't believe no one has caught onto them before now. Personally, I feel all of it takes away from focusing on the team and our first season. All of it is a distraction and our GM should have taken Tucker off the team immediately."

If Holbrook seems familiar to you she should. She is the daughter of retired Dodgers pitcher, Will Holbrook. W. Holbrook retired from baseball after his wife had suddenly passed away in a drunk driving accident. The Holbrook family then moved out to Chicago where Everett Holbrook, Holbrook's younger brother, attends school. The Holbrook family has been quiet over the years until now.

What do you think of Tucker and Holbrook's fake dating scheme? Let us know in the comments below.

Pacey

Pacey threw his glove into the locker. Losing was bad enough but

losing when Emerson's family was watching made it ten times worse.

All he wanted to do was get cleaned up and head back to the hotel. He

was getting ready to head to the shower when Coach called out to him.

"Tucker, I need you for a moment."

He followed Coach into the hallway surprised to see Marcus there on the phone, "What the hell is going on?" he asked.

"Hold on… hold on, I have Pacey right here." Marcus muted his phone, "You're flying back to Vancouver right now. We are pulling you from the roster for now until we can get the situation under control. I need you to shower and ready to leave in thirty minutes."

"What? What happened?" Pacey asked, a sickening feeling filling his stomach, "Where's Emerson and her family?"

Marcus shook his head, "Emerson no longer works for you or the team. Look, I need to handle this, and I need you ready to go in thirty. I will see you on the plane."

His agent began walking down the hall leaving Pacey in shock, "Coach, do you know what is going on?"

"All I know is some kind of story broke online about you and Emerson. You know I don't pay any attention to that shit. Right now, all you need to focus on is getting ready to be on that plane."

Pacey nodded, suddenly feeling numb and then Marcus's words hit him fully.

Emerson no longer works for you or the team.

"Fuck." He rushed back to his locker, searching for his phone.

As soon as it turned on, it started blowing up with notifications. Text messages from friends back in L.A., his mom checking on him, then he got to the article Marcus sent him.

"Oh my god…" Pacey muttered skimming through the short piece on his fake relationship with Emerson.

He pulled up her number calling it, "I'm sorry this number is no longer in service…"

"Fuck!" He yelled, as the guys entered the locker room.

"Pacey, you alright?" Sam asked.

He shook his head, packing up his bag deciding to skip the shower, "No I'm not. Everything is fucked up. Will you do me a favor and get a hold of Emerson? See how she's doing and let me know."

Sam nodded, "Sure thing, but what happened?"

Pacey swung his bag over his shoulder, "I'm sure Coach or Steinberg will tell everyone. If I get a chance, I'll text you later. I gotta go."

"Okay, I'll let you know about Em."

Pacey squeezed his friend's shoulder then headed out the

player's exit where Ben was waiting. He didn't look happy and opened the door for Pacey. Once they were on the highway head towards the airport Pacey broke the silence.

"Did you see or talk to Emerson?"

Ben nodded, "I made sure her and her family made it back to the hotel to collect their things."

"How was she?" He asked fully knowing she was probably as messed up about the whole as he was.

"Not good. Her dad was taking her back to his house until they can arrange to get her things from Vancouver." Ben paused for a moment then glanced back at Pacey through the rearview mirror, "If you have any kind of feelings for that girl then you'll do the right thing and stick up for her."

"What is that supposed to mean?"

Ben shook his head, "Nothing."

Pacey leaned forward, "Bullshit. Tell me."

"I overheard Marcus talking on the phone that they are going to put this all on Emerson. Blame her for everything and make it look like you were none the wiser of her 'plan'."

He could feel his blood boiling, "The hell they are. I will quit and go public with my story before that ever happens. She's not to blame for any of this."

"That's good to hear because if you were going to go with it then I would have had to kick your ass." Ben chuckled.

"I'm going to fix this. No matter what happens to me or my career I will fix this for Emerson."

They arrived back in Vancouver later than expected and Ben took him home. As soon as Pacey opened his door his heart sank to his stomach. Emerson's fruity body spray filled his nose making his chest tighten. Dropping his bag at the door, he headed towards his room only to stop when he found Emerson's door open. Her bed was sloppily made, and she had some dirty clothes in a pile near the closet.

Pacey sat on her bed as his mind ran wild with thoughts of her. What was she doing at that very moment? If she would ever speak or see him again? How suddenly Emerson Holbrook had come into his life and carved out a permanent place within his heart. Running his hand over his chest trying to rub away the sharp ache spreading across it. He lay down and buried his face into her pillow. Breathing in her scent deeply and allowing the tears he held back for so long finally fall.

He woke up from the banging on his door. Not knowing what time, it was he hastily made his way to find out who was on the other side and praying it was Emerson. However, seeing it was Marcus he was tempted to slam the door in his face.

"It's late. Can we do this tomorrow at the stadium?"

Marcus shoved past him, "You don't get a choice in this Pacey. We have to get ahead of this now before it truly blows up in our faces."

His manager went straight to his kitchen where the whiskey was held and grabbed one glass for himself. Pacey was well aware of how much an asshole Marcus was and it was part of the reason why he had hired him. Now he came to regret that decision as Marcus down two shots in a row.

"I'm exhausted Marcus and need the night to process everything that has happened. I'm not asking but telling you that I can't do this tonight." Pacey walked back over to his door to make his decision very clear.

Marcus ignored him, sitting at his table, "Did you fuck her?"

"What did you say?" Pacey's hands clenched into tight balls.

"You heard me. Don't play fucking coy with me. Did you fuck her?" Marcus took a sip from his glass, "I need to know so I can work it in our favor."

Pacey had enough willpower to keep his body was launch at his manager, "I'm not even going to dignify that with an answer. Not get the fuck out of my apartment before I do something I regret."

"Look, I'm trying to fix this whole fucking mess for you. You," Marcus stood, walking towards him then pressed his finger into Pacey's chest, "should show me some respect and be grateful I didn't dump your ass a long time ago."

Pacey's whole body was trembling with rage as he opened the door, "Well Marcus, don't let the door hit you as you leave."

He placed his hand on Marcus's shoulder, squeezing it hard and pushing him out into the hallway. Marcus was turning around to say something when Pacey shut the door, locking it and heading to his room. He could faintly hear Marcus cursing him out as he walked away and for the first time he didn't give two shits about what his manager thought.

The next morning, he had a text from Marcus telling him to be at the stadium at ten o'clock and that movers would be coming for Emerson's things around noon. Looking at his phone, Pacey had exactly an hour to get showered and ready for what could possibly be the hardest day of his entire career. When he was on his way out, he stopped inside Emerson's room again.

The pillow he had clutched to his chest last night was resting on the bed and he picked it up once again bringing it to his face. It faintly still smelled like her shampoo. Cradling it to his chest, he took the pillow back into his room and hid it beneath his own pillows. He knew it was wrong, even a little creepy, but he needed something of hers to be with him. The thought of losing her completely made it hard for him to breathe.

Entering the stadium, Pacey could tell everyone was on edge. He felt everyone staring at him as he walked to Nick's office. He was surprised and hurt when Whitley completely ignored him, opening Nick's door to let him in.

"Pacey, I wish we were meeting under better circumstances." Nick shook his hand.

"Me too."

Marcus scoffed, "Let's get on with this."

The three of them sat down with the Director of Public Relations, Anna, and her assistant taking notes, "Mr. Tucker…"

"Please call me Pacey." He laughed softly, "No reason to be formal."

She smiled, though he imagined it was more out of sympathy than anything, "Pacey then. We all knew going into this that there might be some push back. I have to say, when I first saw you and Emerson together I had a hard time believing you two would even like each other."

"I have the effect on people." He joked, noticing Marcus nodding in agreement.

"I have to say the fact that you two truly seemed like a couple in love makes the fall out of this a little harder to deal with."

Pacey took in a sharp breath as her words hit him. A couple in love? Was he in love with Emerson?

Marcus annoyed tone brought his attention back, "Can we stop with the coddling. The idea was shit to begin with and now we have to deal with it. It's simple. We put the whole thing on her as an overzealous fan who saw an opportunity to take advantage of her favorite celebrity. She used all her womanly prowess on him because he's a dumb jock who thinks with his dick and now his paying for this dumbass mistake."

"Fuck you! Absolutely not! I will not put this all on Emerson!"

Marcus looked unapologetic and unfazed. Nick placed a firm hand on Pacey's shoulder to keep him from reaching over and punching his manager.

"I think we can find a more diplomatic and less offensive way to handle this." Anna said, narrowing her eyes on Marcus, "I think if we come out with the truth and don't point any blame this will all blow over. We might take a hit for it, but I think if we have Pacey sit out a few games, do some interviews with reputable reporters. I truly think this will blow over and we can shift the focus back on the team's season."

Pacey caught Marcus rolling his eyes and could no longer hold it in, "What the hell is your problem? Why are you hellbent on throwing Emerson under the bus? You were the one who wanted to hire her in the first place."

"Oh no, I wanted to hire a real social media manager. I was forced to hire Emerson since she is the GM's best friend's daughter." Marcus looked over at Nick, "If we're being honest here. What do the kids call it nowadays, a safe space."

Nick spoke calmly, but firm, "Watch yourself, Marcus. You don't want to go against me."

Marcus stood up, "Look, if you all want to pussy walk around this then fine. It's your career you're throwing away, Tucker. Between the charges being brought by Lyn and now this little fake dating scandal. You'll be lucky if you get to play ball at all and I don't represent anyone but the best."

"That's fine by me." Pacey seethed, "The hell with you."

Marcus stared down at Pacey, "You don't mean that. You need me."

"I really don't. I'll have my lawyer look over our contract and take care of any consequences from breaking it early. Consider me a free agent now and yourself fired."

Pacey leaned back in his chair smiling as Marcus stood there in shock, "You'll regret this Tucker, I'll make sure of it." With that his former manager walked out of the room.

"Well, we can add this to our list of things to come out with." Anna said, typing out some notes on her laptop.

"I'm sorry. I'm sure I'm a PR nightmare, but I'm willing to hear out any suggestions to make this right for the team. Even if that means I step down for the season." Pacey looked over at Nick, "I don't want the team to suffer from my mistakes."

Nick patted his shoulder, "I know you don't, son. That's why I wanted you on the team in the first place."

For the next hour, Pacey talked with Anna about the next steps he would be taking on his social media accounts. When he arrived back home, he felt a little better knowing the game plan that would keep him training with the team but not playing in games for the foreseeable future. As he watched the movers remove all of Emerson's things from his apartment, he knew the next thing he needed to do was figure out how he could have her back in his life. This time, for real.

Emerson

Emerson slowly opened her eyes hoping, praying that the last week had been a nightmare and she would wake up in Pacey's apartment. The smell of bacon and coffee hit her senses giving her another minute of hope before she pulled her blanket down from over her head. Sighing, the weight of everything that had happened settled back on her chest. The walls surrounding her were covered in band posters and photos from various stadiums around the US. The sounds of her dad and brother talking downstairs pressed the harsh reality that was now her life further into her chest.

"Em! Breakfast is ready." Her dad called up the stairs.

She groaned sitting up in her bed, "Be down in a little bit."

Emerson was staying with her dad until she could get back on her own feet. Her position at the school had been filled and there was no room to add her back into her old department. Looking around, her stuff was scattered among her brother's old stuff from when he lived here as an undergrad.

"Hey."

She looked up to see Everett standing in the doorway, "I'm coming down in a minute."

"I know, I just wanted to let you know that your stuff arrived from Vancouver this morning. Dad and I had the movers put it in the garage for now."

Tears threatened to fall from her eyes, "Thanks. I'm… I'm planning on looking for a new place today."

Everett sat down at the end of the bed, "You know you can stay here as long as you want. Dad would probably love it if you just moved back in altogether."

They both laughed, "I know, but I need my own space."

"I get it. Well, I'm off to the hospital for the day. If you need me for anything just text me. There's nothing I can't rearrange in my schedule."

Emerson leaned over and hugged her brother, "Thanks Everett, I appreciate it."

Walking downstairs behind her brother, she found their dad waiting at the end of the stairs, "I was wondering if you two were ever going to come down. My bacon is getting cold."

After a nice breakfast with her dad, Emerson decided to get dressed and go out looking for a new apartment nearby. She toured a few units that were immediately available for rent, but none of them felt right. It was near lunch time when she stopped off at a little cafe for some food and to get a new game plan. Pulling out her new phone, she decided to check her email in case any employers had replied back to her applications. She smiled when she saw an email from Sam.

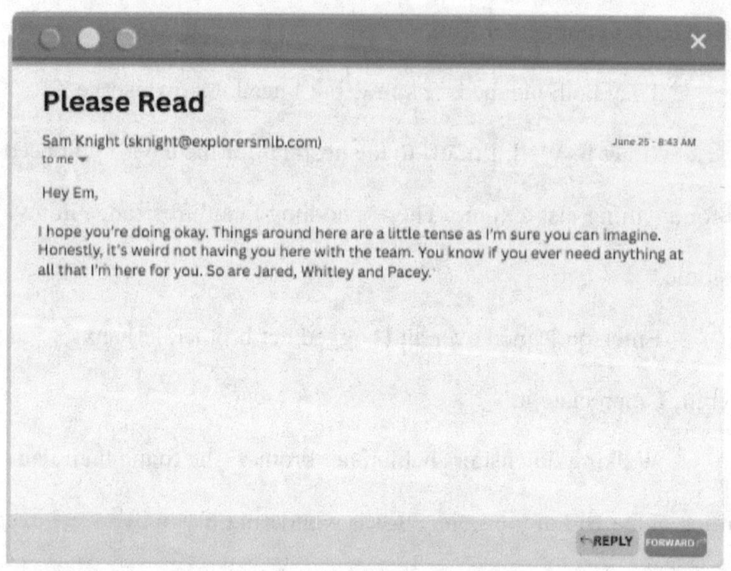

She stopped reading at the mention of Pacey. She was desperate to know how he was doing with everything happening. Most of the Explorers' games were filled with the broadcasters gossiping about Pacey than the game itself. She had noticed that he was not playing any games since their fake relationship came out, but he was still showing up to all of them and practicing with the team. His social media had gone quiet and any posts that were about their 'relationship' were taken down. The only reminders of them being together were currently on her new phone before she deleted her social media all together.

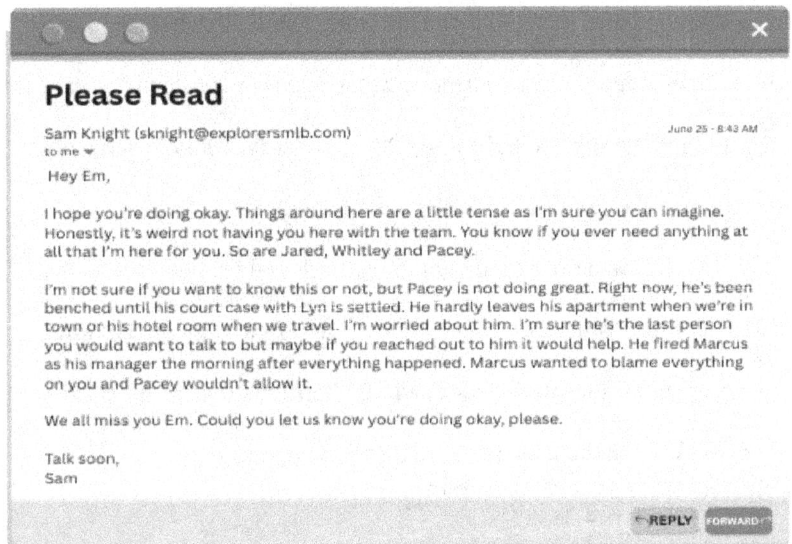

Please Read

Sam Knight (sknight@explorersmlb.com) June 25 - 8:43 AM
to me ▾

Hey Em,

I hope you're doing okay. Things around here are a little tense as I'm sure you can imagine. Honestly, it's weird not having you here with the team. You know if you ever need anything at all that I'm here for you. So are Jared, Whitley and Pacey.

I'm not sure if you want to know this or not, but Pacey is not doing great. Right now, he's been benched until his court case with Lyn is settled. He hardly leaves his apartment when we're in town or his hotel room when we travel. I'm worried about him. I'm sure he's the last person you would want to talk to but maybe if you reached out to him it would help. He fired Marcus as his manager the morning after everything happened. Marcus wanted to blame everything on you and Pacey wouldn't allow it.

We all miss you Em. Could you let us know you're doing okay, please.

Talk soon,
Sam

REPLY FORWARD

That came as a shock to Emerson. She purposely stayed off of the social media figuring they would blame her for everything. They had every right to since it was her idea in the first place. Now, she was curious as to why Pacey would even stick up for her. Sure, they had gotten close and possibly developed feelings for one another, but he had always made it very clear that he was focused on his career.

Emerson looked down at her half-eaten sandwich suddenly not hungry anymore. Sam had emailed her a few times since she left. Mostly checking in on her and letting her know how much everyone missed her. She never replied back. She couldn't bring herself to reply back knowing that it would make it harder than it already was to cut ties with everyone. She had been with the team for less than a year, but they felt like family. To have them all taken away from her suddenly was almost like reliving when her mom had died.

She tossed her sandwich in the trash and headed back to her car. There were still a few tours she was supposed to go on, but after Sam's email all she wanted to do was go home. Sitting in her car for a moment, she grabbed her phone and called her dad.

"Em, you okay?"

"I'm fine, having a moment in my car."

His audible sigh of relief came through before his voice, "What's going on?"

She told him all about Sam's email and how she was feeling about losing everyone out there, "It's like losing mom all over again. One moment they were all there in my life and the now they're not. I know I need to put on my big girl pants and move on with life like I did when mom died." She paused.

"But?"

"But I can't. I just don't have it in me. I need to be an adult, and I just can't."

Tears were slipping down her cheeks as the weight of loss sat heavily on her shoulders. She heard her dad take in a deep breath and prepare herself for the get back on the horse speech.

"Then I think you need to come home and not worry about adulting for a while."

"Really?" She asked completely stunned.

His rich chuckled made her smile, "Em, no one says you have to move on with life a week after losing people you were close to. Come home, I'll make some popcorn, and we can watch the Sox's game on TV. You can try again tomorrow to do what you need to, or you can sleep all day in your bed. Just do whatever is best for you and don't worry about anything. Everett and I got you."

Now the tears were steadily flowing down her cheeks, "Thanks dad. I'll be home in a bit."

"See you soon, Em. Love ya."

"Love you too."

When she arrived home, her dad had a big bowl of popcorn

ready to go and the White Sox game on TV. She changed into comfy clothes and joined him on the couch. Thankfully their broadcasters didn't talk about Pacey or any drama going on with the Explorers. For the first time since leaving the team, she felt happy watching baseball again.

They ordered take out after the game and watched reruns of their favorite TV crime drama. She was mid-bit into her teriyaki chicken when her dad asked her something completely out of the blue.

"Were you and Pacey truly fake dating the whole time?"

She nearly choked on her chicken, "W-Why do you ask?"

He shrugged, "Father's intuition, we'll call it. Seem to me, he may have had feelings for you."

Pacey's voice rang clearly in her head, *"Do you really think this isn't real? That this is all an act? I feel like I'm going fucking crazy. I mean, do you not feel the tether tying me to you? Pulling me to you in every possible way. Feel how natural it is to be around one another."*

"Oh yeah, why do think that?" She nervously pushed her food around on her plate.

"I had a little chat with him when we went to dinner…"

Emerson groaned, "Oh god… wait, Pacey never told me about this."

Her dad smiled, "Good to know he can keep his word. I asked him to keep it between us."

"Dad, what did you say to him?"

"All I told him was that you love people with your whole heart and to not hurt you. I could see that there was more real than fake between you two. I wanted him to know he was damn lucky to have you in his life and not to take that for granted."

She closed her eyes, pinching the bridge of her nose, "I told you before, it was all fake. Just so happens that Pacey is more caring than he lets the public see. Trust me, it was all fake."

"Em, if you need to keep telling yourself that in order to deal with it then that's fine." He placed his hand on her knee as she looked up, "However, from personal experience, if you truly have feelings for him and want to pursue it. You should with your whole heart."

She raised an eyebrow, "Personal experience?"

His smile lit up his eyes, "I was just signed to the Dodgers when I met your mom. I was celebrating out at a bar when she walked in with her friends. She was beautiful, funny and the smartest woman I had ever talked to."

Emerson loved hearing her dad talk about his mom. When she was younger, she had always wished for a man to talk about her in the same way. Seeing the way his eye lit up and his body relaxed as he continued made her think of Pacey.

"I told her that we couldn't be anything serious since I was getting ready to go off to spring training and then traveling for games most of the year. You know what she said to me?"

Emerson shook her head as he chuckled, "She said, Will, if you feel the way I feel then there is no amount of distance or time that could ever change it. I think you're worth it to say no to every guy who comes on to me. Am I worth it to you to say no to all the cleat chasers?"

She laughed, knowing that it would be something her mom would say. She was loving, but brutally honest as well.

"Of course, I told her she was worth it but I didn't want to hold her back. During spring training, she would mail me letters every day and I would write her back. When I got back, I invited her to our home opener where I gave her one of my jerseys to wear."

Immediately, Pacey giving her his away jersey popped into her head. It was folded in one of her drawers buried away to keep her from wearing it all the time.

"Did you get in trouble for giving it to her?" she asked.

"Damn right I did. It was worth it though to see her wearing my number and name. The moment I saw her in that jersey I knew I was going to marry her. That's how I knew this fake dating was more real for him when you came out in his jersey."

"Dad, I don't know what to do. For the first time ever, I feel so lost." She couldn't help the tears running down her face.

He took her plate from her lap and pulled her into his side, "I know you feel lost now, but I think you know what you need to do. What your heart is telling you to do. I think you should listen to it."

"Really?"

He nodded, hugging her tighter, "Yes I do. Now, you just need to figure out if he's worth the fight or not."

"Thanks dad. Who knew you were full of such good advice."

They both laughed before finishing their dinners.

Later that night as Emerson sat in her room, she pulled up her email on her laptop. Clicking on Sam's email, she hit reply and started typing.

Pacey

All his days were blending together. Wake up, breakfast, training with team, watch the games from dugout, home, dinner, sleep. Today was no different for Pacey as he absentmindedly made himself scrambled eggs. He looked at his reflection in the Microwave door. His cheekbones were more defined and his jaw more prominent. Looking down at his chest and stomach his muscles were more toned. The benefits of a constant workout schedule and two meals a day were doing wonders for him physically.

Mentally, he was a fucking mess. He looked back at himself to see the dark circles beneath his eyes and the sullen expression that was permanently etched onto his face. His mind was always running a million miles an hour between his court date with Lyn being up in the air and his career slowly dying a painfully public death. Then there was Emerson. He tapped on the screen of his phone to see her smiling face. The void in his chest grew a little more each time he looked at the picture. His only hope was that eventually it would swallow him whole.

The screen lit up with his lawyer's name, "What's up Jake?"

"Hey Pacey, how you doing?"

"Did you really call me to check in on me?" He sighed, "Sorry, I'm being an ass. I'm alright, you?"

"It's fine, I would expect nothing less with everything you have going on. Honestly, I've been better and wish I was calling under better circumstances."

Pacey plated his breakfast, taking it over to his table, "What's happened now?”

"The court date will be next month on the fifteenth. I've talked with Steinberg and the team's legal team as well."

There was a long pause and Pacey knew what was coming, "Let me guess, I can't train or watch the team."

"I'm sorry Pacey, they're going to be traveling a lot, and I will need you to be in L.A. Her lawyers are going to come at you hard, and I want to make sure we are prepared for everything. I'll need you to fly down to L.A. within the week."

Pacey pushed his plate away from him suddenly feeling nauseous, "I'll get the next ticket out and text you when I'm back at my house."

"Sounds good. Again, I'm sorry Pace."

"Yeah me too." He ended the call, staring down at his phone he could feel the rush of heat building in the center of chest.

Unable to hold it back he picked up his plate throwing it against the wall, "FUCK!"

The plate shattering echoed throughout his apartment. He took a couple of deep breaths before kneeling down to pick up the shards of the plate. He counted each piece to try to calm himself down. Cleaning up the rest of his mess, he went to his home office and called Whitley at her desk.

"Mr. Steinberg's office, this Whitley, how may I help you?"

"Hey Whit, it's Pacey."

"Hi Pacey, did you need to talk with Mr. Steinberg?" she asked.

He could hear her typing on her computer, "No, I was hoping you could help me with something. I need a flight to L.A. as soon as possible. I'm sure Nick will update everyone on what's going on."

"Oh…" He could hear her clicking her mouse then typing, "Is 7:00 am too early?"

"No, that would be great. When do I leave?"

She was murmuring to herself which made Pacey smile, "Tomorrow morning. I'll email you with all the information. Hey, can I ask you something?"

"Sure." Pacey could feel her apprehension through the phone, "Whitley, just ask it's fine."

"Everything between you and Emerson, was it all really

fake?"

He sighed, "Why? Did Emerson tell you something different?"

"I haven't spoken to her or more like she hasn't spoken to any of us. Sam emailed her a bunch of times, and she only replied once. Saying she needed time and space. That's why I'm asking. If it wasn't fake then I don't see the big deal with you two coming out saying that you're a real couple."

He knew Sam had been emailing her, but he didn't say anything about her finally replying back. He would have to talk to his best friend before he left.

"The whole situation is complicated. Thanks for booking my flight, Whitley."

"You're welcome. If you need anything, anything at all, just let me know."

As soon as he was off the phone with Whitley, he sent a text to Sam.

He knew it would be early evening before Sam would get there. He took a look around his apartment then decided to start organizing all his things preparing for the chance he wouldn't be coming back. He packed up the majority of his clothes and any other personal items he had including Emerson's pillow. By the time Sam arrived, Pacey had moved on from packing to drinking the last of his whiskey.

"Come on in, Sammy. Welcome to the pity party." Pacey said, stumbling his way to the couch.

"I think you've had enough of the whiskey, give it to me." Sam grabbed a hold of bottle slipping it out of Pacey's hand.

"Party pooper." He pouted, "Hey Sammy, why didn't you tell me you were talking to Emerson?"

He glanced over his shoulder to see two of his best friend's stiff body, "Who told you I was talking with Emerson?"

"Whit-ley."

Sam sat on the couch, "I should've known… I'm not really talking with Emerson. She replied once and was pretty clear on her wishes."

The whiskey fog cleared a little, "W-What was that?"

"I know I'm going to regret this," Sam pulled out his phone, "Here."

Pacey took his phone, cradling it in his hands like it was a priceless heirloom. Her email was pulled up and even seeing her name pulled at his guilt-ridden heart.

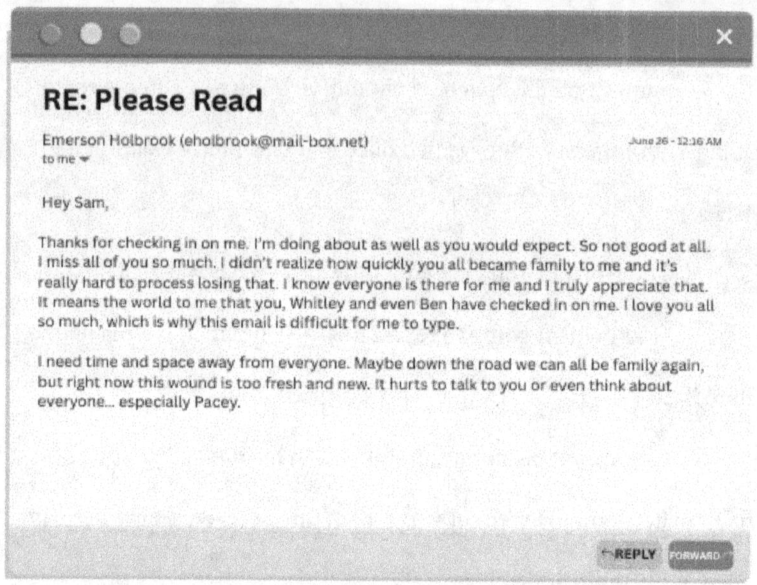

Pacey shoved the phone back into Sam's hands, "I... I can't..."

"Pace, she really-"

He held up his hand, "Please don't finish that sentence."

The whiskey that had been coating his mind with the warm and fuzzies to keep out the cold reality. The ache in his chest was nearly suffocating and he stood up quickly stumbling his way over to his balcony window. As soon as the cool air hit his skin, he tried to take a deep breath in. His lungs burned for the air that the endless void in his chest was taking from them.

"Pacey?"

Sam's voice was so far away as his world began to spin. He grabbed a hold of the railing to keep himself upright.

"Pacey! Hey buddy, sit down right here for me." Sam guided him into one of chairs, "Focus on me and take a breath for me."

He couldn't get his chest to expand, "C-Can't…"

Sam took his hand, placing it on his chest, "Do as I do." He took a breath in.

Pacey focused his eyes on their hands, willing, praying for his lungs and chest mirrored his. The first wave of cool air made him cough as his lungs took it in.

"That's alright, do it again with me." Sam took in another breath as Pacey matched him, "That's great Pace. You okay, now?"

Pacey nodded, feeling the air flowing in and out of his lungs freely. The endless void pushed further down into his chest. He patted Sam's chest before slumping back into his chair.

"Thanks Sam."

"No problem. You gonna be okay? Coach told us you were

headed back to L.A. for a while. Do you need someone to come with you?"

He shook his head, "No, the team is gonna need you more than ever now. I promise, I'll be alright."

"What about Emerson? Are you going to reach out to her?"

Again, Pacey shook his head, "If she needs time and space then we should respect that."

Sam nodded, "I'm worried about the two of you. It's obvious this whole fake dating thing turned into something real. Now, you both are miserable and barely holding on. Maybe you should talk to her and let her know how you feel."

"Maybe one day… when we've both figured out what the hell we're feeling. Right now, it's best I stay as far away from her as possible. I don't want her to get mixed up in all the Lyn bullshit. I don't want to complicate her life more than I already have."

Sam stood, patting Pacey's shoulder, "If you say so. Let me know when you get settled back in L.A."

Pacey gave him a thumbs up as Sam headed towards the door before turning around again.

"For the love of baseball stay the hell away from alcohol while you're back there. Drunk and fun Pacey is fine, but this new depressive drunk Pacey is a fucking handful who needs supervision."

"Got it dad. Now get out of here."

Pacey leaned his head back, closing his eyes as he heard his front door shut. It was taking everything within him to keep the guilt he felt from swallowing him whole. The last person he wanted to be hurt by all of this was Emerson. Realistically, he knew there was nothing he could do to help that. As much as she was in pain, so was he. He wanted nothing more than to reach out to her and make things right. The thought he would cause her even more pain stopped him dead in his tracks from doing anything.

He pulled out his phone, seeing her smiling face on the screen, "I'm so sorry Em."

Pacey opened his Instagram app and went to go to her page. Anna had taken all of their photos off his page already and he was curious to see if Emerson still had any of them. Searching through his followers list he was terribly shocked not to see her name on it. He went to the search tab and typed in her name.

"What the hell…" He mumbled.

Nothing. Emerson Holbrook no longer existed on there. He didn't even know it was possible for his heart to sink even lower be it did. She had deleted her social media because of him. She had to move back home because of him. She had to find a new job because of him. The dam finally broke and tears steadily fell down his face. He didn't know how long he had been outside crying, but Pacey finally pulled himself up and headed to his bedroom.

The morning his head was pounding as he entered the airport. He grabbed a water bottle and some aspirin before heading to his gate. Thankfully, his flight from Portland to Los Angeles was quiet. He listened to his favorite sports podcast and made a note to himself to send Whitley some thank you flowers for taking care of everything.

Being back in Los Angeles felt strange. Normally, he would be ecstatic about being back home. Now, he felt like a stranger in the city of celebrities. As he watched the city go past him, Pacey felt his phone vibrate in his pocket. He looked to see an unknown number calling him and a flicker of hope ignited in his chest.

"Hello, Em?"

A cold laughter on the other end ran shivers down his spine, "Sorry baby, not your little fake girlfriend."

"Lyn. I'm hanging up."

"Wait! You'll want to hear me out. We can end this little court matter before it does some real damage to your little career." She paused, "Still there, Pacey?"

He clenched his jaw, "Start talking."

"Good boy. Now, the way I see it we can easily settled this between you and I. Sadly, if your little cleat chaser had listened to me before then we wouldn't be here now. She should have been smarter and agreed to my deal earlier."

"Get to the point and fast." He said through gritted teeth.

"We can settle this all for one lump sum of ten million and I will happily make this all go away."

He laughed, "Seriously? Is this all about money? Lyn, you make way more than that on one project. Why the hell would you need... oh, I get it now."

"What?" she snapped.

"Hollywood has finally sent you packing. You're out of the

prime-time age and now they don't want you. Is that it?"

He smiled hearing her frustrated sigh, "You know what, Pacey, forget it. I think I would rather see you and your career go up in flames. You'll never play baseball again. You'll be someone's little bitch in prison. I'll make sure to write you every day to remind you that you could have simply made this all go away but instead decided to be an asshole."

"We'll see about that. Goodbye Lyn."

Pacey ended the call and immediately pulled up Jake's number, "Jake, we have a major problem."

Take The Deal...

Unknown (noname1001@mail-box.net)

to me ▾   June 30 - 2:22 PM

Pacey,

I wanted to send you a little reminder of our conversation yesterday. Even though you were completely rude to me, I'm a forgiving and gracious person. I could make your life, your team's life, your precious little cleat chaser's life all a living hell. Or you can man up and take my deal. Honestly, you have no need for it and it would really help me to move on past that trauma you inflected on me.

Now you're probably thinking this is too good to be true. Honestly, it is as simple as it seems. You agree to my terms and I will leave you and everyone around you alone for good. You can go off and have your boring little apple pie life. If not and you want to do things the hard way then I might suggest you check out the attachments below. I can and will make your life a living fucking hell. I will air out every piece of dirty laundry you have out in court. Don't you dare think it will just be me speaking out but every woman you've ever taken advantage of will have my back.

The choice is yours.
Lyn

📎 Attachment 1: Girl #1 - Wrap Party
📎 Attachment 2: Girl #2 - Club VIP Room
📎 Attachment 3: Girl #3 - Away Game Hotel Elevator
📎 Attachment 4: The Cleat Chaser - Home

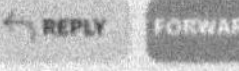

Emerson

Endless hours of applying for jobs were making her head spin.

Emerson felt like her eyes were going to fall out of her head. She had

spent the better part of her day looking at social media coordinator or

manager positions that were working from home. Even though her dad

had told her to take her time and there was no rush for to move out. She

needed some normalcy in her life to keep her mind from wondering too much.

She hit submit on another application before leaning back in her chair and closing her eyes. Today was the first day in a week she had decided to apply for jobs that were not in social or digital media. She thought maybe she would like working with kids and applied to a few teacher assistant positions. She also had applied to work at her local library which was definitely out of her comfort zone. Though the thought of being surrounded by books all day sounded wonderful.

Deciding a break was needed, Emerson decided to browse Twitter for the latest news. Scrolling through her dashboard a lot of the sport reporters were talking about the upcoming All Star game. That's when Pacey's photo caught her attention. It was his professional player photo with the headline, 'All Star Player Missing Big Game'. She clicked on the article and skimmed through the major highlights. She was surprised that it read more like a entertainment gossip article than sports.

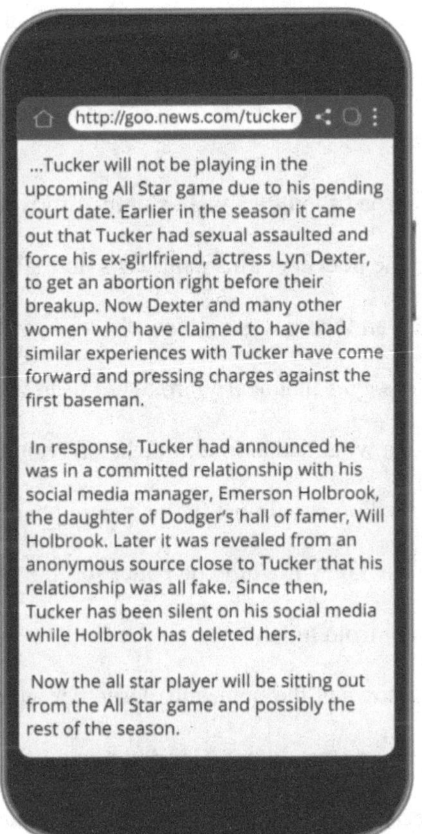

Emerson searched for Pacey's name and court date. Many media outlets were reporting that his court date was coming up within a few days on the fifteenth. Her heart ached within her chest knowing he must have been going out of his mind not being able to play. His court proceeding was being held in Los Angeles, and he had been spotted arriving to his home early last month. She clicked on the paparazzi photo and gasped.

Pacey's broad shoulders were slumped forward, and his hands were stuffed into the pockets of his pants. His normally tanned skin seemed to be paler and there was no hint of a smile on his face. However, it was his eyes that nearly broke her heart. His eyes were dull and downcast like a wounded animal. She hated seeing him like that and the bit of her willpower almost broke pushing her to reach out to him. Deep down she knew it would be better for him all around if she stayed far, far away from him.

Looking down at the time, she closed her laptop and went down to the kitchen to start dinner. Her dad was golfing with some friends giving her the whole house to herself. She turned on her favorite season of Red Moon and gathered all the ingredients needed for her mom's spaghetti. She was just adding the noodles to the boiling water when her phone rang. Not recognizing the number she hesitantly answered it.

"Is this Emerson Holbrook?" The female asked.

"Yes, may I ask who's calling?"

There was chuckle on the other end, "Sorry, I'm Leigh Meyer and you had sent your resume to me about being my client's social media manager."

Emerson let out a sigh in relief, "Yes I did, how are you today?"

"Better now that I'm talking with you. I would like to set up a time for you to chat with my client and I virtually. We were hoping you would be available on Friday at five o'clock."

"Absolutely! I would love to talk with both of you. Five o'clock on Friday is great."

"Perfect! We're both excited to talk with you. I'll email you the link and talk to you on Friday." Leigh said ending the call.

Emerson stared down at her phone for a moment before doing a little happy dance. By the time her dad came home she had their dinner on the table and shared her exciting news with him.

"Em that's wonderful! Do you know who the client is?" he asked.

She shrugged, "I know she's a literary agent and has a few

clients. I can imagine it would be promoting the client's books and any events they may do."

Emerson chuckled as her dad took a big bite of spaghetti before saying, "'ounds 'erfect far ya… Mmm, you make this as good as your momma did."

She smiled, "Thanks dad. I make it anytime I miss her. Today was just one of those days."

"I get it. I miss her every day."

For the rest of dinner, they ate in comfortable silence until Everett arrived. Her brother and dad decided to watch the All Star game while Emerson went back up to her room to check her email for any other job responses. As she sat down at her desk, her phone started to ring again.

"Hello?"

"Emerson, it's Sam. Please don't hang up."

She was stunned to hear Sam's panicked voice, "Sam, how did you get my number?"

Emerson hadn't given her new number to anyone back in Vancouver the only person who knew it was her dad and brother.

"I may have asked Steinberg for your dad's number and called him before I called you."

She rolled her eyes but couldn't help the tension gripping her chest that he went through all that trouble for her number, "What's wrong? Is Pacey okay?"

There was a long pause, "He says he's fine, but I know he's not. Lyn is really dragging his name through the mud, and I hate it. She has this whole army on social media against Pacey. I know he's no angel…"

Emerson laughed, "Now that's an understatement."

"I know, but he doesn't deserve this. It's bad enough that this is affecting his career, but frankly I'm scared he's to his breaking point, Em."

"What do you mean?" she asked.

"I think he's considering taking a plea deal which will mean prison time. Lyn approached him about settling outside of court for ten million, but he refused. I don't think he knew just what she was capable of on social media and dragging him through the mud. I think he's giving up."

She hated hearing that Pacey was hurting and getting railroaded. She also didn't know what she could do about any of it.

"I'm sure you're not calling me to give me an update. There's something you want me to do and I can't fathom what that could be."

"You're right, I need to ask you favor and it's a huge one. Whitley told me that I shouldn't because it's too much to put on you especially after everything that happened. Honestly, I don't have anyone else to go to."

Sam was normally the calm and sensible one between him and his best friend. It surprised Emerson to hear him almost frantic.

"What do you need me to do?"

Emerson stood in front of her mother's gravestone. Kneeling down, she placed the fresh bouquet of tulips in the holder. It had been a long time since she had visited her and now the guilt of that was weighing heavily on her.

"Hi mom…" She wiped away a few wayward tears, "I miss you so much."

When she originally thought about visiting her mom's grave,

she thought she would be fine. Now, sitting in front of her, all she could think about was how messed up her life was right now. She wished more than anything she could hug her mom and ask her what to do.

"Mom, I know you're looking down on me. I'm sure you've had some choice words for the decisions I've made recently especially in the love department."

She thought about Pacey and how charming he could be, "You would have never fell for his charm. You would have put him in his place from the moment he would have said hi." She chuckled.

"Am I doing the right thing, mom? I feel so torn not knowing how I truly feel. Life is so complicated, and you know dad is no help with this."

Emerson looked over her shoulder to see a mom and child laughing while walking down the sidewalk. She couldn't help the smile on her face thinking about all the laughs and tears she shared with her mom.

"If you can mom, let me know I'm doing the right thing. Let me know you approve of this and are proud of me."

"Watch out!" Someone yelled out as she looked up.

A baseball flying towards her and she quickly moved out of the way. A teenage boy ran over grabbing the ball from the ground.

"I'm sorry ma'am. I told my friend not to hit over towards the graves. Are you okay?"

She nodded, "I'm fine, thank you."

He turned around and Emerson let out a small gasp. The young boy was wearing a Dodgers jersey with Tucker and the number twenty-four on it. She smiled looking back at her mom's grave.

"Thanks mom, I love you."

Pacey

Pacey wiped his hands down his dress pants. Today was the second day

of his court proceeding and yesterday had been incredibly emotional

for him. He thought he was going to be able to keep himself under

control and several times as Lyn's lawyer spoke on his character Jake

would have to keep him from lashing out. Lyn's side of the court room was filled with the women who claimed he had abused them in one way or another. A lot of them looked familiar and the guilt from not remembering them all sat on his shoulders.

Ben pulled up to the back entrance of the courthouse, "Damn it."

Pacey looked out his window to see a sea of paparazzi, "Wasn't the courthouse security supposed to keep this entrance clear?"

"Yes, they were. Looks like I get to chew someone a new asshole." He grumbled, "Let's get you inside first."

"Brute force?" Pacey questioned with a small smirk seeing Ben's smile.

"Would you expect anything less?"

No matter how terrible the day would be Pacey enjoyed watching Ben shove, push and facepalm paparazzi out of the way. He met his lawyer in a small meeting room where he had his notes spread out on a table.

"Everything okay?" Pacey asked, concerned about the stressed outlook on Jake's face.

"Yeah, I'm just making sure I'm prepared for whatever may

come out today. How are you doing? Is there anything you need me to know so I'm not caught with my pants down out there?"

Pacey sighed as he sat across from Jake, "I tried looking at everyone on Lyn's side and over the list of names. I don't really remember anything about them. Did I sleep with them? Yeah, I probably did. I partied a lot back then especially after Lyn broke up with me."

"Okay, then we'll just deal with whatever they throw at us. I just need you to keep your temper under control."

He nodded, "I know… I'll try my best."

They went over a few notes Jake had taken before the court clerk came to get them. Walking inside the court room, Pacey looked at the row right behind his seats and his chest tightened. His parents were sitting next to each other for the first time since he graduated high school. Besides his mom was Sam, Jared and Whitley. Seeing his family and friends sitting there in support of him gave him the tiniest bit of hope. The only way it could have been better was if Emerson had been there.

"Please rise for the honorable Judge George Townsend."

Everyone stood, as the judge took his seat, "Everyone may have a seat. We are going to proceed with the prosecution's witnesses."

"Thank you, your honor. We would like to call…"

For the next two hours, Pacey sat through every single woman's testimony of lies against him. By the time they called for lunch, not only was he not hungry but also to the point he wanted to throw in the towel. Sitting alone in the meeting room with Jake, he couldn't even bring himself to go out and talk with his family and friends.

Jake's phone buzzed on the table and his expression went from annoyed to frantic in a matter of seconds. Pacey leaned across the table tapping it with his finger.

"What is it? What's wrong?" he asked.

"Nothing, nothing is wrong. I need for you to go into the family waiting room. I need to go talk with the judge and Lyn's lawyer."

Pacey stood and grabbed a hold of Jake's elbow, "Why? What was that text?"

Jake smiled, "A fucking miracle, now go so I can save your

ass."

He walked across the hall into the room where his parents and friends were all sitting around a table. Immediately his mom pulled him into a hug.

"Sweetie how are you holding up?" she asked as his dad pulled a chair for him.

All he could do was shrug, slumping down into the chair, "As good as anyone who's wild days are on display for the world."

"I would love to know how Lyn got a hold of all these women. Ninety percent of them I don't even recognize, and I was always by your side back then." Sam commented.

Pacey let out a half-hearted chuckle, "Shit, I don't recognize a lot of them. Which helps her case even more that I look like a heartless dickhead."

Fifteen minutes later, Jake walked into the room with his bag in hand, "The judge has called it for today and we will start back tomorrow morning at nine. You all should go home and try to rest up."

"Why did he call it?" Pacey asked as a sinking feeling hit his stomach.

"I asked him to in order for me to prep my character witness for you." Jake smiled as everyone in the room started talking at once.

"What do you mean character witness?"

"Who is testifying?"

"Are you sure about this?"

Jake held his hands up, "I assure you all that this is going to be the best thing for Pacey's defense. This person is one hundred percent the real deal."

Pacey stood up, "Who is it?"

Jake squeezed his shoulder, "We don't want the press to get a hold of their identity. The judge and Lyn's lawyer are the only people who know. They wanted it this way. Trust me Pace, their testimony is going to help you a lot in the long run."

He nodded, "Okay. Well, if you all want to you can come over to my house and stay. I have plenty of room."

Ben was waiting for him outside in the hall to take him to the car. Sam, Jared and Whitley were going to ride along with him while his parents decided to head back to their hotels promising to be there in the morning.

He hugged each of them, "I know you two don't like being around each other. I appreciate you both being here for me."

His dad patted his back, "No matter our differences son, we will always be here for you."

His mom nodded in agreement before they both walked out of the courthouse together. Pacey could have sworn he saw his mom grab a hold of his dad's hand as they were walking. The drive back to his house was solemn as was the mood after everyone had settled in around his living room. Jared and Whitley were curled up on his love seat talking softly to one another. Sam was in the kitchen preparing his famous homemade pizzas.

He stood next to his best friend watching him work, "Who do you think the character witness is?"

"Could be a lot of people. Maybe Steinberg or Coach. Who do you think it is?"

Emerson popped into his mind immediately, but Pacey knew it couldn't be her. She would be the last person who would come to his defense, and he couldn't blame her. He had all but ruined her career and reputation.

"Honestly, I have no idea. It feels like Lyn has turned everyone against me except for those who truly know me."

Sam looked up at him, "Don't let her show of force mess with you. It's like when we played the Yanks or the Cards. It's the ones who are threatened the most who lash out the loudest."

"I think I would rather play a doubleheader against the Yanks than to hear all those women talk about how I abuse them." Pacey looked down at his feet as the shame of his past pressed against his shoulders, "Tell me the truth, Sam. Was I really that bad back then?"

Sam stopped chopping vegetables to face him fully, "I won't say you were an angel back then. None of us were. We were young and dumb. Did you sleep with and leave a lot of girls back then? Yes, but you were trying to fill a hole that couldn't be filled by booze and sex."

"I don't think that void will ever be filled." Pacey murmured.

"I think it was when Em was around. You love her." Pacey's eyes snapped up to Sam as he smirked, "Don't give me that look. You fell in love with her. Honestly, who wouldn't? She's amazing, smart and gorgeous. The two of you are just too stubborn to admit that you love each other."

Pacey stood there dumbfounded then let out a long sigh, "Doesn't matter now. Even if I went to find her in Chicago, I'm pretty sure her dad and brother would kill me for breaking her heart."

Sam wiped off his hands before gently squeezing his shoulders, "She's worth it though, right?"

Pacey nodded as Sam continued, "Then don't give up yet. Get through all this Lyn bullshit then go get your girl."

"Since when did you get so smart about life and love?" He chuckled.

"Fuck you, I've always been the smart one. Plus, now maybe you won't give me shit about the romance books I read. Now get out of here so I can cook dinner." Sam pushed him out of the kitchen.

Pacey headed towards his bedroom, sitting on the bed and allowing the heaviness of the day to sit on him. Each woman's testimony replaying in his head as he closed his eyes and laid back.

"He forced me onto the bed, pinning me to it and ripping my clothes off."

"He threw me against the wall where I hit my head really hard. I... I don't remember how I ended up underneath him on the

bed."

"He left his hotel room without a note or even waking me up. I had no idea where I was and then the manager made me pay for everything for the time Pacey was there. It was thousands of dollars."

"Pacey would call me any time he was back in L.A., and we would go out to the clubs. He would encourage me to drink and take pills. When I asked him about getting serious he told me all I was to him was a piece of ass to use."

His fists clenched at his sides as each of their voices echoed in his mind. He couldn't get their tear-stained faces from playing like a movie reel over and over. Pacey couldn't recall a single moment that each woman told the judge. He had a lot of blackout moments back in his younger days, but that's why he always stayed close to Sam. He never let Pacey go home with anyone when he pushed his drinking too far. He sat up when there was a knock on his door.

"Hey Pacey, food is ready." Whitley called through the door.

"Thanks, I'll be right there."

He quickly changed out of his suit and headed back to the living room with his friends. The friendly banter and jokes took the edge off for him. Looking around, he found a whole new appreciation for his teammates and baseball family. Finally, being able to relax enough to let himself laugh and feel the smallest bit of hope that everything would be okay.

When Pacey arrived at the courthouse the next morning, he was directed to go into the family waiting room until a clerk came to get him. Jake had been radioed silent even when Pacey had texted him early in the morning. Walking into the courtroom, Jake was already at their table and scribbling down notes on his pad.

"Is everything okay? Not like you to not answer my texts?"

Jake nodded, "Everything is good. Hey, when your character witness comes in please try to keep yourself neutral in response. We don't want to give Lyn's lawyer any kind of reaction that he could use against you."

Pacey nodded having a million questions as to who they were, but the bailiff came in announcing the judge's arrival.

"Mr. Carter, you can call your witness now."

Jake stood up, "The defense would like to call to the stand, Miss Emerson Holbrook."

Everything around Pacey suddenly slowed. The doors opened and in walked Emerson. Her long hair was pulled back into high ponytail with some framing her face. She wore dark brown dress pants that clung to her like a second skin paired with a pair of ankle boots. The solid olive blouse made her warm amber eyes shine and were focused straight ahead of her until she reached his table. She glanced over to him as her naturally rosy lips pulled into a soft smile. His rapid heartbeat drowned out all the murmuring from the gallery of people behind him. She stepped up on the stand taking her oath then sat down as Jake walked up to her.

"Thank you for being here, Miss Holbrook. If you could please provide your testimony of your time with Mr. Tucker for the court."

"First I would like to thank the court for allowing me the opportunity to share my testimony. I feel it's important to hear from both sides of the story especially in situations like this."

The judge nodded, "Go on, Miss Holbrook."

"Mr. Tucker's team hired me to help manage his social media. Entertainers, celebrities, athletes, they all have a persona that is for the world to see. They are typical archetypes that you would find in your favorite movies, shows or books. Mr. Tucker was known for being a bit of the playboy or bad boy in his early career."

"Objection, how can she testify to what he was like in his early career." Lyn's lawyer shouted out.

"Overruled. Please continue."

Emerson squared her shoulders back, sitting up straighter, "I would know because I have been a fan of his since the beginning of his career. My dad is a retired professional baseball player who played for the Dodgers. We are still hardcore Dodgers fans, and I remember the first time I saw Mr. Tucker head out onto the field."

She looked over to him, "I remember my dad being impressed by him and anyone would be a liar if they didn't say that he's an attractive man. I started following his career from that day and remember all the tabloids tracking all his wild nights out. When I first met Mr. Tucker, he was a jerk to put it nicely. He was stand offish, rude and his ego could fill this entire room. I was disappointed that my hero, a man I admired was nothing but a complete douchebag."

Pacey hung his head low as his lawyer leaned against the

stand, "So he made a bad first impression?"

"Yes he did," she chuckled, "However, I soon found out that it was all an act. His bad boy, womanizing persona was all an act for the world. Running his social media meant that I was around Mr. Tucker a lot. The more I was around him, the more I learned that he is actually one of the most caring, protective, loving people I have ever met."

She looked back at Pacey, who couldn't help staring at her, "Once Miss Dexter started dragging his name through the mud of public opinion, I came up with an idea to counteract her claims."

"This is when the fake relationship came about?"

"Yes, I was the one who came up with the idea that we should be in a fake relationship. At first, Mr. Tucker wasn't sure about going along with it. He didn't see how it could help show his fans how he truly is with women."

"Miss Holbrook, could you tell us how he was with you during your fake relationship?" Jake asked.

Pacey leaned forward on the table curious to finally hear her inner thoughts about him.

"He was always a gentleman, and I mean that in every sense

of the word. When fans started harassing me, he insisted on staying with me or having security stay with me. When they vandalized my home and got a hold of my personal phone number Pacey moved me into his apartment. In the months that I lived with him, never once did I ever feel unsafe or pressured to do anything."

Jake walked back to the table standing in front of Pacey, "Miss Holbrook, my next question is going to be extremely personal and private. I apologize for the invasiveness, but it's important for us to know. Did you and Mr. Tucker ever cross the line to having an intimate relationship?"

"No, not that the temptation wasn't there. When I first brought this idea to him, his only rule was that I couldn't fall in love with him. At the time, that wasn't going to be a problem. The longer we were together, and I got to know who he was as a person and not Pacey Tucker the MLB all star." She smiled at him, "I couldn't help to fall in love with him."

"Why is that?"

"He is a caretaker. He takes care of those around him and tries to protect them no matter what the cost is to him. He stands up for those who can't stand up for themselves. He respects people's opinions and most importantly their privacy because he knows what it's like to not have any. There were moments when we were together, and he could have easily pressured me into doing something. However the moment I told him that it was better that nothing happened between us, he immediately backed off. He respected my wishes and never once made me feel guilty or bad for not wanting to cross that line."

Emerson looked at Lyn, "I don't know what Mr. Tucker was like when he was with Miss Dexter, but I do know that the man he is now is not the man she is claiming him to be."

Pacey

"Thank you Miss Holbrook. You're dismissed." The judge said as the door opened with Jake's assistant running in.

Pacey watched as Emerson walked past him and to the back of the gallery sitting next to her dad. He hugged her as she wiped away tears from her cheeks. He wanting nothing more than to go to her, but

Jake's voice brought his attention back to why his assistant had rushed in.

"Judge, may we approach the bench?"

"Ladies and gentlemen of the gallery, we are going to take a recess until tomorrow morning at 9:00 AM where the defense can present their new evidence." The judge stepped down from his seat and headed back through the door to his chambers.

Pacey turned to Jake who was collecting his things, "What the hell just happened?"

"Let's get back to the meeting room and I'll explain everything."

He looked over at Lyn and her lawyer seeing them in a heated conversation. She was upset about whatever had just happened and Pacey suddenly had a spark of hope ignited in his chest. He quickly looked over to the seats where Emerson and her dad were sitting only to see them empty. Disappointment spread down his body like cold water. He started to walk out of the courtroom when Jake grabbed his shoulder.

"I know you want to go after her, but you can't. We need to go talk about this new evidence now."

"Why didn't you tell me Emerson was testifying for me? Did you reach out to her?" He needed to know if she did this on her own or if she was compelled to by his lawyer.

Jake smiled, "She came to me. Apparently she saw some articles on the trial and wanted people to know her side of the story."

They walked inside the meeting room where his parents, Sam, Jared and Whitley were waiting. Pacey couldn't help his shoulder slouching slightly when he didn't see Emerson in there as well. Jake took out a small packet handing it to Pacey.

"Can you guys tell me what you know about your teammate, Hunter Rowe." Jake asked.

Everyone's eyes shot up to him as Sam spoke, "Was he the one who leaked Pacey and Em were in a fake relationship?"

Jake nodded, "Yes. He's been seeing Lyn Dexter for a little over a year now. Apparently, her career is tanking, and he was supposed to be the star player on the Explorer's team. When Nick Steinberg went with Pacey, Hunter and Lyn started coming up with a plan to not only drag Pacey's name through the mud but also get as much money out of him as possible."

Pacey knew Hunter had beef with him, but he never thought it was anything more than locker room ego. He couldn't believe that one of his teammates would actually do this to him. Suddenly, his anger and betrayal collided at once.

"Fucking bastard!"

"Pacey Tucker!" His mom shouted, "No reason to use that language."

Pacey started to pace the room, "Sorry mom, but I think there is. I always knew Hunter had a problem with me, but I never thought one of my teammates would stab me in the back. There's always ego in the locker room but we push it aside the moment we hit that field."

His dad nodded in agreement, "I agree. The camaraderie and brotherhood of a team is sacred. Even when Will and I had our fights we never would do anything to one another that would harm them in anyway."

"Apparently that memo never got to Hunter until now. He came forward only after Lyn dumped him and said since she did all the work he wasn't entitled to anything she would get from this case. He wasn't happy so he gave his statement about everything. Between his statement and Emerson's testimony, we have a really good shot of getting this whole case dismissed." Jake patted his shoulder.

Pacey let out a sigh, "So now it's all up to the judge?"

Jake nodded, "Yep, now we wait. Hunter will come in to make his statement in court then the judge will make his ruling."

That night as his friends slept at his apartment again, Pacey sat up on his balcony unable to keep his mind off of seeing Emerson. He had begged Jake to give him her contact information but understood when he didn't. He didn't want to break her confidence with him. He looked up at the moon wondering if Emerson was also sitting up wherever she was looking at it as well. Running his hand over his hair, he pulled out his phone and brought up his Instagram. Scrolling through the mindless notifications, he stopped suddenly seeing a familiar name on there.

He immediately went to her page and followed her back. It was her personal Instagram and not the one she had created when their fake relationship started. He scrolled through her pictures getting a true look of who she was. Photos with her dad and brother, her with students and friends at school. The last photo was of her from an Explorer's game wearing his jersey.

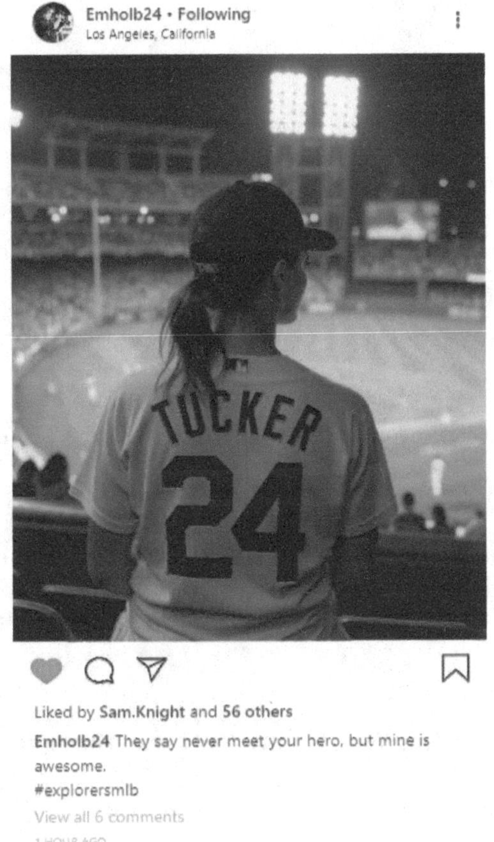

His heart did a double beat rereading her caption and looking at her photo. No matter what happened with the trial, if he was able to go back to playing baseball or not. One thing Pacey was a hundred percent certain about. He was going to tell Emerson Holbrook that he was head over heels in love with her.

The next morning when he walked into the courtroom Pacey was shocked to see Emerson sitting in the second row beside Sam, Whitley and Jared. Her dad was in the same row next to his parents. She gave him a soft smile as Jake tugged on his elbow to their table. He glanced over to Lyn who was looking particularly pissed off at the world.

"Please rise for the honorable Judge George Townsend." The bailiff announced.

"You may be seated. Mr. Carter you entered a sworn statement from Mr. Hunter Rowe. Is he here to make his statement before the court?"

Jake nodded, "Yes, I would like to call Hunter Rowe to the stand."

Pacey watched as Hunter walked in, not looking at either him or Lyn. He took his oath before sitting down on the stand. Jake approached him with his statement in hand.

"Mr. Rowe, is this your statement given two days ago to the court officer in Vancouver, Washington?"

"Yes it is."

Jake handed the statement to Hunter, "Would you please read it out loud for the judge and gallery to hear."

Listening to Hunter's statement infuriated Pacey but also he couldn't help to pity Hunter for falling for Lyn's deceptive game. He explained how Lyn had cornered him at a party and their whirlwind love. She had first told him the story about Pacey forcing her to get an abortion after the announcement Pacey was going to the Explorers. From there her story about the abuse and sexual assault only got bigger as she became obsessed with dragging Pacey's reputation through the gutter. When Hunter threatened to leave Lyn, she finally told him that she had plans to have charges brought against Pacey and force him to give her a large settlement of money that they could split evenly.

"Mr. Rowe, is this the document you provided to the court officer that you found in Miss Dexter's apartment?"

"Yes." Hunter looked at the sheet of paper then handed it back to Jake.

"I would like to submit item 4A into the evidence of a doctor receipt of a procedure that took place In February 2016. On the document you will find the basic notes of the procedure requested by Miss Dexter and the date of the request five days earlier with her signature."

Pacey's eyes widened as he looked over at Lyn. She was furiously talking with her lawyer as the judge looked over the document. Five days, she had gone to the clinic five days before and he never knew. For five days, she lived with their child growing in her knowing she was going to take them away. He suddenly felt sick to his stomach then he felt a hand on his shoulder. He looked over to see his dad squeezing his shoulder. That's when he noticed the tears sliding down Emerson's face as her eyes narrowed on Lyn.

"Mr. Rowe, you can step down." The judge said, reading over his statement, "I would like to take a recess for thirty minutes then we can reconvene for my final verdict."

The next thirty minutes was the longest of Pacey's life. He had tried to go to Emerson, but Jake had pulled him away into their meeting room while Emerson went with Whitley and Sam. It was driving him crazy to be this close to her and not being able to talk to her. When they went back into the courtroom, he found her sitting in between Sam and

Whitley. She was talking to Whitley about something that made her beautiful smile appear.

"Please rise for the honorable Judge George Townsend." The bailiff announced.

Suddenly, Pacey's stomach started twisting uncomfortably as the judge sat in his seat. This was it, the moment that would change his life forever.

"Please be seated," The judge pulled out his notes review them as everyone sat in their seats, "After considering the testimonies of everyone and the evidence provided I have made my final verdict. If the defendant would please stand."

Pacey's legs were trembling as he stood up beside Jake.

"In the case of Dexter versus Tucker, I hereby dismiss all charges filed against Mr. Tucker with prejudice. Miss Dexter, it is obvious to me that you felt the need to make this court your final act performance of a well planned drama. However, you will not be rewarded for your performance in my courtroom. You are dismissed."

Everyone behind Pacey started cheering as Lyn broke down into sobs. Pacey hugged Jake nearly picking him up off the ground. His parents pulled him into a big hug as Will Holbrook patted his back.

Sam, Whitley and Jared were next to envelop him into a group hug.

"I knew she wasn't going to win! Tonight, we celebrate!"

Jared said.

Pacey pulled back looking at Sam, "Where's Emerson?"

His friend looked behind him, but she was nowhere to be seen,

"She was right here…"

Pacey rushed past his friends making his way out the front

entrance of the courthouse. Reporters were swarming Lyn and her

lawyer as they exited the building. That is when he spotted Emerson

walking with purpose towards his ex.

"Hey Lyn!" She called out as Lyn turned towards her.

Emerson drew her hand back and slapped Lyn across the face

with a resounding echo silencing everyone around them.

"That's for trying to ruin Pacey's life and career. Stay out of

his life or you'll have to deal with me."

Pacey's jaw dropped as he watched Emerson walk away

toward the sidewalk, "Emerson!" He yelled.

Before he could see if she heard him the group of reporters

were surrounding him. Ben suddenly appeared from what seemed like thin air and ushered Pacey towards the black SUV. He caught one last glimpse of Emerson and her dad getting into a cab and driving in the opposite direction that he was.

Emerson

Emerson was slowly packing her things for her early morning flight back to Chicago. Her dad was going to stay in Los Angeles for a little longer to visit some old teammates and visit her mom's grave. The thought of switching her flight to a later one had crossed her mind more than once since leaving the courthouse. Video of her slapping Lyn was going viral and all she wanted to do was get back home. She sat down on her bed, picking up her phone to scroll through her Instagram feed.

The first post was from Pacey's page. Whoever was running it had shared a post from ESPN stating that Pacey had been cleared of all charges and would be reporting back to the field within the next week. She double clicked the post to like it skipping over reading the fan comments. Before she left her mom's grave Emerson had decided to follow Pacey again on social media. No matter what happened between them, she would always be a fan of his.

As she was scrolling, an incoming phone call popped up. Emerson stood up nervously seeing it was Leigh's number.

"Hi Leigh."

"Emerson, wow girlie you have one hell of a slap." She chuckled, making Emerson grimace.

"Yeah… my emotions may have gotten the better of me." Emerson sighed, "I understand that everything going on right now looks bad for me. I get it if this call is to let me know you're considering someone else for Raelyn's social media manager."

Leigh scoffed, "Please, if you think this will scare us away you apparently have never dealt with a whole fandom constantly being all over your client and her boyfriend."

Emerson had almost forgot that Raelyn Barton was dating the most handsome man on television, Austin Jameson. She couldn't imagine having to deal with the Red Moon fandom who are all very intense about their actors and show.

"True, though I am one of those fans. I love Red Moon."

"That's good because Raelyn and I would like to offer you the position. You would be able to work out of Chicago or really from anywhere. We'll have weekly meetings over Zoom and will fly you out to any events that need to be covered for her book release. I'm going to send you all the nitty gritty details as far as when we would like for you start and salary. If anything doesn't seem right or you want to change any of it just let me know. We're both really excited to work with you if you accept our offer."

Emerson was smiling ear to ear, "I'm sure it will all look fine, but I'll review the offer and let you know within the next couple of days. Is that alright?"

"Absolutely, take your time. Raelyn said to tell you that she'll throw in a Red Moon convention all-inclusive experience if you say yes. Don't let that sway your answer though." Leigh laughed.

"I don't know meeting Austin Jamison and Jackson Powell again might be worth saying yes right now." She chuckled, "But I'll give the illusion that I might say no and read over the offer."

"See this is why we think you're the perfect fit to work with us. I look forward to hearing from you soon." Leigh ended the call.

Emerson immediately went to go call her dad as a knock came from her door. In her excitement of being offered her dream job, she didn't check the peep hole and opened the door. She was shocked to see Pacey standing there still in his suit with his tie loosened around his neck.

"P-Pacey…"

"Hi Emerson, could we talk?" He asked, looking past her into her room.

She stepped aside to let him inside then leaned against the door, "Is everything okay? Please don't tell me there was fall back from me slapping Lyn."

He chuckled, "Not that I'm aware of but the video of it is all over social media."

"So, what did you want to talk about?" she asked, looking down at her feet.

"First, I want to say thank you for coming forward with your testimony. You didn't have to do that, and it made a world of difference. It also meant a lot to me, so thank you."

She pushed herself off the door sitting on the bed, "You don't need to thank me. It was the right thing to do and I should have come forward earlier. You shouldn't have had to face that alone. Plus it was my horrible idea in the first place, so really I should apologize to you. I'm sorry for everything Pacey."

He shook his head, "Don't apologize. I don't regret a single moment of you being with me."

"Really? You're weren't exactly welcoming at first, however if you ever get tired of the whole baseball thing then you should really go into acting."

He looked over at her, "You think I was acting?"

"Well yeah," she scoffed, "Hence the whole fake dating. You were acting like a boyfriend, and it was convincing. My dad thought we had crossed the line and were really dating. Kudos to you."

Emerson was surprised to see hurt expression filtering over his face.

"It may have started out fake, but I really did… I mean I do have feelings for you."

Her heart thumped against her chest, "W-What? Pacey, I know it may seem like you did but you don't. It's common for someone acting to think the feelings are real but they're not."

"They're real for me. I mean, if you don't return them then just say that and I'll respect that. Don't tell me my feelings aren't real when they are." He walked over to the window, looking out to the ocean.

Emerson walked over to him, "Come on Pacey, guys like you only fall for girls like me in books and movies. I'm not saying that in the moment the feelings weren't real, but it's been a couple of months now. I'm sure they'll pass, and you'll be off dating someone more suitable for you."

He turned towards her, "What the hell does that mean?"

"I mean someone who can be photograph cheering you on at

games and going out to clubs to celebrate wins. An equal to you. That's all I meant."

Pacey rolled his eyes walking back toward the middle of the room, "I really wish everyone would stop putting me up on such a high fucking pedestal."

She walked up in front of him, "I wasn't putting you on a high pedestal. You were already up there and part of that is your fault. Acting like you're god's gift to the world. I'm just stating facts based on the image you've created for yourself. So, don't blame me for it."

"Emerson, I'm just a regular guy. A regular guy who fell in love with an extraordinary woman. I wasn't expecting to fall in love with you, but I did. Now, I'm here trying to tell you that and you just keep telling me that it's all fucking fake. It wasn't fake for me!"

Suddenly his hand was behind her neck, and he was pulling her lips to his. His touch like fire immediately searing into every part of her.

"This isn't fake." He whispered against her lips before dipping down and grabbing her thighs picking her up off the ground, "None of it was fake. I was just too scared that I wasn't enough for you. That I would never be good enough for you."

He laid her down on the bed, hovering over her body, "I still don't think I'm good enough for you, but I can't stay away. I need you. I need you cheering for me at games. I need you wearing my jersey. I need only you."

Tears were slipping down the side of her face as he spoke. She ran her fingers down the side of his cheeks cupping them.

"You should have started with that." She smiled as he chuckled resting his forehead against hers.

"I love you, Emerson Holbrook. I'm not perfect, far from it. I'm going to mess up. My schedule is crazy, and I'll be gone a lot of the time but I want to make this work. I want this more than anything else because I love you."

Emerson pressed her lips against his, "I love you too, Pacey Tucker. I want this too. I want us. I want you."

Pacey's smile was breathtaking, "Really? Truly?"

She laughed, matching his smile, "Yes."

Emerson kissed him again but this time without hesitation. She ran her fingers through his hair as their kiss deepened. She pushed his jacket off his shoulders as he untied his tie tossing it off to the side. His lips returned to hers briefly before beginning a trail down her neck. His hands slid up her body beneath her shirt leaving a scorching trail in their wake. Pacey pulled away from her just enough for his eyes to search hers.

"Are you sure?" He asked.

Emerson nodded, "Yes, more than ever before."

Pacey looked down at his and Emerson's fingers interlocked together. Their night together was playing on repeat in his mind making his smile a permanent fixture on his face. Emerson was reading over her new job offer as they waited for her plane to be called. Pacey was flying out later in the morning back to Vancouver while she was flying back to Chicago. There were a few things she needed to take care of there with her dad and brother then she was going to fly to Vancouver.

"I have to say, their offer isn't as good as the one from the Explorers but it's close."

He chuckled, "You can really work from anywhere?"

She nodded, "Yep. Most of it will be online so as long as I

have a good internet connection then I'm good. I'll have to travel for events and conventions which will be a lot of fun. Sam is going to be jealous."

Pacey laughed, "I don't know how I feel about my girlfriend running off to fangirl over some actor."

Emerson looked up at him then kiss him, "Don't worry, I promise to not fangirl too much over Austin and Jackson. Not to mention they are both happily taken."

"Good to know." The announcement for Emerson's flight come over the intercom, "I believe that's you."

She put away her laptop and they walked hand in hand to her gate. He hated saying goodbye to her but knew it would only be for a week or two. Knowing she would be back in Vancouver after that made the pain in his heart worth it saying goodbye now. When he looked down at her, Emerson was wiping away a few tears rolling down her cheeks.

"These next couple of weeks will fly by and next thing you know you'll be heckling me from the family box." He ran his thumb over her cheek.

She sighed, "I know. I don't want to leave you, but know I need to. When is your post going up?"

Pacey pulled out his phone bringing up his Instagram, "It's up now, so be ready for the interrogation when you get home. Please try to convince your dad and brother to not break my face."

"I make no promises, but I'll try." She pushed herself up kissing him, "I love you. Text me when you're back in Vancouver."

He pulled her into his arms, hugging her tight, "I will. I love you too, fangirl."

She smiled before walking up to the gate and disappearing down the ramp. Pacey looked at the picture that was posted fifteen minutes earlier. He and Emerson were sitting in front of the large windows as a plane was taking off. After reading the blurb one last time, he started making his way down to his gate.

Liked by **Emholb24** and **10K others**

Pacey.Tucker Started out fake dating and fell in love for real ❤

#theallstarandthefangirl

View all 9.4K comments

15 MINS

Emerson

October - NLCS Game 4

Emerson was pacing in front of the seats in the family box. Whitley was chatting with her brother and her dad was talking with Pacey's parents. Meanwhile, she was trying to walk off the bundles of nerves knotting in her stomach. The Explorers were up three games over the St. Louis Cardinals to head to the World Series. The first two games had been in St. Louis where her boys barely pulled out two wins. Game three Jared hit a homerun bringing in two runs and winning them the game in the ninth inning.

"Em, you have to chill out." Her dad said gently as if she were kid again.

She shook her head, "It's the bottom of the ninth, they're tied, and he's last at bat. I know if Pacey doesn't hit a homer he'll be so disappointed."

"If they lose then they can still win it in game five." Pacey's dad said, taking a drink of his beer.

"I know… however Pacey will blame himself for the loss."

"Now batting, first baseman, number 24, PA-CEY TUCK-ER." The announcer called out.

Emerson watched her boyfriend walk out to the plate. His broad shoulders were tense and his eyes were focused on the pitcher. The first pitch was a fastball straight into the catcher's mitt. Pacey shook out his arms then returned to his stance.

"YOU GOT THIS PACEY!" Emerson yelled.

The second pitch was a changeup skirting right past Pacey's bat. He took a step back, hitting his bat against his cleats. Then he looked up right at Emerson and she blew him a kiss. She could have sworn she saw him smirking. The final pitch was a curveball with a resounding crack Pacey's bat connected with the baseball. The whole stadium watched in silence as the ball flew through the air towards left field. The left outfielder for the Cardinals ran towards the wall watching the ball as it began its descent. Flying over his head, it landed in the glove of a fan and the crowd went wild.

"EXPLORERS WIN! EXPLORERS WIN GAME FOUR AND NLCS!" The announcer yelled.

Everyone in the family box was screaming and jumping in excitement for their win. Emerson watched as Pacey ran around the bases, his team waiting for him at home plate and lifting him into the air after his foot landed on the plate. Tears were streaming down her face from the overwhelming joy flooding her body. She felt someone tugging on her arm and turned to see Whitley pulling her into a hug.

"Come on, Ben is taking us all down to the field so we can go celebrate our boys win."

Ben pulled Emerson and Whitley closest to him so fans wouldn't try to pull or push them out of the way. Their families were close behind them as they walked out onto the field. Jared was first to find them immediately picking Whitley up and kissing her. Sam found her and she give him a tight hug.

"Congrats!" She said next to his ear.

"Honestly, couldn't have done it without you Em. You're the one who gave Pacey focus and inspiration to get us here. So, thank you!" He said pulling her back into a hug.

He let her go then turned her around to see a path clearing to reveal Pacey. Emerson ran to him; he grabbed her around her waist lifting her into the air.

"You did it Pacey! I'm so proud of you!" Emerson said before Pacey's lips crashed to hers.

"We did it fangirl!" Pacey twirled her around before letting her feet touch the ground and kissing her again, "I couldn't have made it this far without you."

She shook her head, "You were born to do this, but I'm grateful to be a part of it as well."

Coach walked up to them slapping Pacey's back, "Come on Tucker, we've got a horde of press wanting to hear from you."

Pacey nodded then turned back to Emerson, "I'll see you back at our place then we can celebrate properly."

"I'll be the one in bed wearing absolutely nothing." She smiled as Pacey groaned kissing her one last time.

She hooked her arm with Whitley's as they watched their team walk over by the dugout. Emerson noticed their dads also talking with the press about the game. Looking around the stadium filled with people chanting Pacey's name, watching him wave at fans and sign various items for them. She couldn't imagine her life without it now.

The next morning, she was up before Pacey which was an oddity. Normally, he was the one up and ready for the day before she could even form a thought. Between the celebration with the team in the locker room, their celebration in bed and playing a hard game, Pacey was still sleeping soundly. Emerson made him some coffee and her tea then started on breakfast. Once she had a plate filled with bacon, she headed back into their room to wake up the homerun king.

Emerson set his favorite cup on the side table then leaned over kissing his lips gently, "Time to wake up sleepy head."

A low growl rumbled within his chest, "Why? No work today. No games. No wakey-wakey."

"Pacey, we have to meet up with everyone at noon. It's almost ten o'clock and we both have to get ready. So, time to get up." She was getting off the bed when an muscular arm snaked around her waist pulling her back onto the mattress.

Pacey pulled her firmly against him, feeling how awake other parts of him were, "Oh, I'm up fangirl but no need for us to leave this bed."

She rolled her eyes, "Oh my god Tucker, do you ever think with your upstairs brain and not your dick?"

"Nope, especially when I have a sexy girlfriend to live out all my wildest fantasies with." He lifted himself up, settling between her legs.

A small moan escaped her lips as he kissed his way down her neck and chest, "Pac-cey… everyone will be waiting for us…" She let out a breathy sigh.

"Let them wait. I need you right now."

His dark, lust filled eyes bore into hers and Emerson knew she would cave in to him. She pulled his lips to hers and fell into a blissful oblivion.

Their family and friends had given them a lot of grief when they arrived to Jared and Whitley's house over an hour late. After a few drinks and a barbecue filled lunch everyone was lounging outside. The crisp fall air was a stark contrast to the rare sunshine filled day. Emerson was sitting with Whitley and Sam while Pacey tossed a baseball with their dads and Everett.

"So what episode is he on?" Sam asked.

She laughed, "Pacey is on episode ten of season one."

Sam eyes widened, "Ah, so Ash is making her debut."

"Are you talking about my lovely she-wolf?" Pacey asked, walking towards them and sitting next to Emerson, "She's hot when she goes feral."

"I hate to break it to you, but your girl is definitely dating Jackson Powell on and off screen." Emerson patted his hand.

Pacey's shoulder slumped forward then his eyes snapped up to hers, "Wait... spoilers! Ash and Tibs? Really? Oh, I bet Rhys has some words for him dating his little sister."

Emerson started laughing, "You know you can ask Austin about that whenever we go to New Orleans for their convention."

"What?" Sam scoffed, "You're taking Pacey with you to a Red Moon convention. I feel betrayed."

"Awe, we'll bring you back an autograph for you." Pacey teased as Sam flipped him off.

Emerson held her hands up, "I'm sorry Sam. I'm sure I could see if Raelyn could get me one more ticket."

Sam shook his head, "No, that's okay. I'm pretty sure I'm out of town that weekend visiting family. However, I do expect an autograph now. Y'all heard Pacey he would get me one."

"I was-" Emerson cupped her hand over his mouth.

"We will absolutely bring you back all the autographs. Right Pacey?" She narrowed her eyes at him.

He nodded, "Yes fangirl."

"Is Raelyn the one who is releasing a book soon? The one you manage social media for?" Whitley asked.

"That's her. Her book Project Fanfic was inspired by her real life romance with Austin Jameson" She pulled up the latest post with the cover reveal, "I read an advance copy and it's good. The romance swoon worthy and the spice in hot."

Whitley pulled out her phone, "I'm going to pre-order it right now. Hey, have you ever thought about writing?"

Emerson shook her head, "I used to love writing and thought one day I would be a published author. After my mom died, all my inspiration left, and I haven't written anything since."

"Maybe you should think about it again. I mean, take a page from Raelyn's book and write about your love story."

She looked over at Pacey talking with Sam and Jared, "I don't know… I don't think it would be all that interesting."

"What wouldn't be interesting?" Pacey asked returning his attention to the girls.

"I was telling Emerson she should try writing again and write about your love story. I mean I would read it in a heartbeat." Whitley turned her attention to Jared.

Emerson chuckled, but then saw Pacey staring at her intently, "What?"

"Well… would you write something like that?" He asked.

She scoffed, "Really? I haven't written anything in over a decade. I would be better off letting Raelyn write it. Plus, would you really want our love story out there for all the world to read?"

Pacey shrugged, "I don't know, I think if it's something you would be interested in doing then I'm all for it. Plus, the fake dating trope is all the rage on the fanfic sites."

Emerson busted out into laughter, "Oh my god, I've created a monster. You're on the fan sites now? Oh, wait until I tell Sam."

"Wait, wait, wait… no need to tell Sam about this."

"Sam! Sam! You'll never guess that Pacey is on the-"

Suddenly, her mouth was covered by Pacey's, "Shhh… that can be our little secret fangirl."

"Hmm… fine, but only if you give me another kiss."

Pacey smiled before kissing her once more, "I love you."

"I love you too." She smiled truly feeling happy for the first time in a long time.

Emerson

Present Day - Convention Panel

"When Pacey and I went to New Orleans, I spoke with Raelyn about writing her story, writing in general and she gave me some really solid advice as to where I should start."

Raelyn put on her best bashful act, "Awe shucks, stop it.

Honestly, Emerson had a solid idea for a story. I only guided her a little bit and she took my little nugget and turned it into an compelling love story."

Delaney smiled, "All three of your books are epic love stories. I mean, you three are really living out every fangirl's fantasy from celebrity romance to rockstar romance and we all know that sports romance is taking over the romance genre."

"That's all very true, but also I think our books stand out because their deeply rooted in the love that inspired each of them." Laurel said glancing off to the front row where all of their guys were sitting, "These stories are about women who have some real trauma and mental health struggles, the men who see them for who they are and love them for it. They don't try to change them or fix them but lift them up as who they are. We need more men like that nowadays."

The crowd cheered as Delaney nodded in agreement, "I don't know about the audience, but I know I would love to experience a love like the three of you have experience and written about. As a fan of your books they give me hope that I'll be able to find my own epic love story."

Emerson leaned forward, "Ohh, so Delaney who are you a fan of that you would potentially fall in love with?"

She loved the newest client of their agent. Emerson still manages all of Leigh's clients' social media now including Delaney. She had gotten to know the debut author since she lived near her brother in Chicago. Often visiting her at her indie bookshop and talking about her book coming out within the next few weeks.

"Oh, I don't know…" Delaney's cheeks turned a deep shade of pink, "Probably the closest person I would be considered a fan of would be A.J. Graham."

Laurel brought her mic up, "That name sounds familiar."

Delaney smiled, "He's a New York Times Bestseller for his thriller series. He is famously known for never doing press or promotion tours for his books. No one has even seen him in public for nearly a decade. He never has an author photo so a lot of people assume he is a pen name for another famous author."

"Ohhh, intrigue and mystery." Emerson said then remember talking to Delaney before the panel about an upcoming event at her shop, "Wait… is this the author who is coming to your bookshop?"

Raelyn piped in, "Oh yeah, if you guys didn't already know. Delaney has an amazing indie bookshop that you all should support. It's the cutest bookshop I've ever been to."

"Thank you, I really appreciate that and yes Emerson, I will get the chance to finally meet my favorite author of all time."

Emerson reached over patting her hand, "Then you still have a chance to live out your own fangirl love story."

"We'll see, but for now I would love for everyone to give a round of applause for Raelyn Burton-Jameson, Laurel Adler and Emerson Holbrook!"

The panel ended and all four authors walked off stage to the backstage area. Raelyn, Laurel and Emerson all stopped when they saw their guys talking with Thomas and Leigh.

"We are some lucky fangirls." Emerson said, making the others laugh.

Austin was first to notice them walking over, "Great panel ladies."

"I don't think I'll ever get used to sitting in front of thousands of people." Laurel said as Zeppelin slipped his arm around her shoulders.

"I pull you up on stage in front of tens of thousands of people all the time." He kissed his temple.

She rolled her eyes, "Yes, but they could care less about me and are there to see you. Everyone here today, was here to see us which is baffling."

"It gets easier the more you do these panels. I felt the same way during my first few panels." Raelyn looked up at Austin, "However, I'll say that I had help from an expert on convention panels."

Emerson smiled up at Pacey, "What'd you think?"

"I think that us men should take our amazing ladies for a celebratory dinner and drinks. What do you guys say?"

They all nodded as they made their way towards the green room to grab their things. Emerson stayed in her spot watching as her friends were laughing and joking with one another. Pacey wrapped his arms around her waist and rested his chin on her shoulder.

"Penny for your thoughts?"

She smiled shaking her head, "No thoughts only vibes."

He laughed, "You've been watching too much BookTok again."

"No such thing." She kissed his cheek, "I never thought I would be able to be this happy and I'm grateful. That's all."

"Awe, my fangirl is feeling her mushy feelings. That's adorable."

Emerson pushed Pacey away playfully, "Get off me Tucker. You're ruining my vibe."

He caught her elbow and twirled her back into his arms, "How this for a vibe…"

Pacey pressed his lips to hers nearly taking her breath away. When they parted for air she chuckled.

"Now those are vibes every fangirl wants."

Sneak Peek

Book 4 in the Fangirl Series

Coming Out In 2026

When they landed, Delaney and Emerson made their way towards the main entrance where they found Quinn dressed in a black suit, white button-down shirt, tie and chauffeur's hat. She was holding a sign with their last names on it. Emerson started laughing as Delaney wished for the earth to swallow her whole.

"Miss Holbrook, Miss Bishop you're chariot awaits." Quinn bowed, holding out her arm towards the door.

"Oh, I like her… she's my kind of people." Emerson chuckled as they followed Quinn out to her car.

"If you like her that much then she's yours. Free of charge."

Delaney winced as Quinn smacked her arm, "You couldn't give me up. You love me too much and would miss me."

"Mmhmm…" Delaney smiled as she put her things in the trunk, "But really, Emerson, if you want… OW!"

Quinn took off her flip-flop and smacked her, "Stop trying to give me away! You're stuck with me."

She rolled her eyes as Emerson continued laughing getting

into the backseat.

"Hey Emerson, do you think the Fangirl authors would ever be interested in doing an event at Scattered Pages?"

Delaney narrowed her eyes at her best friend, "I think they have a full convention schedule and you they have books to work on or content to create for multiple platforms."

"Of course we would! Are you kidding me? Raelyn would do it just to visit your shop again. She really does have a thing for small town bookshops. I think it's a great idea."

"I told you so." Quinn not so quietly whispered.

Emerson placed her hand on Delaney's shoulder, "Did you think we wouldn't do it?"

Delaney shrugged, "I'm always surprised when authors say yes to an event at our shop. If I keep expectations low then I don't get my hopes up."

She felt her squeeze her shoulder, "We'll have to work on that, but yes I think once we all have our next projects done or thought of then we should gather for an event here. You should definitely tell Leigh about it and I'm sure she would work with Quinn on setting it all up."

Delaney felt her shoulders squeezing in towards her ears, "We'll see. I want to get through A.J. Graham's event first. It will be the biggest event we've ever had and if we can get through it smoothly then I'll be more open to having fangirls flood our shop."

Quinn pulled up in front of the Scattered Pages and Delaney

relaxed feeling at home finally. Their bookshop was a corner, two story building. Large windows with displays of books were on either side of the main lobby doors. The lower level was the retail store with books, selected movies and merchandise for sale. The upper level was office space and event area. They could fit up to two hundred and fifty people in the space but had never had an event to fill it completely.

Currently, the store front was decorated for fall even though mother nature was insisting that summer have an extended stay in the Chicago area. Thankfully, they were close enough to Lake Michigan that the cool lake breeze cooled their small little town just outside of Evanston. Even though Delaney would love to live alone in a cabin in the woods, all her pride and joy was sitting in front of her now.

"Em!"

The three of them looked over to see a man running across the street towards them. As he got closer, Delaney recognized Everett Holbrook from photos Emerson had shown her. The siblings hugged as Quinn nudged her in the side.

"Who's the hottie?"

Delaney rolled her eyes, "That's Emerson's brother, Everett. He's finished up his second degree at Northwestern. Yes, he's single and yes he's off limits."

Quinn huffed, "You never let me have any fun."

"Almost like I know you or something. Also, I thought you were talking with some guy online?"

"I like keeping my options open, but yes we've been trying to set up a time to meet up. He travels a lot for business." Quinn put on her best smile as Emerson and Everett walked towards them, "Are you sure he's off limits?"

Delaney noticed that Everett was obviously checking her friend out. She would never stand in the way of her friend dating a great guy, but she didn't want anything to affect her relationship with Emerson.

"For right now, yes."

Quinn sighed, "Fine, but if he asks me out then it's all fair game."

"Deal." Delaney waved to Everett as Emerson pulled her into a hug.

"We're taking off. Dad is cooking and I need to go make sure the house doesn't burn down. Hopefully we can hang out the next time I'm in Chicago."

Delaney nodded, "Absolutely, I would love that."

"Let me know how your event goes, especially if you get to have your own fangirl love story." Emerson smiled.

"I doubt that will happen, but I'll let you know. Have a safe drive to Elmhurst." She waved goodbye then followed Quinn inside the shop.

They were normally closed on Mondays in order to restock and freshen up the displays. Today, Quinn and Delaney were working on finalizing all the details for A.J. Graham's event. Quinn was working on her questions for the events while Delaney double and triple checked her order for his books. They were to be delivered three days before the event and in case of an emergency she had an in with a local book distributor that could get her books fast.

She was changing out the front table display with all of his backlist titles when Quinn decided they needed to call it a day.

"Come on, we are going to go home, order our favorite Chinese takeout and drink wine. Then you can tell me all about the convention and what Emerson meant by fangirl love story."

Delaney groaned, "Fine, but we're going to need bourbon for that."

Quinn chuckled as they locked up and walked out of the shop, "Don't need to twist my arm."

Homeruns & Hearts Playlist

Top 10 Songs

1. Legends Are Made -Sam Tinnesz
2. I Can Do It With a Broken Heart -Taylor Swift
3. Last Man Standing -Livingston
4. Before You Go -Archers
5. Right Kind of Trouble -Radio Company
6. Hall of Fame -The Script
7. Centerfield -John Fogerty
8. Anti-Hero -Taylor Swift
9. Vigilante Shit -Taylor Swift
10. Right Now -Van Halen

Check out the full playlist by scanning the QR below!

Acknowledgements

I want to thank my friends for always putting up with my crazy writer ways. You all have provided me with endless support and love. I'm forever grateful to have you all in my life. Paul, Megan, Kat, Zee, and Jen. I love you all.

To J.A. the man who inspires, the constant joy and light you give to the world through the roles you play and the music you create is immeasurable. Thank you for sharing your many talents with all of us fangirls.

Finally, I want to thank the woman whose unconditional love and support drives me every day. Thank you Mumsie for making me into the woman I am today. My silly little love stories wouldn't be here without you. I love you!

About The Author

About The Author Nikki Rae Nikki Rae resides in St. Louis, Missouri. She spends her days as an administrative assistant for a public middle school. She loves to read, play Dungeons and Dragons, attend concerts, fan conventions, and snuggle with any one of her three cats that deem her worthy of their time.

Fangirl Series

The Fangirl Series is a contemporary romance, interconnected standalone series with happily-ever-afters. Tropes featured include celebrity romance, he falls first, found family, rockstar romance, childhood friends to lovers, love triangle and more.

REBLOGS & HEARTS
Available on: Amazon, Kindle and Kindle Unlimited

Raelyn Burton blends into the background safe behind the protective wall she built around her. To deal with the solitude, she escapes into the fantasy world of her favorite TV show. Inspired by her favorite character, she begins to write fanfiction online for her newly found family to enjoy. As her popularity grows online, she catches the attention of one particular fan who begins knocking down the walls guarding her heart.

Austin Jameson has been portraying the same character for ten years on TV. He loves his life, his fans, the people around him. However, something was still missing. He takes solace in the anonymity of being among his fans online and reading the stories inspired by his show. When a particular fanfic catches Austin's attention, he cannot help to reach out and begin building a friendship with the writer.

Soon fantasy collides with reality creating the perfect storm of heartbreak and passion that could only be true in the world of fanfiction.

SUMMER TOURS & HEARTS
Available on: Amazon, Kindle and Kindle Unlimited

Laurel Adler has always been living inside the shell of a quiet, reserved bookworm. She would rather spend her time writing or reading fantasy worlds filled with true love and heroes. When her best friends push her out of her comfort zone Laurel finds herself in the middle of an epic love triangle that could ruin the lifelong friendships that mean everything to her.

Zeppelin Foster's lifeline has always been music and his childhood best friend. He always believed fame would make his life perfect, but he was wrong. Falling into the world of sex and rock 'n roll, Zeppelin finds himself on the edge of controversy that could end his career. When his manager comes up with a plan to help keep him on track, he will find himself in the middle of fighting for the one he loves and not destroying the friendships that mean the world to him.

Sometimes you have to face the music forcing you to leap into the mosh pit and never look back.